Chain of Command

Colby Marshall

Chain of Command
©2012 Colby Marshall
All Rights Reserved

ISBN 978-0-9849070-5-2

Visit Colby online:

www.ColbyMarshall.com

STAIRWAY≡PRESS

The Armchair Adventurer

An Armchair Adventurer book
STAIRWAY PRESS—SEATTLE

Cover Design by Guy Corp www.grafixCORP.com
and Simon Paul www.SimonPaulDesign.com

www.stairwaypress.com
1500A East College Way #554
Mount Vernon, WA 98273

For my Mom and Dad,
who never once doubted this day would come.

CHAPTER ONE

Zero Hour
California

HIS HEART RATE never rose above sixty as he looked through the scope of his .50 caliber sniper rifle at the unfortunate soul caught in his crosshairs.

He kept his breathing even. He inhaled deeply, slowly, so he could hold his breath as long as it took when the moment came. Then, he controlled his exhale equally. Hold. Breathing when he pulled the trigger could affect the shot's precision. He had done this a time or two. Actually way more, but this one was different.

This one he knew.

Still, no reason to worry. Stick to the protocol.

He fixed on the target's head in the center of the scope. The perfect kill shot. Just the way the United States military taught him.

Beside him sat a cell phone, the prepaid kind you could pay cash for in any discount store so it couldn't be traced. Only one person had the number to this phone.

He sucked air into his nostrils, noting the feel of the air temperature as he watched the glowing face of the phone, the clock flicking in time from 8:59 to 9:00 PM. The phone vibrated against the cement. He turned it on and listened in his earpiece.

"You good to go?"

"Yep, have to go now. Target locked."

"On my three," said the voice.

It was important their shots go off at exactly the same time so the message would be unmistakable.

1

He heard the voice count it off at the other end of the phone. "One..."

His finger tightened on the trigger. His eyes bored into the skull of the man he was about to blow apart. He was lucky he still had a clear shot, but then again, the plan was perfect. Amazing something so incredible and horrible could be counted off in the same manner as ripping a Band-Aid off of a five-year-old kid's knee.

"Two..."

His finger tensed just the right amount and held there, ready to fire.

"Three."

As he squeezed the trigger, he heard the shot at the other end of the line. *A blast right on top of my own. That's a new one.*

Even as the recoil slammed his frame backward, he was already back on his feet and disassembling the rifle. He thrust the pieces into his case in less than thirty seconds, then ran down the stairwell, calm but rushed.

And he was right to be in a hurry. He'd not only just heard the gunshot that killed the President of the United States.

He had just executed the Vice President.

Day 1: Early Morning
Washington D.C.

The phone rang. The shrill cry of her mockingbird ringtone crowed in the air demanding an answer. Try as she might to ignore it, it wouldn't stop.

"All right, all right!" Fifty-three-year-old Elaine Covington rolled over in her bed and pulled the receiver to her ear. This had better be good.

"What?" she barked into the phone. The numbers on the clock beside her four-poster bed read 12:44 AM. Who the hell would be calling at this hour, and what was so important they felt it warranted waking her?

"I'm sorry for the lateness of the hour, Madame Speaker,"

said the voice on the other line, tension seeping through his tone. His first words were too fast, his last too slow, as if he didn't know what to call her. "But it's an emergency. This is Bert Royal."

She knew him, though her staff spent more time with him than she had. There weren't many occasions when her position required her to interact with President Seymour's Chief of Staff. Elaine clutched the phone tighter as Bert spoke.

"The president and the vice president have been shot. Both are dead. Madame Speaker, you're the first Congressperson, um, former Congressperson to know."

Through the white hailstorm in her mind, the lists of what to do, what to say, in what order, and to whom battled for dominance. She had to get dressed, had to get out of this room, out of bed, damn it. "Give me ten minutes. No, make it fifteen. Get that new bimbo press secretary we just hired. Meet me at the office."

"No, Madame Speaker. I'm sorry. I've got orders to send a car with a special detail to take you to a secure place."

She swore. What her exact words were she doubted she'd remember. She agreed to be ready within the hour. Knuckles still white from clenching the phone, she dropped her cell back on the nightstand.

Elaine lay back on her pillow. Surely she was in the middle of a dream. A nightmare. Congress would assemble; she'd have to preside for hours over a debate about whether or not to attack the country responsible.

Suddenly, her eyes flew open. She sat up straight in her bed. She hadn't been asked to show up at the Capitol. She had been told she'd be taken to an undisclosed location where she would be debriefed.

It was as if she'd been slapped across the face the same way her grandmother smacked her once when she talked back to her at age ten.

President Seymour was dead.

Vice President Tifton was dead.

The Constitution dictated the next person in line.

Elaine Covington blinked twice. She was now the President of the United States.

Elaine's heart pounded as she was ushered into an unmarked black sedan. It sped through town without yielding to a single traffic light or stop sign and pulled into an underground parking garage. Other than that, Elaine couldn't tell where they were. She'd tried to follow the maze of turns the car made from the moment the Secret Service closed her inside, but she'd lost track. She only knew they hadn't driven too far, so they must still be in DC.

Two Secret Service agents hustled her into a dark corridor. The men on either side of her were supposed to make her feel safe, but somehow they only put her on edge. Sweat seeped into the silk blouse she'd thrown on underneath her charcoal gray suit. She fought to breathe evenly. To present a calm facade.

As she came to the end of the tunneled hallway, low lights streamed into the corridor from one side. The agents steered her inside the room, where she found herself standing face to face with President Seymour's Chief of Staff, the president's National Security Advisor, the Secretary of Defense, and a handful of other people she didn't recognize right away. A rip tide of whispers surged around the space. Nervousness crept up her neck like a wild electrical current threatening to catch fire.

Another person standing in the room caught her eye, though he was off to the side and not part of the general buzz of conversation. He stood next to the wall in his Navy uniform, alert. The briefcase he held was handcuffed to his wrist. Elaine's chest clenched, but somehow she swallowed the moan that threatened to escape her lips.

The nuclear "football" was a forty-five pound briefcase that held, in essence, the ability of the President of the Unites States to unleash a nuclear response to any threat to the nation. The briefcase, always handcuffed to a high-ranking military officer, was never more than a few feet from the president at all times.

And now, the power to detonate those weapons was in this

room, only a few feet away from Elaine Covington. This was no dream. No action movie scenario. This was real.

The briefcase still held Elaine's attention when a voice reminded her others were in the room.

"Madame President," Ronald Garrety, the National Security Advisor, said.

The silver hair receding from Garrety's round face swam in Elaine's vision. Some part of her understood his words addressed her, but hearing him refer to her this way made it harder to pay attention to what followed.

"I know this must be a difficult evening for you, but we have much to discuss." He gestured to a chair across the table. "Please."

"Of course," she said, straightening her jacket. "Ladies. Gentlemen." She sat down, giving a nod to the two other Cabinet members who'd not yet spoken to her.

Elaine licked her lips. What would a president say?

"Do we know anything?" As soon as the words tumbled out of her mouth, her face burned with how stupid she sounded.

Bert Royal slumped in his chair. The short, dapper man looked for once like he had dressed in the dark, thrown on whatever clothes he'd worn the previous day. Bert had not only worked as President Seymour's Chief of Staff; he was also a good friend. This couldn't be easy for him, having to continue to do his job and act as if his emotions weren't all over the place.

The National Security Advisor shot a glance toward Royal, but then quickly returned to facing Elaine. "Not a lot yet," he said, "but our people are on it, covering it from every angle. Vice President Tifton was killed as he was leaving an auditorium at the University of California, Berkley, where he spoke to some college students. President Seymour was shot getting into his car. He'd just returned to Washington from his trip to visit the region in Alaska hit by the earthquake." Garrety's eyes once again flicked toward Bert Royal, then back to Elaine.

"And other than that?"

"That's all we know. We know it was professional. Deliberate. The timing was too precise to have been a coincidence, so the two shootings must be connected. We're going to have to wait for further investigations to yield some results. At this point we have no leads. All we know is we're dealing with two sick bastards who are damned good shots."

"Terrorists? Foreign country involvement?" she snapped back.

"Given the plotting and precision of the attacks, you'd think so, but we can't be sure. No one has claimed responsibility. We haven't picked up on any communications, though we're watching that situation closely."

Bert Royal, who until now had been sitting at the end of the table, silent, finally piped up. "Isn't that unusual? Plenty of whack jobs should've lined up by now to tell us it was their brilliant idea to kill the president and vice president simultaneously."

"What that tells me," Garrety said, "is this wasn't an attack on the American way of life. These aren't your typical terrorists who want martyrdom and infamy. The killers wanted to get the job done without getting caught."

Garrety leaned forward, folding his hands on the table between them. "Most demented bastards who pull stunts like this want their names in the paper. They're proud of what they've done. Our killers aren't like that. They executed their mission and disappeared. Which means one of two things: they were guns for hire, or they have another agenda. Maybe both," he said.

"In other words," Bert said, "professional assassins."

"Exactly," Garrety replied.

CHAPTER TWO

Day 1: Morning
The New York Herald

THE SUN WASN'T even up when McKenzie McClendon arrived at her office at the *New York Herald*, but the flurry of activity inside was the kind reserved for days like this. Big days.

Her roommate, Pierce, sat on the edge of her desk. Even though he worked on another floor in the same building, she rarely saw him at the office. This situation usually meant one thing: gossip.

Somehow, his usual bowtie didn't match the day. He shifted his skinny frame, handed her a cup of black coffee. "Morning, Morning Glory. Feeling any better?"

"Before you start, Pierce, don't," she answered. She already knew what had happened, dreaded having to talk about it with anyone. Stunned didn't cover it. The guilt pitted in her stomach over feeling so selfish at a time like this didn't help.

She stared at the copy of the *Herald* on her desk. The headline said: "A Nation Shocked: President and Vice President Assassinated on Opposite Coasts."

One stupid migraine and she'd lost the scoop of a lifetime.

"I'm only here for moral support. I wasn't going to say a thing. Besides, I'm well aware that all our conversations at this desk are heavily monitored."

McKenzie glanced toward the ever-annoying crack between her cubicle and the next. Sure enough, the coworker at the next desk averted his eyes. She grabbed a tall, twisty piece of black-lacquered "artwork" and shoved it back in front of the gap in between the thin plastic panels. That thing was well worth the five bucks she'd paid for it at a garage sale a few months ago.

"I thought I told you not to break down my defenses when you sit on this desk."

"I was only trying to spy on the other angles for you. You know this'll be plastered across the papers for months. Getting a leg up early can't hurt."

She sighed, staring back down at the picture of a younger, smiling President Seymour in the sidebar of the front page. A world-changing event, and she'd slept through the whole thing. "Where were you?"

"Upstairs debugging syntax in the code of an incompetent moron," Pierce answered.

"In English?"

"The new guy is trying to write the Great American Novel of computer code without knowing how to spell."

"Right. Co-workers are fun."

She skimmed Jessie Cartwright's front page article about the assassinations, unable to help wincing at the horse-like blonde's penchant for ending paragraphs on heartstring-pulling quotes. If you liked that kind of thing, fine, but McKenzie'd always thought Jessie's little quirk toed the line of objectivity. Then again, she was probably the only one who noticed.

"I have no doubt you could've written it ten times better," Pierce said.

"At least *you* know that."

Pierce hopped off the edge of her desk, then grabbed his satchel from the floor. "Perk up, Pumpkin. It's not the end of the world."

"I hope not. I'd hate to think the last random pet name I'd ever hear you call me would be something as generic as 'Pumpkin'."

He pecked her on the cheek. "I have to get back upstairs before they realize I'm missing. See ya, Artsy Fartsy!"

She watched Pierce walk away. When he was out of sight, she turned to the memos on her desk. Her smile flat-lined. Super.

Today, she'd be writing about Park East Elementary School selecting a new principal.

Now, that's news that'll change the world.

Why don't they just cut me with a butter knife? It would be more efficient.

Son of a bitch. She and Jessie had been at the *Herald* for the same amount of time. Did she suck so much at writing that her editor thought the only things she could handle were glitter and glue projects?

The emotion in the office was so thick it was almost palpable. "He had children," the woman in the cubicle next to her sniffled as she spoke. "I know they were in college, but it doesn't matter how old you are or if he's the president. Losing a parent is unbearable."

McKenzie shot a quick text to Pierce:

> *What does it say about me that it's the morning after an unprecedented national crisis, and all I can think about is myself?*

The talk around her ranged from intense and emotional to the obvious political discussions. Some speculated the assassinations were an act committed by an activist angry about President Seymour's recent pick for the Supreme Court. Others waved around conspiracy theories suggesting the Democratic Party wanted to rub out two Republican leaders.

"It seems a little too convenient that *none* of the Secret Service protection was able to save *either* of them," one woman ventured. "Maybe they were in on it, too!"

McKenzie's phone vibrated in her lap. She flipped it open and read Pierce's reply:

> *It says it's a normal Tuesday morning.*

Most of the suspicions were so over the top they couldn't be taken seriously. One man announced this was a sign of the start of

Armageddon. How did she end up sharing an office with these idiots?

She typed back:

Ass.

McKenzie was almost as sick of the supposition as she was of seeing co-workers stop at Jessie's desk to congratulate her.

Most of the comments ran along the lines of, "It's history." McKenzie quickly tired of Jessie's fake smile and simpering response of, "I hate that my big story had to come from something so tragic."

"And *I* hate it when my breakfast threatens to make a second appearance," McKenzie mumbled under her breath.

At six-thirty in the morning, Morton Gaines waddled into the office. A squat, bald man, McKenzie's boss would've resembled Mr. Clean if it weren't for the fact that he was missing the earring and weighed about two hundred pounds more than the white-clad advertising icon.

He wore his pants pulled up far past his waist with his tie, as usual, tucked into them.

"Listen up, people," he said in his trademark growl. "The White House has set a press conference for nine AM. Jessie—" he nodded toward the blonde "—the chopper's standing by."

McKenzie's glare shifted to Jessie, and she squeezed the pencil she held, willing it to snap. Of course, it didn't. That splintering crunch would have been much too satisfying for it to actually happen.

"As for the rest of you, we need some other angles on this press conference. A few well-placed people are saying they have details on the assassins. Find whatever you can on whoever it is. I want their mother, their grandmother, their high school English teacher, their kindergarten girlfriend…anything and everything. I have Jessie covering the main story. Everyone else, we need the deep background and the local angles, and we needed them yesterday. Get to work!"

McKenzie groaned as she opened her internet browser. A new take on the assassinations was about as likely as she and Jessie taking a trip to Disney World together. God, if only the assassin would dial her personal line and offer her an exclusive interview.

She Google searched Elaine Covington, the Democratic Speaker of the House who, as of this morning, was the President of the United States. Information on the former governor of Colorado was scarce. Amazing how someone could be third in line for the presidency, and McKenzie, along with most of America, had no idea what she stood for.

McKenzie found a few photos of Elaine Covington on the campaign trail, her tight, brunette up-do a bit too chocolate brown for her age, her expensive, tailored suits smart. The search yielded a couple of interviews on Covington's attempts to halt meth production in Colorado and transcripts from various press junkets. Elaine Covington's father had died of a heart attack five years ago, her mother of cancer when she was seven. She had one brother, but other than that, no family. She was a widow. Her husband had been killed in a car accident the same year she ran for the House of Representatives.

Sympathy vote.

After two hours researching, McKenzie knew not much other than that Elaine Covington was pro-choice and a snappy dresser. There was no First Family to cover, so that ruled out a piece on how Elaine's nonexistent children would be affected. Unfortunately, the new president had never done anything too wild, like run nude through a department store during a fur protest. Now *that* could've topped Jessie.

The owner of the desk next door peeked around the cubicle. "Want to go with me to Conference One and watch the press conference?"

McKenzie dropped the pencil nub she'd been drumming on her desk and ran both of her hands through her hair.

What a choice. I could compile questions for the current assignment, which is sure to be the journalistic masterpiece of the year.

On the other hand, I could mope over a press conference I'd die to be at with a guy who owes his eyesight to the fact that the closest pencil sharpener in the office is a good hundred yards away.

"Sure," McKenzie answered. "It's not like I have anything better to do."

CHAPTER THREE

Day 1: Morning
The White House

ELAINE HADN'T EVEN had time to stop for her usual mid-morning diet Coke since she'd been awakened at o-dark-thirty that morning. Everything since that phone call blurred together like a dream sequence in a television sitcom.

Her swearing in as President of the United States took place in a quiet ceremony at the White House while the sun came up. She would take a public Oath of Office later, but it was important she be installed right away. If any of the country's enemies saw the United States leaderless and on shaky ground, they might decide this would be the opportune moment to launch an attack.

After the formal procedure, she'd met with more advisors than she could count. They discussed everything from her options about how to proceed with her Cabinet to what color she should wear for a press conference later in the day.

Although a hell of a lot of people were telling her what to do, no one seemed to know exactly how to move forward. The chain of command had never been put into action past the vice presidency.

Elaine chose to keep President Seymour's Cabinet in place for the time being. The administration was haywire enough without replacing officials in the midst of the most devastating tragedy since September 11. In fact, this day reminded her very much of that particular sunny Tuesday morning. Everywhere she walked, people whispered, tears falling. The White House staff was in shock.

Elaine drank in her surroundings. The cream and gold stripes on the walls of the Oval Office complemented the gold draperies. The staff photographers, recording the entry of the first female president into the Oval Office, had been shooed away. She stood in the middle of the eagle-and-shield emblem on the carpet.

My office. I'm the President of the United States.

She considered taking a seat on the sofa but opted for the power position in the black leather chair behind the desk. The Director of National Intelligence was on his way up with Bert Royal to brief her on a new development in the case.

"Mr. Royal, Mr. Garrety, and General Helms to see you, Madame President," Katherine said over the intercom.

Elaine asked the secretary to show them in. She stood from behind the huge desk, the same one used by almost every president since Rutherford B. Hayes. The Resolute desk was made from remnants of a British arctic rescue ship. *Too bad no one can rescue me right now.*

"Madame President, may I introduce the Director of National Intelligence, General Grafton Helms," Bert said as he entered the room, gesturing toward a man whose graying hair was cut so close to his head it was almost invisible. His broad nose coupled with his stature reminded Elaine of a rhinoceros ready to charge when provoked.

"Madame President." General Helms gave a curt nod.

"My pleasure," Elaine replied. She was the ranking officer in the room, yet somehow under the gaze of this man who had actually served in the armed forces, she had to fight looking at her feet. Her insides trembled like she was a teenager chosen to play principal for a day in high school who now had to address the real headmaster.

Still, she hooded her eyes to mask her lack of confidence. She could put on a show if she had to. "What do we know, General?"

"FBI Director Leighton Collins has informed me that this morning, a team entered a room at the Five Points Hotel in Los Angeles rented to one Lieutenant Cody Randolph, a former-SEAL who was discharged from the Navy back in '02. Housekeeping screamed bloody murder when they went in to clean and found him dead. Hotel called the locals. Local cops called in the Feds after going in and finding Randolph shot once in the head. They also found his .50 caliber rifle and about a hundred recon photos of the vice president in a briefcase in the hotel closet," the general said.

Elaine glanced at her watch. "We're sure this guy shot the vice president?" Elaine asked. She sounded dense, but such a fog clouded her head that she had to double check.

General Helms continued. "There's a lot to look into, including ballistics on the rifle, but I'd say a dead SEAL carrying around photos of the vice president is a decent bet. He's the guy. Same old story. Disgruntled ex-military man. A doc decided Randolph was mentally unfit to continue as a SEAL, so the Navy gave him a medical discharge. Guy has issues. Nightmares every night about watching teammates blown to kingdom come. His team was on an operation in Afghanistan in '02 when they ran into a bunch of local militant whackjobs. Slaughter doesn't begin to describe it. Mayday came in, rescue attempt failed. Just this guy and his partner made it out, but not because of anything we did. Maybe Randolph held a grudge. No idea what stalled the evac team, but if Randolph and his partner had waited on 'em, we'd have had two more families to notify and wouldn't be having this conversation at all. Instead, they escaped, found some other soldiers, hunkered down, and hitched a ride home."

"So did the partner shoot the president?" Elaine asked. Could it be that simple?

"Well, it would be the easy jump to make," the general said. "But it doesn't look like it. The partner was at a bar in New York City all evening last night, as confirmed by more than fifty witnesses. We're still questioning some of them, but it seems airtight."

"I guess that settles that," Elaine said. Her heart thudded into the recesses of her chest. "I suppose whoever killed the president here in Washington hopped a flight to California and took care of Randolph?"

The general shrugged his shoulders. "Or he hired someone to do it. Either way, whoever shot the president didn't trust Randolph enough to leave him alive, which most likely means Randolph knew the killer."

Elaine turned to Ronald Garrety. "So, do we hold onto what we know until we have a second suspect, or do we release the information?"

"Madame President, we have to make the knowledge public if for no other reason than to show people we're making headway with this investigation. Even though Randolph's dead, public opinion would be more favorable if we looked closer to apprehending the president's killer. Twenty-four hours can't go by without us having any leads. There'll be panic."

"We'll take a lot of flack for one of our own military turning against us," Bert piped up from the corner chair. His voice cracked, supporting the red-eyed evidence of recent tears.

"Not as much flack as we'd take if it looks like we don't have a clue who did it," Garrety replied.

She couldn't let Bert's grief influence her right now. She faced Garrety again. Elaine nodded. "I agree. Tack it onto the press conference," she said. She locked eyes with Bert. "I want to make it very clear that the persons responsible will be brought to justice."

"Yes, Madame President," Bert said, making a note on his clipboard.

"And the press conference is scheduled for?" Elaine asked.

"1000 hours," Bert answered.

"Let's try to have more information by then, shall we, gentlemen?"

CHAPTER FOUR

Day 1: Morning
LAX, Los Angeles, CA

THE MAN GRABBED his beer off the bar and took a swig. Nice thing about airports: everyone minded their own business. No one gave him a second look. They were all too busy watching the TV in the corner, which was running continuous coverage of the assassinations.

What would his mother say if she could see him now? "What kind of person drinks before they've even had breakfast?" she'd ask.

He'd answer, "The kind that shoots the President of the United States and doesn't leave a trace." But then again, he'd never have to answer that question from her, because he'd put bullets into both his parents' heads years ago. They had it coming for being such pains in the ass growing up.

Too bad his accomplice couldn't be here to have a beer with him. It wasn't possible though, so his solo celebration would have to suffice. At least the TV wasn't tuned to one of those mindless game shows or so-called talk shows where the white trash of the world came on national television to air the paternities of their children. God, this country was ridiculous. People would say anything on television for a few minutes of fame.

The newscasters' voices and the chitchat of other passengers waiting for flights droned in the background while he zoned out for a little while. He'd been restless cooped up in the apartment for so long. The four walls had been making him crazy. But growing careless was a rookie mistake. Notoriety was the *last* thing he was looking for. As soon as he got home, he'd hang out and wait for the public outcry to fizzle like with any news scandal.

Suddenly, his eye caught the corner TV as a new face flashed to the screen. He took another chug of his beer.

Well, hot damn. A presidential press conference.

The woman standing behind the Presidential Seal looked unruffled to the amateur eye. Uptight black suit made for bitches with a permanent stick up the ass. Prim hairdo his grandmother would've worn. Even so, she wasn't as calm as she came across. The look somewhere behind her eyes permeated from the hollows of the pupils.

Fear.

"It is with deep sadness that I speak to you today, not just as a leader, but as a fellow citizen shocked and dismayed by the tragedy that has befallen our nation. Last evening, President Matthew Seymour and Vice President Bernard Tifton were killed on opposite coasts of our country. Our nation now faces the loss of not one, but two great leaders. As Speaker of the House of Representatives, it falls to me not only to take over the duties of the presidency, but also to ensure the persons responsible for these despicable acts are brought to justice."

She detailed the finding of a suspect's body in California, though she didn't admit the dead guy was a former SEAL.

You wouldn't have discovered him if I hadn't found him for you.

She had to be sweating underneath that dark suit. If only he could put a finger to her throat, he knew her blood would be racing like a skittish rabbit's.

It was the same speed Randolph's pulse reached a few hours ago when he'd shown up at the former SEAL's hotel. "It's just business," he'd said to Randolph right before he pulled the trigger. "Nothing personal."

"This I can assure you," the president continued, "the FBI is working in coordination with the CIA to locate and arrest the culprit. We're pursuing several leads and are confident the perpetrator will be apprehended very soon."

At this, he laughed out loud, raising his beer. No one in the bar noticed. They wouldn't, of course. They were of the same mold as the rest of the country.

"Here's to the bullshit leads," he muttered under his breath. "You've got no more leads than a pig in a snowstorm. Unbelievable."

After Elaine Covington's brief address, the Presidential Seal was removed from the podium, and the press secretary took her place. Andrea Orellana's practiced voice spoke into the mic. "I'll take a few questions only. Ms. Cartwright, up front please."

McKenzie's jaw plummeted as she watched her rival stand amidst the gaggle of reporters.

Unbelievable.

"Thank you, Secretary Orellana. Jessie Cartwright, *New York Herald.*"

First Gaines chose Jessie to go to the press conference, and now the frickin' press secretary picked her for the first damn question. This could not be happening.

Jessie wore an easy smile, but McKenzie knew that look too well to think it innocent.

"Is it true," Jessie said, "the alleged assassin found dead was a former United States Navy SEAL?"

McKenzie wished she could be sucked right into the gaping hole that was her mouth. How the *hell* did Jessie come up with *that?*

"No comment." Orellana scanned the crowd of news hounds, seemingly oblivious to the near constant flare of flashbulbs and whir of camera shutters. "You. In the striped tie."

Another reporter stood, and the press secretary answered a few more questions about the funerals, how the state of affairs would affect upcoming Senate votes, and a smattering of other logistical inquiries, none of which were nearly as interesting as the one Jessie had ventured. Was it just McKenzie, or had the press secretary looked increasingly uncomfortable since the initial question?

"That's all for now," the press secretary said shortly after

19

answering a question about possible foreign involvement.

McKenzie glanced at the clock. The whole thing had lasted only a few minutes. Way less than normal.

She stared at the screen as Andrea Orellana exited the White House Press Room. The picture flickered back to the news anchor behind the breaking news desk, but his voice was nothing but disjointed buzzing in her ears. The press secretary hadn't confirmed Jessie's accusation, but she didn't have to. The way Orellana's face had gone rigid, she may as well have had the confession stamped across the front of her blue blazer. Jessie was right. The vice president's killer had been in the United States military.

Something tickled at McKenzie's brain. She took off back toward her cubicle.

Of all times to leave my phone at my desk.

As soon as she had her precious phone back in hand, she punched the buttons in quick succession and scrolled through her contact list.

"Yes!" she breathed, hitting the call button. After a couple of rings, a voice picked up on the other end. "May I speak to Detective Becker, please? I'm his niece. Yes, I'll hold."

A moment later, a man picked up. "Uncle Sal, it's me, McKenzie," she said as if they talked all the time. In reality, she hadn't seen her mom's brother face to face in almost two years. Still, he was family, and regardless of distance, she had the "favorite niece" card on her side.

"Well, hello there, Bumble Bee. Long time no see."

Despite her concentration, a smile spread over her face. Ever since she was little, he'd kidded her about being too busy to keep him up to date on her life.

"I know, I know. Before you ask, no, I haven't lost my phone. No, I'm not allergic to e-mails. And no, I'm not dating anyone."

"That's good to know. I'd hate to think some tawdry affair was what was keeping you from calling and not *Jag* reruns."

"Ouch," she replied. If only he was wrong. "How's Levi?"

"Not dating anyone, either," Uncle Sal replied.

McKenzie bit her lip. She had to remember to call more. "Yeah, he's a tad young for that."

"I don't know. The way he tells it, the first grade is swimming with foxes," he replied, chuckling. "To what do I owe the pleasure, McKenzie?"

This would be tricky. "Uncle Sal, you know I'm working for the *Herald* now, right?"

"Oh, dear," he sighed.

"It's only a tiny favor," she pleaded. "I need to know his name." She waited a moment while he was silent. "The SEAL's," she added.

"I knew what you meant," he said, but no more.

"Uncle Sal, my job is on the line here. This story could make my career."

"McKenzie, this isn't just any murder case. It's the President and Vice President of the United States, for God's sake."

"Don't you think I know that?"

The air he blew out came over her end of the phone as static. Other than the crackles, Uncle Sal was so quiet that for a frightening moment, McKenzie was afraid he'd hung up on her.

"You have to swear no one will know where you got this information," he whispered.

"I'm a professional journalist, Uncle Sal. We never reveal our sources." Her pen hovered over her notepad.

"Don't make me regret this, McKenzie."

He'd said the same words just before he let her jump on the bed when she was five years old. She'd stayed with him for the weekend while her parents were out of town. Uncle Sal had said, "Go ahead and jump, but don't make me regret it." She'd tried to do a split in the air. The box springs had never recovered.

"I won't," she promised.

She heard him take in a sharp breath. "Cody Randolph," he said. The click of the phone let her know this time, she'd better not break her word.

"Thanks, Uncle Sal," she said into the off-the-hook signal

bleating in her ear.

She opened a new document on her computer. If nothing else, the piece had the potential to have people talking. In journalism, buzz was ninety percent of the goal. The letters of her title appeared on the screen: *Are We Creating Killers?*

CHAPTER FIVE

Day 2: Morning
New York City

MOVE.

He slid the already-packed duffle bag out from under the twin bed, ripped his cell phone from the wall charger, and was out the door. He exited the stairwell at the second floor, turned right, then followed the hallway until it dead-ended at apartment 9B.

Ten seconds to jimmy the lock, ten more through the living room into the bedroom. Luckily for the girl who lived here, he'd watched her purely for the tactical advantages of her apartment.

Even though they'd left hours ago, he knew the Feds were probably camped outside, waiting for him to run. Out the front door.

Five seconds to unlock and lift the window. Thirty-two seconds later, his feet slammed the pavement in the alley behind the apartment building. It was four blocks to the nearest subway tunnel, but he walked twelve blocks to an entrance he didn't frequent on a regular basis.

As the train rumbled through the New York City underground, he unfolded the newspaper from his bag and pretended to read it. He'd found in the past few months that his intense gaze seemed to unsettle people for some reason. He wasn't even looking at them usually, but that degree of focus apparently does something to your eyes.

Now, he stared at the newsprint as he reviewed the op in his mind. They'd be watching. He had to have a way out, but he also needed an extra pair of hands. No way he'd involve his family in this bullshit. He didn't have friends. Not anymore.

Thankfully, this morning while he sat in his apartment to lull the wonderful FBI agents outside into thinking he was staying put, the newspaper had been dropped on the doorstep.

"They buried it! Page nine, right next to an article about a possible UFO sighting in Central Park!" McKenzie fumed. "Does this coffee shop have anything stronger than espresso?"

"Aw, buck up, Little Speciest," Pierce said, offering her half the chocolate biscotti on which he'd been munching.

"Did you meet me down here to check on me or to be condescending?" She snatched the biscuit out of his hand. "I have nothing against aliens, but that article was supposed to yank me from the depths of journalism hell. It's now in the corner of a page only read by retired old men who have time to comb the thing cover to cover. You want me to 'buck up'?"

Pierce shrugged. "Either that or put a gun in your mouth. Bucking up will keep your shirt cleaner. Would it make you feel better if I hacked into the *Herald*'s servers and corrupted Jessie's hard drive?"

"Tempting, but they'd probably know it was me no matter how good you are. I'd lose my job. Be prosecuted. You know, all sorts of fun stuff."

He reached across the table and squeezed her shoulder. "I better get back to the office. If anyone notices I'm not there, you won't be the only one in need of a stiff drink tonight."

McKenzie muttered, "Bye."

After Pierce rounded the corner and was out of sight, she slammed her fist on the newspaper. She yelped as her caramel latte splashed into her lap. "Damn it!"

She shoved back from the table and stormed toward the restroom in the back of the coffee shop. Her skirt dripped a trail on the floor behind her.

She snatched a handful of paper towels from the dispenser and tried to blot her skirt dry. The hand dryer on the far wall yielded even less success. She held her skirt away from her skin and under the dryer as best she could, but the stupid machine kept cutting off every few seconds. She jammed the start button, but just before the dryer whirred to life again, she heard an unmistakable *chink*.

She glanced underneath the stall doors, checking for feet. "Hello?"

No response. She must have imagined it. She restarted the dryer a fourth time, but something peculiar about the restroom entrance caught her eye. The hook was secured in the clasp on the wall, effectively locking the main door.

What the hell?

McKenzie eased back from the dryer. A hand clapped over her mouth. A strong arm locked her into place in front of someone who had at least fifty pounds on her. She tried to scream, but the sound was nothing but a muffled whimper into her attacker's palm.

Hot breath brushed against her ear as a deep voice spoke. "Quiet. I'm not here to hurt you."

She struggled against his grip, but the more she fought, the tighter he squeezed. She tried to suck oxygen through the tiny gaps between the guy's fingers, but all she inhaled was skin and her own salty sweat.

"I told you, all I want to do is talk. But I'm not letting go until you promise to stand still and shut up. Now, if you'll do that, nod."

McKenzie bobbed her head up and down, angry tears stinging her eyes. His hand loosened from her face, but he kept a firm grip around her middle. She took a few deep breaths as she fought the urge to scream for help.

Instead, she choked out, "Who are you?"

"Cody Randolph's partner."

It took McKenzie's brain a few seconds to make the connection. Her eyes widened. Cody Randolph. The dead SEAL who shot the vice president. Beads of sweat formed on her upper lip.

25

"What do you want?" she whispered.

Do I really want the answer to that?

"To talk to you about your article. That's all."

His boulder of a bicep clenched around her shoulder said otherwise. "You can't just follow women into public bathrooms without anyone noticing," she hissed. Hopefully, that was the truth.

"Ms. McClendon, I was a Navy SEAL for seven years. I've made it in and out of war zones without anyone knowing I was there. No offense, but the ladies' room isn't exactly a fortress."

McKenzie's chest heaved underneath his arm. "I might be able to talk better if my lungs weren't being crushed."

His grip slackened the slightest bit, but his hand moved to her left wrist. He whirled her to face him as if they were doing some kind of violent tango. His tousled light brown hair matched the stubble on his chin. "Lieutenant Hutchins," he said. His ice blue eyes bored into hers.

"I'd introduce myself, but clearly you already know who I am," she said, out of breath.

His face twisted into a half-smile. "You're right. I suppose we're past the niceties."

Just like that, he released her arm. She stumbled backward into the wall.

Her cell phone was in her purse. Any chance she could reach it? Probably not. His hands would pound her skull to dust by the time she unzipped her bag. She used her thumb to wipe the lipstick smeared across her face. "*Lovely* to meet you, Mr. Hutchins."

"*Lieutenant* Hutchins. And yes, the circumstances suck, but you of all people should understand why I didn't want to saunter into the *Herald* building."

"A phone call would've been nice," McKenzie snapped before she could stop herself.

"Surely you don't think lethal androids like me do normal things like use phones?"

So, her news article had drawn him to her. McKenzie had

not only accused the United States military of turning its soldiers into remorseless robots, but she'd also implied that despite witness testimonies, the person standing before her may have shot the president.

Serious damage control required. "You misunderstood, *Lieutenant* Hutchins. I only suggested that perhaps investigators abandoned a profitable route of inquiry too soon. I didn't mean to offend you."

Really, really didn't mean to, considering your thumb is larger than my windpipe.

"I believe you said, 'Do the drunken testimonies of bar patrons satisfy the FBI? Are we one hundred percent sure the former partner of the assassin had nothing to do with the murders?'" His eyes dared McKenzie to contradict him.

Damn. He had the thing memorized. Talk about pissed. "Look, it's my job. Again, no offense, but it's nothing half the country isn't thinking. Plus, it makes a good story. It wasn't personal."

"Well it's personal to me." Anger flashed in his eyes.

The door was yards away. Someone would hear her if she called for help. However, if he shot the president, he'd probably be willing to bump off a reporter no problem. That, and he could easily grab her if she tried to run. She wiped her palms on her skirt.

Think, brain! Think!

"It's a good ten paces to the door, but I'll give you a head start."

McKenzie's attention jerked back to Hutchins. "What?"

"If you're thinking of running," he replied. His eyebrows arched. "You can sprint. You might have a chance. The lock might slow you up, though."

McKenzie knew her eyes went as big as saucers. In the next second, the SEAL smirked.

"Hilarious," she replied. "So, I take it you didn't sneak in here to shoot the breeze."

"My partner was a lot of things, but he wasn't a mindless

killer," Hutchins said, the growl in his voice as comforting as that of an uncaged Siberian tiger.

McKenzie held back the retort on her lips and instead forced out, "What do you mean?"

"I can't let people think he was something he wasn't. I know what the evidence says, but I knew Cody. I know he didn't do this. I'm going to prove it. So, take it back. Come with me and search out the real story. You said I killed the president in one of the biggest papers in the world, for God's sake. It's the least you can do for me."

McKenzie shook her head. "I had every right to say what I did."

Hutchins grabbed her wrist again. "Oh, really? Been sued for libel much?"

"Been arrested for assault much?"

The SEAL's lip curled. "Touché. Still, do you want to try me? Think your position at the paper is secure enough that they'd support you if someone filed suit?"

McKenzie stepped backward to put distance between the two of them, but he closed in, running her into the bathroom wall. "I'll retract my statement about you and imply further investigation is warranted. That's the best I can do."

"Not good enough."

"What do you care what people say about him as long as they know you had nothing to do with it?"

"First off all, Mac—"

"McKenzie," she corrected.

"*Mac*," he said again. "You said it yourself. Who cares that fifty people saw me in a bar? Cody and I were partners, so until I clear him, I'm suspect number one."

McKenzie gritted her teeth and looked at his fingers clasped around her wrist. "Gee. I can't imagine why anyone would think you were capable of something like that."

He followed her gaze toward her arm. His fingers unfurled, but he leaned his face into hers, keeping her trapped against the wall. "He was my partner. For years, I trusted him with my back.

I don't want him to be that guy everyone only knows because they think he committed the worst crime this millennium."

He backed away a step. McKenzie exhaled the breath she hadn't realized she'd been holding. She examined the spots where the tile pieces ran together on the floor. Cody Randolph's name was the worst kept secret on earth right now. In Jessie's newest front page article, she'd read all about the pictures of the vice president taped around Cody Randolph's hotel room, the same hotel room where the police found his sniper rifle. She looked back up at Hutchins. This man wasn't ready to believe the truth, but she couldn't blame him. His teammate was a traitor.

"The problem is he *did* commit the worst crime of the millennium."

"Well, I guess I'm through here, then," Hutchins said. He turned his back on her.

McKenzie closed her eyes.

Slow down, heart. We're in the clear.

In the next instant, however, her eyes flew open. "Wait!"

It was too late, though. Her chance at the interview of a lifetime—and the front page—had walked out the bathroom door.

CHAPTER SIX

Day 2: Late Morning
Washington, D.C.

MR. HAROLD GRIMSBY turned the key in the apartment door. He'd knocked at least twelve times, but there'd been no answer. The folks in this building had been complaining about the water pressure, and he'd been instructed to check every single pipe. The complex couldn't afford the water damage bills if one burst. An oversight might cost Harold his job. Even so, using his key made him nervous. He always worried the tenant might be in the shower or something.

He called out to the tenant, a Mr. Benson, as he stepped onto the square of linoleum that served as the foyer. The apartment was quiet and the lights were all off. The twelve-inch T.V. set in the living room was unplugged from the wall. Harold headed through the bedroom and into the bathroom. He'd check the pipe, and Mr. Benson would never even have to know he'd been there.

As he crossed the bedroom, he spotted a shiny black briefcase sitting in the open closet. It looked kind of like one of those in the movies bandits used for ransom money. Harold shook his head. He was acting like his wife's nosy sister. He needed to move along with what he'd come here to do.

He knelt down in the bathroom, opened the cabinet under the sink, and fished through bottles of cleaner and rubber gloves to examine the plumbing. His knees creaked like rusty door hinges. Della Ray was right. It was probably time for him to retire.

Back when they'd married, he'd promised his wife the world

wrapped in a bow. He'd been sure he would put himself through school, become a policeman. Maybe a detective. Still working as a maintenance man at this age had never occurred to him.

Harold sighed as he finished tightening up the pipes. If any leak had existed, it was fixed now. He panted, hoisting himself off the floor by holding onto the counter. He picked up his tools and stuffed them into his belt.

As he walked back through the bedroom, that shiny black case caught his eye again. It wasn't his business, but the nineteen-year-old budding detective inside him wondered if maybe, just maybe, he should take a peek. What could it hurt? Of course it was nothing, but it was fun to imagine an adventure at his age. Maybe a little girl was trapped in an abandoned stockroom nearby, and she could be saved if only the police knew her kidnapper was here at Terrace. He could see the headlines now: Harold Grimsby, Local Hero.

He was being silly, but still, he eased himself onto the floor again. He cracked open the clasps on the case. Now that he was up close to it, this case was different than a briefcase. Bigger, and it was hard, as if made to carry something heftier than papers and file folders.

When he slid open the lid, fear gripped his chest. "Oh, my sweet Heaven." He lowered the top back into place, careful to snap it shut exactly like it had been before he opened it. After what he'd just seen, letting Mr. Benson know he'd been inside his apartment would be a huge mistake indeed.

Day 2: Late Afternoon
New York City

"I told him I'd retract my statement implicating him," McKenzie fumed to Pierce as they sat over dinner in their shared apartment. "What more does he want from me? I'd be a laughing stock if I said I was wrong about Randolph. The rest of the world says he's the killer, including the Feds and the CIA. Jessie would be taking sound bites from the president, while I'd be back to covering the world record for most sneezes in an hour."

"There are worse stories," Pierce said through his bite of meatloaf.

"Whatever. Either way, I can't say I think Randolph didn't do it. I don't care how much I pissed off *Lieutenant* Hutchins."

Pierce seemed to consider her statement as he chewed and swallowed. "I don't know, McKenzie. I think you might be going at this thing all wrong."

"Meaning what?"

"Meaning," Pierce said, shoveling a bite of mashed potatoes into his mouth, "this guy intends to try to clear his partner's name, right?"

"Right," McKenzie conceded.

"Well, go along with him. 'Helping him' learn the truth is even more golden than an interview. After all, he knew Randolph better than anyone. You know, inside knowledge of what made the assassin tick, profile of a killer, that sort of thing."

"You actually think I should run around the country with a guy who *might* have assassinated the president?"

"Must we always be such a Negative Nancy?" Pierce asked, shaking his fork at her in a scolding gesture.

"I don't know, Pierce," McKenzie said, sliding her peas from one side of the plate to the other and back again. "This guy would just as soon slit my throat as give me any more ammunition to use against his friend. Randolph may have shot the vice president, but Hutchins is loyal to him. That's the whole point. He doesn't want his partner's name to go to complete shit."

"So, play along about trying to clear his friend. We know it's a crock to think Randolph didn't kill the vice president, but you can still let the dude think you're helping him. No matter what, you get inside info about the killer's life. Then, if by some chance it turns out Randolph *was* innocent, you have a cover story."

Hutchins was a complete stranger, but a part of McKenzie was reluctant to betray or mislead the SEAL. It wasn't just because he could kill her with one well-placed jab to the nose, though imminent death was reason enough. This was a scoop for her, but it was real life for him. Not only had Cody Randolph been his friend, but Hutchins' own reputation was at stake.

She said as much to Pierce.

He pushed his chair away from the table, scooped up his dishes, and headed toward the sink.

"Well, tell him the truth. Tell him you don't know if you can help him, but you'd like to try," Pierce said. He plunked the dirty plate and silverware into the basin. "See you in a couple hours."

McKenzie finally put down her fork. Food and a nervous stomach didn't mix well. "I'll do the best I can," she said.

The problem with a Navy SEAL is it's damn hard to find him if he doesn't want to be found. She'd been at it all afternoon and into the evening, but all of McKenzie's usual methods of tracking down interview subjects—including but not limited to internet searching—had failed. As a result, she'd resorted to the most despicable tactic in all of investigative journalism: the white pages.

The last name "Hutchins" was listed more than eighty times in the New York City phone book. With nothing else to go on, McKenzie settled in at the kitchen table and started dialing numbers.

The first twenty phone calls yielded no results. She had a few people ask what she was selling, and one man even offered her a donation, assuming she was with a charity.

She picked up the phone to dial number twenty-one. The number was bound to be close, right? She punched the first three digits.

"What the hell am I doing?" She jammed the button to end the call, and instead, she opened a new text to Pierce:

Lieutenant Hutchins. Phone number. Any help?

Her phone dinged with his reply:

First name?

She laughed and shook her head:

> *Would you like a random one or an educated guess?*

After a long minute, the phone chirped again. She read:

> *Sure. I can find a guy with no name. And maybe Wile E. Coyote can loan you an ACME rocket to bust him with when you find him.*

McKenzie slammed the phone shut without responding.

Damn it!

Half an hour and two dozen numbers later, McKenzie held the phone book right in front of her face. "You worthless piece of shit!" she screamed, hurling the thing full force at the door.

"What the—" Pierce said, ducking as the phone book sailed over his head and through the open door. He twisted his key out of the knob, wandered into the hallway, and retrieved the object of McKenzie's frustration. He closed the door behind him and cocked his head. "Rough day?"

She snatched the book out of his hand and dropped it unceremoniously into the trashcan. "If I ever see another one of those God-forsaken compilations of dead trees again, I'll lose my mind."

Pierce's stare lingered on the garbage can. "You've always been a people person."

"Just because you spend your time waltzing with old ladies at the nursing home, suddenly you're a social butterfly."

"First of all," Pierce said, ticking off the note on one of his fingers, "it's not a nursing home. It's the Seniors Center. Second of all, it's not the waltz. It's salsa."

McKenzie folded her arms across her chest. "If I said I hated you, would you hold it against me?"

"No more than usual," he replied. "Still, you might want to look at this before you burn me at the stake."

He fished in his pocket and produced his business card. "Here you are, Lovely."

"How thoughtful," McKenzie mocked, but then she spotted the scribble on the back.

A phone number.

Pierce held up both hands. "Please, please. No need for applause. Regular bowing will do the trick."

McKenzie hit his arm playfully. "No way. Is this his number?"

Her roommate rubbed his bicep, feigning injury. "Well, I'm not quite *that* perfect. A friend of a friend who may or may not be a technical analyst with an important governmental agency looked into a record or two for me. No 'Hutchins' of the accurate age group listed in the city, but she did find a hit for a couple in their fifties with a son who'd be around that age. It's a shot in the dark, but at least you'd be aiming in the general direction."

She was already dialing. "You're a genius" she said, squeezing his hand with the one not holding the phone.

He squeezed back, then walked into the kitchen and opened the fridge. His back to her, he said, "You only want me for my brains."

"Oh, shut it——" her reply to Pierce caught in her throat when a woman answered on the other end of the line. "Yes. May I speak to Lieutenant Hutchins, please?"

The female voice stuttered. "Lieuten…um, I'm sorry. There's no one here by that name."

Click.

McKenzie let out an exasperated half-laugh.

You have to be kidding me.

"That went well," Pierce observed from behind the kitchen counter. "Please don't throw your phone, though. It might prove less resilient than the phone book."

She collapsed her head into her hands. "Any thoughts for a plan B?"

Pierce shrugged. "Chocolate. Whiskey. Cyanide."

She opened her eyes and peered at him between her middle and forefinger. "Cyanide?"

"Yeah, well. Chocolate goes to your hips, and whiskey leaves you with a hangover."

She let her head droop to the table. "You're right. I'll take the cyanide."

CHAPTER SEVEN

Day 2
Central Makran Mountain Range, Pakistan

UHLIG BEGGED HIS legs to carry him up the stairs, though today they were more like piles of bones picked clean by the vultures. And while dread dragged on his body, that same dread forced each foot to climb one step higher and higher. Matters would only grow worse if he were to bring bad news *and* not be punctual.

The door opened before he could knock. A slight, shapeless form moved out of the way for him to enter. He recoiled as he smelled the stale bread and cigarette smoke he associated with this room and everything that went on here. The only worse smell had been that of the barn near the house where he'd grown up.

A twig of a man reclined on the sofa. Before he could stop it, Uhlig's gaze flickered to the figure at the man's feet.

Al-Musari drew back the sleeve of the girl on the floor and put his cigarette out on her olive skin. The girl shrieked in pain, and her fingers clawed wildly at the floor.

The man tossed his cigarette butt onto the crumb-filled saucer in front of him. "Uhlig, I take it you have been working on our little problem." Al-Musari paused to sip from his water glass. "Tell me, where does our progress stand?"

"I spoke with the election official in Kabul we discussed," Uhlig said, but the muffled cries of the girl on the floor scattered his thoughts like sand in a windstorm. "He was reasonable, but..."

His voice trailed, and his gaze shifted.

Al-Musari grabbed the woman's hair through the dirty cloth

covering it and wrenched her head back. Her neck twisted in the same grotesque way a chicken's did just before it snapped. He held her face an inch away from his. With every gasp she took, the veil screening it curled in toward her nose.

"Quiet," he commanded.

He flung the arm holding her, slamming her to the floor. "You were saying, Uhlig?"

The silent lump that was the girl stirred on the ground, then leaned on the leg of the table.

Uhlig forced his eyes to remain on his own feet. "The official in Kabul was rational and open to what I had to say, but unfortunately, he feels most others will not be."

"Of course," Al-Musari spat. "They, too, have been swayed by the luxuries provided by 'freedom.' I suppose they are emboldened by the absurdity of the current American situation. What of Najjar? Almasi? Can we count on their votes?"

"Sir," Uhlig breathed, wiping the sweat from his upper lip with the back of his hand, "Ikram Totah has gained too much ground. Her path is only fueled by the controversy surrounding her candidacy."

Al-Musari slammed the water glass on the table. The girl huddled below jumped and scurried away on her knees. "Someone will see reason!" he shouted.

"There is nothing I can do," Uhlig replied. "Please, sir. We have run out of people we can buy."

Or threaten.

Another amorphous figure appeared with a pitcher, refilled Al-Musari's water glass, and disappeared without a sound. Body odor filled Uhlig's nostrils, and his stomach rebelled.

Al-Musari dipped his fingers into the water glass then stretched his palm out over the floor. His eyes followed the droplets, which trickled onto a splash of the first girl's blood.

"Very well, then," he rasped. "Kill her."

CHAPTER EIGHT

Day 3: Morning
New York City

HUTCHINS WATCHED THE five-foot-three girl drop her keys trying to lock her apartment door. *Dexterity: none.*

No time to be picky, but he'd have to have a serious talk with this girl about the pencil skirts before they left. No way she could run in those things. And that bunch of auburn hair needed to be in a ponytail or something so it wouldn't block her vision. She had nice eyes, though, even if they'd been spitting fear and fury at him last time he'd seen her.

She turned around, but her eyes were on her purse in an effort to return her keys to their spot.

"You should watch where you're going," he said just in time to keep her from walking into him. *Awareness of surroundings: zero.*

"Jesus Christ!"

"No. Lieutenant Hutchins, but thanks for the vote of confidence."

In what appeared to be a reflex, she gripped the key in her hand like a blade and pointed it toward him. "What the hell are you doing here?"

"I heard you were looking for me," he said truthfully. He'd called his mother last night to tell her he was okay so she wouldn't worry, and she'd informed him a girl had called asking for him. Of course it was the reporter. She'd asked for Lieutenant Hutchins.

He nodded to McKenzie's "weapon." "How about we save the heavy artillery for the road, Mac."

Colby Marshall

Her nostrils flared. "McKenzie."

Fight instinct: check.

"Get packed, Mac. We have a plane to catch."

Day 3: Morning
The New York Herald

McKenzie tapped on Morton Gaines' door.

"In," her boss barked.

McKenzie opened the door to find him sitting at his desk eating a donut. No wonder the "diet plan" his wife put him on wasn't working. She tried to blink away her disgust as a trickle of white powder fell from his chin. "Mr. Gaines, I need a few days away from the office to chase a lead."

She closed her eyes. He would be denying her request in three seconds. Two seconds. One.

"What kind of lead could you have better than what we already have rolling?"

"I'm going on a trip to get an inside story, and I need funds."

McKenzie tensed, bracing herself for the blowback.

Finally, he shook his head. "Jessie uncovered that a SEAL shot the vice president. She has the story under control. She scooped you, McClendon. Get over it, and move on."

McKenzie clenched her fists at her sides. She would *not* scream at her boss and end up without a job. "But, sir, this is something Jessie couldn't possibly have. What if I could blow this thing wide open?"

"What are you talking about, McClendon?"

And I thought I hated hearing my parents say my last name knowing they'd picked this screwed up double M-C thing. God, she hated it when he referred to her by her last name but used Jessie's first. How had Jessie become his pet? Did she *bring* him those donuts in the morning? Give him something *other* than donuts? It was hard to imagine any other reason Jessie could find herself in Morton Gaines' good graces. Wasn't like she was *that* talented.

"Trust me. I'll bring you one of the biggest stories you've

40

ever had."

"If you want money for a trip, you have to give me a little more than pretty please, McClendon," Gaines replied as he wiped his white-powdered hands on his slacks.

McKenzie folded her lips. A good journalist wouldn't reveal her source. Still, if she wanted the cash, she had to play her trump card.

"I have the SEAL's partner," she said quickly before she had time to overthink.

If Gaines' mouth had been a pit of surprise before, it was now wide enough for him to swallow the entire contents of the donut box as well as the container itself. "You're joking."

"Mr. Gaines, do you honestly think I'd joke about something like this?"

Though Gaines wasn't a pushover, he was no fool, either. She'd come in here requesting not only time to take a trip but funding for the expedition. He had to know she was confident she could deliver.

He held out one of the company credit cards. "You can buy airline tickets with this."

"Thanks, Mr. Gaines." He was actually giving her his blessing—and money.

"McClendon, you'd better not disappoint me, or I swear you'll be writing obituary columns for the next year."

"I won't, Mr. Gaines." She took the credit card and left his office, unable to suppress her grin.

Two hours later, McKenzie dragged her pink suitcase on wheels through LaGuardia Airport. Even if her skinny jeans and boots were fashionable enough, it didn't matter. The damn suitcase looked like someone puked Pepto-Bismol all over it. Every time she carried it, she felt as conspicuous as a polka-dotted zebra bumbling through the airport. She hadn't bought the brightly colored case because she was a girly-girl. She chose it because it was easy to spot at baggage claims.

Hutchins hovered near one of the ticket lines, a khaki duffle bag slung over his shoulder. He nodded toward the counter, so she wove through the maze of roped-off space that seemed almost comical when the airport wasn't crowded. When she finally stepped in behind the last person in line, Hutchins simply ducked under the tape to stand beside her.

"I guess you're the type who ignores the signs, huh?" McKenzie said, shaking her head.

"What signs?"

"The ones that point which direction you should go. You're supposed to follow the things. They're called rules."

Hutchins pulled out his wallet, which, when flexed, revealed a wad of bills. "There are two types of people, Mac. Some follow, and the others are efficient." He glanced at McKenzie's purse. "You got a credit card?"

She blinked twice, processing. "Yeah, the company—" she muttered as she removed the card from her purse.

He swiped it. Then, in one quick motion, he twisted her hand and entwined his fingers into her own.

"Yes, we'd like two tickets to Las Vegas, please." Hutchins shifted his eyes toward McKenzie and lifted their clasped hands just enough for the fifty-something woman behind the counter to see. "Your quickest flight out."

"Aw," the lady sighed. "Newlyweds?"

Hutchins smiled, closed-lipped. "No, ma'am, but we will be when we come back," he replied, winking.

McKenzie let out a nervous laugh, which the lady smiled at knowingly.

Yep. I'm such a sweet little girl in love. With my career.

A few moments later, they waited in the security checkpoint line, boarding passes in hand. "What's in Vegas?" McKenzie asked.

"Slot machines."

"I'm serious—" she said, but stopped to shift focus to the belt that would take her carry-on through x-ray. She slid out of her boots and loaded her suitcase onto the table.

Her chest seized up as she fumbled to get her laptop into a bin. She'd already held up the line as she took off her belt and fished through her bag to remove the argyle-print pouch containing her three ounce containers of lotion and body wash. Now, the line groaned behind her while she sped to unzip her laptop case, then the *second* case within. Why did the damn companies insist on making the sleeves *just* large enough for the computer to fit?

She ripped the sheath off the laptop's corners.

Behind her, the SEAL dropped his entire bag onto the belt without removing anything.

"Showoff," McKenzie muttered under her breath when they were on the other side of the metal detector. She repacked her laptop.

"Low-maintenance," he countered. "Come on."

She shuffled behind the SEAL as if she were a stereotypical subservient handmaiden. After the two of them boarded the plane, Hutchins stuffed his bag underneath the seat in front of him. He reached for McKenzie's suitcase, but she snatched it up. "I've got it."

He didn't argue but sat down and folded his hands in his lap. He thumbed through a magazine from the back of the seat, but even so, she felt his eyes on her as she hefted her suitcase into the overhead bin. On her toes, she gave the ugly pink bag one final shove to pop it into the narrow space. Huffing, she collapsed into the seat next to Hutchins.

"Don't say a word," she said.

"About what?"

The plane bounced along the runway, the engine screaming as it mustered the momentum to climb. Outside, the ground fell away from them, the people and planes becoming smaller and smaller. The buildings of Manhattan looked like scattered toys left out on a playground.

She winced.

"What's wrong?" Hutchins muttered.

"Just my ears. They pop during takeoff and landing. It'll go away in a minute. Always does."

"You have gum?" he asked.

"Why do you ask?"

"'Cause there are two ways to make your ears better, and one's easier than the other."

"Care to share?"

"Valsalva maneuver," he answered. "Close your mouth, pinch your nose shut, breath out hard through your nostrils."

"Won't that bust my eardrums?"

"Could, I guess, but it works for military ops at high altitudes. However, if you prefer the tamer version..."

He reached into his bag and produced a pack of sugarless sticks. He handed her a piece. "Chew hard."

She chomped on the gum, and the pressure in her ears dissipated. "Where'd you learn that one?"

His eyes returned to the magazine page he'd been staring at since they boarded. "I know a thing or two about altitudes."

"I thought you were a SEAL," McKenzie said. "Aren't they in the water?"

"SEALs. SEa, Air, and Land. SEAL."

"Hmph. I never knew it stood for anything," she said.

"Thankfully you jump out of the plane before you have a chance to worry about your ears."

McKenzie glared at him. "*You* jumped out of planes?"

"Once or twice," he replied, still looking down. "Don't worry, though. I think you're reasonably safe on this commercial flight."

McKenzie stiffened. She hadn't even noticed her hands reaching to tighten her seatbelt buckle. "Right," she whispered. "So, one more time. You still haven't told me what's in Las Vegas."

"Sure I did."

Her fists curled. She let her chest fall one millimeter at a time. "Let me try this a different way. When we arrive in Vegas, what next?"

Finally, Hutchins shut the magazine and faced her. "Let's get one thing straight, Mac—"

"McKenzie."

"*Mac.* We're running this op exactly as if it was military. Tactical information will be divulged on a need to know basis only."

"But I—"

Hutchins picked the magazine back up. "Need to know basis."

CHAPTER NINE

Day 3: Early Afternoon
The White House

THE RED PHONE only rings in case of severe emergency or imminent attack. When the handset at Elaine's side in the Executive Residence buzzed, she knew it signified her first big test.

Elaine had returned to the Residence to change her clothes between meetings. Regardless of whether or not she was in charge of a nation, she couldn't stand the itchiness of her wool pinstripe pantsuit another second. The tiny window of privacy was one of the few times when Bert Royal or one of her secretaries couldn't barge into the room to update her on something about the day's schedule.

Now, her blessed five minutes of peace was being interrupted by the bleat of the red phone.

"Madame President, this is Ronald Garrety. We have a situation. A civilian ship has exploded in the Mediterranean Sea. I would appreciate it if you would meet me in the Situation Room at 1300 hours."

"I'll be there," she said, her blood racing in her veins. Up to now, it hadn't felt real. More like she was playing White House. But now, the time had arrived for her to take on an obstacle as Commander in Chief.

She scooped up her cat, holding Macy away from her body so as not to get cat hair on her fresh clothes. "Am I ready for this?" she asked.

Macy stared at her, purring away.

On her way out of the Executive Residence, she nearly ran

into Hayley Seymour, the former First Lady.

"I'm terribly sorry," Hayley mumbled, her eyes on her feet. "I thought you were out. They said I could take a few moments to come up and make sure I've collected all of my things. Do one last look over."

Elaine shook her head, squeezed the meek lady's shoulders. The poor woman had lost her husband and her home in one fell swoop. "No. Please, take as long as you need, Hayley. There's no rush here."

Hayley Seymour's eyes lifted, and a thin-lipped smile crossed her face. "Thank you. This has all been...quite a shock."

"It has to us all. I can't imagine what you must be going through. I'm so sorry for your loss," Elaine said.

Hayley Seymour once again turned her focus to the ground. "So am I."

Elaine gave the former first lady a final pat on the shoulder before leaving her to comb the Executive Residence for any missing personal belongings. As Elaine walked out of the safety of the Executive Residence, one of the Secret Service agents posted outside the Residence said into his headset, "Glass on the move."

Elaine entered the Situation Room. It was like walking into the airlock on a spaceship. The table in the main conference room stretched almost the entire length of the space. An extra layer of chairs lined the wall in addition to those surrounding the table. One flip of a switch, and the windows fogged. The walls included protections against unsecured or unwanted text messages, cell phone calls, or the tracing of either. The room was made for shitstorms.

Ronald Garrety and Bert Royal already stood around the table along with the Secretary of Defense and the Deputy of Homeland Security. Intelligence analysts and other strategists flipped through papers, hovering near the chairs at the wall. General Helms held the position across from Garrety, watching one of the six flat screens on the wall, his snubbing of her obvious.

"Gentlemen, ladies," she nodded, taking her seat. The rest of the room took its cue and sat as well. "What do we have?"

"Suicide bomber," Garrety said, his voice flat. "American civilian ship, but some important people on board. Ikram Totah was killed."

Elaine blinked in disbelief. The woman who'd been the rallying point for reform in Afghanistan, the woman whose name would be on the ballot for their presidential election this year. Gone.

"What do we know about the bomber?" She swallowed hard.

The Deputy of Homeland Security spoke. "Not a lot. The guy was in port dressed in normal clothing. Witnesses saw him lurking near the debarkation exit, but they say he appeared to be with the group getting off the boat. He looked more lost and confused than anything else." He shrugged, loosened his tie as though describing the scene was enough to make him nervous. "Probably part of his ruse to hang around without attracting attention until Totah was near. Those close enough to tell us exactly how it went down aren't in any shape to talk, but one sixteen-year-old girl walked away without a scratch on her. She's shaken up and hasn't been able to give us much other than he was 'foreign-looking'. Average height, average weight. That narrows it down to, I don't know, over half the planet."

"Thank God we have a reliable witness," Elaine said with a sneer. "Anyone claim responsibility?"

"Loads. Nothing credible so far," Garrety responded.

"What's the status of the vessel?"

Garrety's eyes met hers. "Completely destroyed, Madame President."

"Casualties?"

"Fifty dead so far. Forty-seven American citizens. Emergency workers are calling in every few minutes with updates."

Images of shrieking and flames, the smell of burning flesh sizzled in Elaine's mind. Almost fifty Americans dead. "Schedule a press conference this afternoon. We need to issue some kind of statement."

About the people killed. About Totah.

The advisors stood as Elaine left. Ronald Garrety fell into stride with her.

"Madame President, I would advise you to rethink the press conference until we have further information." His beady eyes squinted with disapproval. "Even insinuating that we're supportive of Totah's platforms could spark an unfounded conflict. With all due respect, we have enough problems."

Elaine rolled her eyes. "Right, Ronald. I called up God this morning and asked him, 'Could you please have a suicide bomber blow up a civilian ship today? I'm feeling a bit bored.' I know it's not convenient timing, but we can't exactly ignore an international incident. We can extend condolences without being stupid about it. That way, we keep favorable opinions on all fronts. It's all about phrasing."

"I'm not suggesting we ignore it," Garrety replied. "But there's a huge difference between issuing a statement and conducting a full scale press conference. Conferences set us up for all sorts of *questions* we aren't prepared to answer, if you haven't noticed. Frankly, I don't trust Orellana to handle them."

Elaine stopped and faced him, her eyes narrowing. "If the press secretary and my other advisors do their jobs, we won't have a repeat of the last press conference debacle. Orellana will be fine as long as she actually does her research on the reporters in the damn Press Room like she should. If she doesn't, I took office a few days ago. I'm completely within my rights to appoint a new Cabinet as I deem necessary. I've kept Seymour's in place to streamline this abrupt change of administration, but that choice doesn't have to be permanent."

Garrety searched her face. "Madame President, I understand your frustration, but Orellana is dealing with a media wildfire no one in her place has ever had to navigate. Slack might be a recommended course of action."

Elaine let out a dry laugh. "Yes, because I know *nothing* about coping with stressful, unprecedented situations. Goddamn it, Ronald. You have to be kidding me. You cut a third-grader some slack for forgetting to study for a spelling test. This is the White House, for God's sake. I'm going to make decisions based on competency, not on the emotional needs of Andrea Orellana or you or President Seymour's favorite tennis buddy. I'm sorry the ship was blown to smithereens. I am. But I won't apologize for wanting a more recent image in the minds of the public other than the last press conference where we were made to look like a bunch of bumbling idiots caught with their pants down."

She resumed walking, painfully aware of her voice bouncing back at her from the walls.

Garrety clearly noticed their tones had become louder, too. He caught up to her and lowered his voice as he glanced back at the Secret Service agents on their heels. "I'd also advise on a more personal level that we step lightly around any implication that the assassination investigations won't continue to be our first priority. Yes, we need to relieve some pressure in the press. I also understand it's your right to appoint new Cabinet members as you see fit. However, for the moment, it's vital to remember that people around you lived and worked beside the president. They care whether or not his killer is found even more than the general public. Many of them are people you want to keep on your side right now. Bert Royal is among them. He was one of Seymour's closest friends."

Elaine looked straight ahead as they neared the staircase leading toward her office in the West Wing. "Thank you, sir, but I can assure you, Bert Royal's feelings about President Seymour are low on my list of concerns. As far as advising me on a personal level goes, I'd advise *you*, on a personal level, to back off. Have a good afternoon."

CHAPTER TEN

Day 3: Early Afternoon
Washington, D.C.

HE'D BEEN HERE too long. It would be nice to lay low another couple weeks—hell, another couple *days*—but he was afraid someone had been in his apartment. It was a gut feeling, but he'd learned long ago to trust his instincts. Besides, he had a new job to start.

His next hit was a British mogul named Ian Davies, the Donald Trump of the United Kingdom. Ten million dollars had already been wired into his offshore account. The other twenty million would be paid upon completion of the job. He'd be a fool to pass up an offer like that.

He wore the rubber gloves from under the sink as he scoured the apartment with bleach and polished all surfaces, leaving no chance of fingerprints. Hair follicles were an occupational hazard he took care of long before they became an issue. He kept his head—as well as his body—waxed in its entirety. Still, he swept to make sure he left no fibers, then double-checked every single inch of the place. Something as small as a sock or a dollar bill left behind could be disastrous.

No mistakes.

Maybe being cooped up in this apartment the past few days was making him paranoid. Still, even if someone *had* been in his rental unit, they couldn't know enough about him to identify him.

Ever since the maintenance call when he'd opened the black case in the closet, Harold Grimsby had watched Mr. Benson when he could, though Mr. Benson didn't leave the apartment much. Harold kept intricate notes, including a physical description and details of what he'd seen in the apartment. He'd asked around about Mr. Benson to the other renters in the building. All of them described him as quiet, a loner.

Harold was nearly ready to go to the police, but he wanted one more thing: another look inside that case. If he knew the models of the weapons in the container, the police might not think he was some crazy old man when he told them his suspicions. They might even thank him for his help, mention him in the paper.

So he planned to go back into Mr. Benson's apartment the next time the man left. The risk was huge, but he had to make sure he'd collected as much information as possible. If he was right in what he was thinking, he could very well be onto something so important it could change his and Della Ray's lives forever.

When Mr. Benson left, Harold managed to sneak into the main office and grab the key to Mr. Benson's apartment. He only had a few minutes. Mr. Benson's trips were never long.

He rushed up the stairs as fast as a pair of eighty-year-old legs could climb and plunged the key into the door. His hands shook so hard he had to brace his right with his left to unlock the door.

He headed straight back to the bedroom and opened the closet door where he'd last seen the mysterious case. He slid it out, his trembling fingers working the clasps. He fumbled the lid twice. How many minutes had it been?

Finally, he propped the top open and reached for his notepad to take down the model numbers. Again, he put his left hand to his right wrist to steady it as he wrote.

The smell of beer fluttered through his nostrils.

"You should mind your own business, old man," Mr. Benson whispered into his ear. "Why are you here?"

"I—" Harold stuttered. "I was checking a pipe. This shiny case caught my eye. I apologize for my curiosity, sir. I didn't mean to intrude."

But Harold knew he'd seen too much. Mr. Benson had no way of telling this was Harold's second look at the case, but anyone in the world right now need only see the contents of that case once to be a threat to Benson.

Harold closed his eyes. Della Ray's face rushed to the forefront of his brain. Benson's hands grasped either side of his head, but Harold didn't try to fight back. After all, what could an old man do against such reckless evil? Harold took a deep breath and exhaled slowly, savoring the air he knew would be his last.

And then, with one quick snap, Harold was gone.

CHAPTER ELEVEN

Day 3: Noon (PST)
Las Vegas

HUTCHINS' GAZE WHIPPED across the smattering of people waiting for their own flights as he exited the gate at McCarran Airport in Las Vegas. A girl in ripped jeans listening to an mp3 player, a black guy in a suit with his Netbook. No one appeared to take special notice of him and the reporter. No one was pretending *not to notice* him and the reporter. Good.

He sped through the main terminal, the sound of McKenzie's suitcase whooshing along behind him to let him know she was keeping up. Her boots might be designer, but at least they were functional. Even without the noise, the scent of her perfume— something light and flowery—would've told him she was there. He pushed through a group of tourists to reach the slot machine- lined wall. Bypassing the games, he went straight for an alcove that held an ATM.

"Card," he said, still scanning the people around him.

"Huh?"

Hutchins turned to face the reporter, who stood with her arms crossed. Her face was sharp, her chin coming to a point almost like a SOG, one of the SEALs' specialty knives. "Your debit card. Give me your debit card."

The woman flinched, seeming to notice the ATM for the first time. "How do you know I have one?"

"You took out your wallet at the ticket counter."

"Yeah, but I didn't use my debit card," she argued, her copper eyes wide.

"Let's just say observation is one of my strong suits," he replied. "Now, card. We're wasting time."

She unzipped her purse, pawing through its contents in search of her wallet. Her fingers fought to free the piece of plastic from its niche, her chest lifting with tiny gasps of frustration.

Three. Two. One.

Hutchins swiped the wallet from her hand, plucked the card, and slid it through the ATM in another three seconds flat. "Punch the PIN."

When she did, he hit the button to extract the maximum amount the bank would allow.

"Whoa, dude. You didn't include cleaning out my bank account in your description of this trip. I have the company credit card, remember?"

Christ watching the home shopping network.

Executing an op was a lot easier when your teammates followed orders. "We need cash, and I need you to trust me."

She folded her arms again. "Trust has to be earned."

"Says the chick who accused me of murder."

Her nostrils flared again. "How do I know it's just an accusation?"

They'd been standing here a good five minutes now.

The longer you're still, the greater the chance people will notice you.

"You don't."

The money fell into the dispenser, and the reporter retrieved it. "What now?" she asked, but he was already walking.

Through the terminal and to the lockers. He twisted the combination lock. Eight. Forty-three. Sixteen. He reached inside. His hand wrapped around the manila envelope he knew would be there.

"I thought you didn't have cash," McKenzie said from behind him.

"I don't," he said. He ripped open the envelope addressed to Mr. Neil Fredericks and sifted through the contents. Wallet, driver's license, passport, key.

Good.

Hutchins took off through the terminal again. The reporter shuffled behind him, struggling to keep pace. He veered into the coffee shop to his right. "Laptop."

"Not even a please?" she replied, but she was already extracting her computer. "What now?"

"Two tickets to Miami. Use your company card."

She glared at him. "Vacationing, are we?"

"I told you. Need to know basis."

"All right, all right." She pecked away at her computer for a few minutes, finally reaching the page to book a flight. "From Vegas to Miami, correct?"

"Yes."

She looked from the screen to the manila envelope and back again. "What name?"

"Here," he said, pulling the laptop toward him. He entered his information into the computer and extended his hand for the credit card.

McKenzie passed it to him. "This is getting old."

Moments later, they were set with two tickets on a plane to Miami leaving in the next hour, courtesy of the *New York Herald*. Now, phase two.

Hutchins wove through the crowded airport. He walked past their gate to the next, a plane bound for Heathrow International Airport.

"We passed our gate," McKenzie huffed from behind him.

"I'm aware. Just shut up and pay attention."

Hutchins found seats next to a middle-aged man who'd been making futile efforts to calm a toddler. The kid, red-faced and crying, had run away from the guy. She was now on the floor, cracking eardrums with one long continuous scream. The man scooped up the girl as he muttered apologies to the crowd around him.

All eyes were on the spectacle before them. Hutchins unzipped the front pocket of the backpack next to the man's chair and dropped his old wallet in. Two seconds later, the bag was zipped again. Most likely, no one would remember what the two people sitting next to the man with the screaming kid looked like or even that they were there at all. Better than throwing the wallet in the trash any day. If anyone was tailing them, they could always forage through garbage. Sending a wallet over the pond might cause some confusion when it was discovered, but at least it wouldn't be found by anyone who mattered.

Hutchins set his sights on the ticket counter but stopped when he failed to catch the shuffle of the reporter's boots on his heels.

What now?

He spun around to see her standing smack in the middle of the walkway, blocking the flow of traffic.

So much for blending in.

"What are you doing?"

"I'm waiting for you to tell me, if we aren't going to Miami, where the hell we *are* going."

Sweet cartwheeling Jesus.

He rushed back toward her, braking when his face was an inch away from hers. "*Mac.* We don't have time for this bullshit."

"Look, Mr. Personality." She paused, holding puffed air in her cheeks.

At this, Hutchins couldn't help the smile that crossed his lips. She looked just like that screaming little girl from moments ago.

The reporter released the breath she'd been holding and spoke through clenched teeth. "I'm not moving one more inch until you tell me where we're going."

He backed a step away from her. Too many eyes.

"California. Now, move your ass."

CHAPTER TWELVE

Day 3: Afternoon (EST)
The White House

IF IT WAS POSSIBLE, General Grafton Helms had become even more intimidating than when Elaine first met him. As he entered the Oval Office, Elaine reminded herself that despite being a woman and despite never having served in the military, she was his superior officer.

It was a concept he obviously did not enjoy. His jaw was set in a firm line, his eyes burning into hers. He sat down across from her, the knife-edge crease in his uniform trousers an indictment against her wrinkled skirt.

"Let's get right down to it," she said, wanting nothing more than to take control of this meeting. "Do you have any updates regarding the assassination investigation, General Helms?"

"With all due respect, Madame President, are you sure you wouldn't rather wait for Mr. Garrety to arrive?"

Elaine bit back her snarl. "Mr. Garrety is my National Security Advisor, not my babysitter, General Helms. I'm sure you can catch him up."

Helms glanced at the door as though hoping the president's administrative assistant, Katherine, would burst in with Garrety at that exact moment. She didn't. He turned to Elaine. "We've had a couple of things turn up. First of all, the hotel manager of the Five Points Hotel where Cody Randolph was holed up was found dead. He lived a block away in another building he managed. No family or close friends, so they only found the poor bastard when he started to stink up the place."

Helms cleared his throat, studied Elaine. If he was waiting for her to beg for more details, he'd be waiting a long time.

Finally, Helms spoke again. "The M.E. narrows time of death to within a few hours of when Randolph was killed. I'm guessing the killer disposed of the manager because he could identify him. Probably talked to him to find out where Randolph was. No sign of forced entry at Randolph's hotel, so the killer might have obtained a key from the manager. Then again, I don't doubt Randolph *knew* the killer, so it wouldn't be much of a jump to think Randolph let him in, either."

Elaine nodded. "Was there anything about the hotel manager's death that might point us in the right direction?"

"Ah, now there's where things get more interesting," the general said, sitting back in his chair and stroking his chin. "The manager wasn't shot like Randolph. He struggled. He'd pushed furniture up against doors and in front of windows inside his apartment. The killer entered through a broken bathroom window. How the hell he squeezed through that porthole beats me. You wouldn't have thought a cat could force its way through that thing."

The general shook his head before continuing. "So, the manager was expecting trouble. He fought and went down with a slit throat. Here's the kicker." He paused for what may have been dramatic effect. "The wound started out straight for about two inches, but it showed signs of serrations at about the third inch before becoming straight again. Could be a coincidence, but the pattern of that cut suggests a certain kind of knife. The laceration looks like it came from one of the Emerson CQCs."

Elaine stared at the general. She knew nothing about special makes of knives or what this new evidence implied, but she wasn't about to admit it. He'd get far too much perverse satisfaction from knowing something she didn't.

He didn't disappoint. His smug wink made Elaine want to throw the book atop her desk at him. "The Emerson CQC is one of the SEALs' specialty knives. One SEALs prefer, in fact."

It wasn't anything to be jumpy about. The killer could've

easily taken the knife *from* Randolph. Or bought it on eBay. Still, the possibility of another former SEAL—or worse, an *active* SEAL—being the president's assassin made her nauseous.

"Anything else?" she asked, filing the information away deep in the recesses of her brain. She'd ponder it later when she had some time alone.

The general's mouth turned down at the corners. "Randolph's former partner is taking himself an impromptu vacation," he said, again taking an arrogant pause to relish in having the upper hand.

Then, as an afterthought he added, "With a reporter from the *New York Herald*."

This time Elaine couldn't help raising her eyebrows. "Really?"

"Yep, a McKenzie McClendon. Seems Miss McClendon wrote a small article on Randolph in the *Herald*. Something about how SEALs are little more than government-trained killers. It's weird, too. She could've kicked both Randolph and Hutchins—"

"What did I miss?" Garrety said loudly as he strode into the room. He nodded to Elaine and then to Helms. His eyes met Helms' for a fraction of a second longer than seemed normal.

What was that?

The National Security Advisor settled into a chair across the desk from her, extracting papers from his briefcase. His rigid jaw line relaxed, and his fists unclenched.

"I was telling the president that Ms. McClendon, the reporter, could've kicked both Randolph and Hutchins in the balls and been less offensive than she was in her article." Helms turned back to Elaine. "I don't know what to make of their rendezvous, but we're keeping an eye on them."

"See that you do, General," she replied. "I want to know everything, even if it seems unimportant."

Day 3: Early Afternoon (PST)
Oxnard, California

Hutchins pressed a tiny key into her palm. "No one will ask you any questions, but if they do, breathe normally. Don't talk too much. Liars give themselves away by over-talking."

McKenzie squirmed.

Easy for him to say.

"Don't you know the worst thing you can do if you want someone to breathe normally is to make them think about breathing?"

"Controlling your reactions is—"

"Something SEALs train for for years," she said.

"Not years," he answered.

McKenzie scowled. "Okay. Fine. It's something SEALs train for. Period."

Hutchins started the rental car. "Well, you're not a SEAL. Now, if they ask anything, you're Danny Herndon's sister. He died in a car wreck two weeks ago. You've been too distraught to settle his affairs until now."

McKenzie stared at the driver's license and death certificate for Danny Herndon in her hands. Surely this wasn't normal.

"What if they want my ID?"

Hutchins' eyes shifted toward her. "Then you give it to them. They won't, though."

"Give them my *real* ID? And how can you be so sure they won't? There has to be some kind of procedure to check out a person trying to empty someone's safety deposit box."

"You have the key and a death certificate. People don't question grieving people enough. Trust me."

McKenzie rubbed the plastic and the paper documents together. "You didn't answer me about my ID."

The bank sat a block down and one across from where Hutchins parked. "You're right. I didn't."

McKenzie curled her fist around the key and the papers. "I'll take that as a good luck."

* * *

Christ carrying a Menorah.

Hutchins had planned a lot of ops in his time, but this was without a doubt the worst. Assess, handle, get the hell out. That's the way he was used to doing it. It was what worked. This time, however, he'd managed to skip a few crucial parts of the first step.

Way back during BUD/S training, his Officer in Charge ordered his team to run down the beach to the marker, come back, and do nothing else. Hutchins' team ran hard to the marker and was back before any other team.

As they stood at attention to wait for further instructions, the OIC stood in Hutchins' face. "Hutchins, why did your team not take your boat to the marker? Are you lazy, son, or do you just not like hard work?"

Hutchins stared straight ahead. He sucked the salty sea air into his lungs, which were flaming from the early morning sprint. "You said to run to the mark and do nothing else, sir."

"Everyone else took their boat, Hutchins. Why did you not take your boat?"

"Your instructions were to run to the mark and back, sir. Nothing else, sir."

The officer stalked back and forth in front of him. "This team is the only team that did not carry the boat to the mark, Hutchins. Are you sure about your call, sailor?"

Hutchins could feel his teammates' eyes on the back of his head. They'd all suffer if he'd led them wrong. They hadn't questioned him, as they knew not to. It was his job to make sure they didn't fuck up, and they trusted him.

"Yes, sir," he'd said, his breath never catching. "Positive, sir."

Attention to detail.

He'd been right.

Now, he sat out front of the bank. He'd just sent in a woman who had no idea what she was doing or how to handle situations under pressure. She had no reaction time, no stealth, and zero concept of not drawing attention to herself. Her cover was about as solid as a sumo wrestler's ass, *and* she could identify him. He had absolutely no control over what happened once she was inside that bank, but that wasn't even the worst part.

Jesus and his brother on a twice-wrecked four-wheeler.

The worst part was, he hadn't told her what to expect. He was about to find out how well she followed direction.

CHAPTER THIRTEEN

MCKENZIE APPROACHED ONE of the desks inside the bank, all the while trying not to blink so maybe her eyes would burn.

Damn that tube of waterproof mascara.

"Can I help you, Miss?" asked the heavyset black man seated behind the desk.

"Yes," she said, and her voice quivered. "I'm here to—"

How the hell do you say you want to get your dead brother's stuff?

"—to clear my brother's safety deposit box. He passed...he, he..."

Her eye twitched, but she didn't give in. A tear blossomed in its corner, obstructing her vision.

Yes!

The employee glanced to McKenzie's hand. She clutched the manila envelope containing the fake documents tighter.

"I'm so sorry for your loss," he said. He reached across the desk. "Wesley Howard. I'll be happy to assist you, Miss—uh—"

"Herndon," she supplied. "Nadine Herndon. Thank you."

He crossed behind his desk and extracted several forms from a drawer. "I take it you're joint owner of the box if you'll be removing its contents." Fluorescent highlighter streamed over several blanks requiring her signature. "I assume you've brought copies of the proper paperwork, as well?"

"Yes, sir," she answered. In reality, she had no clue what the proper paperwork was or if a joint owner had come with him to open the box. Surely the SEAL had done his research.

The forms contained a lot of complicated legal language, which she pretended to skim before finally arriving at the signature line at the bottom. She let her pen hover above it for a moment before she signed: M. Nadine Herndon.

The man took the forms and the death certificate. He made copies of each before stapling them together. "Now, Miss Herndon, if I could just have a quick look at your license, we'll be all set."

Every muscle in McKenzie's body stiffened. With a calming breath, she commanded them to relax. *Do not react.*

"Sure thing," she muttered. Her hands shook so hard that she had trouble with the zipper on her purse. "Stupid thing always sticks."

Howard smiled knowingly and slid a box of tissues toward the edge of the desk. "Take your time."

McKenzie nodded and gasped, then plucked a tissue from the box. She dabbed at her eyes and grabbed a second tissue to blow her nose. Inside, her thoughts pinged around like the metal orb in a pinball machine.

Shit, shit, shit.

Then, in one perfect, desperate second, she knew what she had to do. Somewhere in her never-plan-further-in-advance-than-one-day head, she'd known she'd have to do it all along.

Her fingers closed around her wallet, and she said a silent prayer. This was never going to work.

McKenzie made a show of pulling at the corner of her driver's license, channeling the same trouble she'd genuinely had extracting her debit card at the airport. With every tug, she let out a frustrated groan. She shook her head side to side. She was about to be caught. Would he just let her go, or would he call the police? *Shit.*

Real tears streamed down her cheeks.

Wesley Howard spoke in a soothing voice. "Don't worry about taking it out. I can look through the plastic."

McKenzie wiped her eyes with the back of her hand.

If this works, I swear I'll go to church every Sunday and never again think about poking out the eyes of the guy in the cubicle next door.

The sniffling hid her increased breathing rate. She pressed

her thumb firmly over the first part of her last name. Under the guise of wiping her nose once more, she chanced the quickest glance she could at the license to make sure the necessary portion was covered. As she looked down, though, all she saw was her thumb before feeling so conspicuous that she snapped her head up again.

She held the license, safely tucked underneath its plastic sheath, toward the bank manager. Sobs racked her frame, and her shoulders trembled.

Please leave it in my hand. Please leave it in my hand.

Through the blur, she saw Wesley Howard cast his eyes downward and immediately back to her. He patted her hand awkwardly. "Let me take you to your brother's box. Shall I?"

The arm holding her wallet jerked back as if he'd threatened to cut it off. She threw her wallet into her open purse and compensated for her sudden movement by "needing" another tissue. "Yes, please."

McKenzie walked in a haze through the hallway as Howard led her, following him into a windowless room. She stood motionless as he exited the room to retrieve "her brother's" box. When he returned, he set it on the table, turned his own key into the box, and stepped away. "No need to rush. I'll be right outside."

He pulled the door closed behind him. McKenzie turned to the table. There was a second lock underneath the one the bank manager had keyed. She dumped the little silver key out of the manila envelope and twisted it in the other keyhole. With a click, both locks were open. The lid moved freely when McKenzie lifted it.

Her mouth fell open at the sight that greeted her. "You've got to be fucking kidding me."

A gun lay in the box, wrapped in plastic and cushioned in cloth so it wouldn't jostle inside.

The fear that made McKenzie terrified to touch it was the same fear that urged her fingers toward it. Heart racing, she traced the top, not letting her hand anywhere near the trigger.

Damn it. She didn't even know how to check to see if it was loaded.

Her hand curled instinctively around the small pouch beside it. She removed the box within the pouch. Bullets.

She squeezed her eyes shut. She could call out to Howard, tell him what she'd found and that she had no idea it would be there. He'd probably call the authorities, but she could confess, say she'd had no idea what the SEAL had put her up to. Apologize.

But this was the story of a lifetime.

Pulse hammering, she shoved the box of bullets into her purse. She forced her hand to grasp the gun and dropped it in, as well. God, she had to pee.

Deep breaths, McKenzie. You have this.

Before she had a chance to change her mind, she jerked the door open and faced Howard. His forehead wrinkled as he seemed to be taking her current emotional temperature.

He didn't step away from her, but his torso leaned back ever so slightly as if he was bracing for her to faint or cry or attack. "All done?"

She nodded, biting back the urge to detail all of the things she'd "found" in the deposit box that didn't include a weapon. Hutchins had warned her of this one, the bastard.

Liars talk too much. Don't talk.

Howard walked her all the way to the door of the bank, where she thanked him and said goodbye. She practically ran the block to the car, half-expecting to be cornered by policemen at any second.

The cops didn't come, though. She wrenched the car door open. Hutchins didn't even look at her.

"You get it?" he asked.

They were already backing out of the parking spot. "Screw you," she replied.

"Can't, Mac. Have to drive right now. Did you get it?"

McKenzie felt her face heat up. She tapped her leg three times with her palm to force down the tirade that threatened to stream from her mouth.

"You're lucky I don't know how to use it," she shot back. "Where to now?"

"To get the bazooka, of course."

She flipped him the bird.

CHAPTER FOURTEEN

Day 3
Central Makran Mountain Range, Pakistan

IT WAS NEVER supposed to be like this.

Uhlig lay on the cold stone tile of the bathroom, his face pressed to the side of the toilet. This wasn't the way his life was meant to go.

Damn them.

He gripped the sides of the commode and dragged himself up over it again. His gut twisted and furled as he dry heaved. There was nothing left. All of the contents of his stomach had already been flushed.

The stench of vomit haunted his nostrils, but he was too weak to move. He collapsed again, his head clacking against the wall. Phone. Where was his phone?

The untraceable cell phone lay on the ground just inside the door. It must've fallen out of his pocket when he'd first come in. Hauling himself to his knees, Uhlig crawled toward it, finally making it near enough to close his fist around it.

He had to call, had to hear the voice to remind him. Sometimes, he needed to remember why he'd come to this place to work for this infamous man. His fingers found the speed dial button. He listened to the music playing on the other end.

Uhlig had returned to the house today to give an update on his search for Totah's allies. While he waited for Al-Musari, one of the young and heavily veiled servant women brought him tea. Her hands shook as she poured it, and the liquid splattered his forearm. She jumped back from him as though bracing for a strike. It was then that his leader entered the room and slapped the girl hard across the misshapen blob of fabric that would have been her face. She fell in a heap, and Al-Musari shoved her away from him with his foot.

They'd discussed the hit on Ikram Totah, who would have been running for the presidency in the democratic election in Afghanistan. Al-Musari seemed pleased, particularly with the excess damage to the American elite onboard the ship. That turned the topic to the reaction of the United States, and of course, to the recent string of events that had taken place there.

"I'm torn, Uhlig. As much as I feel like a pig rolling in shit to see those two cowards shot in the streets, to see a woman take up the office…" Al-Musari had puffed on his cigarette, blowing the smoke in fine waves out the corner of his mouth. "Know this, Uhlig. When you do what it is that I do, you know things. There are only five men alive who could pull off what was done in America this week. One is dead. Another retired after being driven insane by the death of his son. Of the three still active, one works mostly out of the Palestine area, feeding off of the religious conflict there. The second is an enemy."

Uhlig scooted to the edge of his chair. The girl on the floor stirred at his movement. "And the last?"

Al-Musari took another long drag and exhaled downward toward the girl. "American," he supplied, irritation licking at the tone of his voice.

"Hello?" came the greeting from the phone's other end, drawing Uhlig back to the present.

He sucked a deep, rattling breath. Memories flooded him. His chest clenched in pain. This was that moment between pulling the lynch pin on the grenade and throwing it. The moment of not turning back.

"Hello?" the voice said again, this time louder.

Another voice in the background, one Uhlig was sure he'd heard before even though he couldn't place it, said, "Who's that?"

Panicking, Uhlig ripped the phone from his ear and ended the call. He cradled his knees to him and rocked himself. "I'm sorry. I'm so sorry."

Another sob escaped him. He opened the phone again. He pressed the numbers, this time reading them from his own scrawl on a piece of paper. After the automated greeting from the main line, he gave the extension. As expected, the reporter picked up right away.

Uhlig closed his eyes. "I have information you may find useful."

CHAPTER FIFTEEN

Day 3: Afternoon (PST)
Los Angeles, California

AS THEY TURNED into the driveway of Cody Randolph's family's home, another car peeled away from the curb. Other than that, the driveway in front of the tidy bungalow was empty. Hutchins parked the SUV in the circular drive, and they hopped out.

"Where *is* everyone? This place should be swarming with reporters, news vans..."

The door flew open, and a wild-eyed woman with a shotgun stormed the porch. "I told you people this morning, get the *hell* off of my property. If you think I won't do it because it'll be the next big story, you might want to think again. I don't care what you think of me, my son, or my dog, but I'll be damned if you're going to disrupt this grieving family for one more—"

"Mrs. Randolph, it's me," Hutchins called, hands lifted.

"Noah!" Cody Randolph's mother squealed.

Noah?

The woman wrapped her arms around Hutchins. She squeezed him for a long minute until finally, she let go.

Mrs. Randolph left her hands on his shoulders. "Now, let me have a look at you," she said.

McKenzie noted that her eyes were streaked with red, her gray shirt wet with tear stains and the black smudges of mascara. Tell-tale signs of recent tears.

"You look tired, Noah. And what's all this?" She prodded at the stubble on his chin. "I think a piece of peach pie might be just

72

what you need." She dropped her fingertips from his face and grabbed his hand, not even sparing a glance for McKenzie.

Mrs. Randolph released Hutchins' hand as they crossed the threshold into the kitchen, a small red-painted room adorned with roosters of all sorts. Noah took it upon himself to sit at the table, and McKenzie followed his lead. Mrs. Randolph shoveled runny pie onto dishes. There were three plates. She must've noticed McKenzie's presence after all.

"Oh. This is my friend Mac, Mrs. Randolph," Hutchins said, apparently remembering his manners at last.

"McKenzie," McKenzie corrected, smiling and extending her hand.

"Nice to meet you, Mac," Mrs. Randolph replied, too busy with the pie to notice McKenzie's outstretched hand. "Ice cream with your pie, Noah?" She stopped short of the freezer and reached back to the counter for the remaining two plates.

McKenzie took her cue and remained quiet while they all ate. When Hutchins had cleaned the last morsel of crust from his plate, he set down his fork. The clang echoed, breaking the prickly silence.

"How are you holding up?" he asked.

Tears welled in her eyes, but Mrs. Randolph fought them back. "As well as can be expected, I s'pose. I don't really want to talk about it, Noah. It's just too hard. When you said you were coming, I thought I could do this, but having you here is tougher than I thought it would be. Can't even have a proper memorial for my own son. Everyone would just make it out to be a freak show. No idea when I'll get his ashes back, either. No one cares that *I'm* mourning. It's all about their investigation. Then there was the article in that New York paper by some awful reporter who wouldn't know truth in journalism if it bit her in the—"

"Could I have some more pie, Mrs. Randolph?" Hutchins asked.

"Of course," she replied.

As she turned her back to fetch more, Hutchins glared at McKenzie. She tightened her grip on her fork, and something flashed across Hutchins' face.

Was that a smile?

"Seeing you brings back so many memories," Mrs. Randolph said. She set Hutchins' plate back in front of him. "I don't think I can talk about him."

The quiet suffocated the conversation. Hutchins seemed to be focused only on the food. For all the skills the SEAL had, handling a grieving woman didn't look like one of them. McKenzie reached across the table and touched Mrs. Randolph's arm. "I know this is difficult for you, but it would be really helpful to us if you could talk about Cody."

McKenzie glowered at Hutchins.

Now would be a great time for you to say something, here.

He put down his fork. "I don't believe Cody did what they say, but someone sure wanted to make it look like he was a killer. I'm trying to figure this thing out, but I hadn't seen Cody in years." Hutchins paused, his eyes shadowed as if the wrong words might betray weakness. "I don't have a clue where to start to prove he didn't do this. Help me. Help *us*."

Mrs. Randolph used the hand that wasn't enfolded in McKenzie's to wipe away a falling tear. "He was a good boy," she sobbed, her chest heaving. "He couldn't have done this."

"I know," Hutchins said.

"To be honest, Noah," she said, composing herself, "I didn't know that much about him anymore, either. I didn't see him as much as I used to. He didn't really like to be around people." Her head twitched a little. "I mean, he seemed depressed sometimes, like he was holding double his own weight on his shoulders. When he came home from Afghanistan, he folded into himself like he thought we wouldn't understand what he'd seen. He was probably right." She wept into a napkin. "I should've tried harder."

"Afghanistan was rough for him. That doesn't mean he was a murderer," Hutchins replied.

"Oh, I know that, Noah. I know he didn't do those things. I'm only saying he pulled away from us. I guess he'd rather be alone than be around people he thought looked at him like he was crazy because of the PTSD." She stopped, leaning toward McKenzie as if confiding a shameful secret. "PTSD is Post Traumatic Stress Disorder."

McKenzie nodded and let Mrs. Randolph continue.

"Sometimes he'd have flashbacks, shake uncontrollably. Everyone worried, but our concern might've come across like we were afraid of him. I don't think he could bear the thought of us seeing him not in complete control." She sniffed, blowing her nose into the wrinkled paper towel again.

Noah gave her a moment to get her bearings, then asked, "So was there anyone he *was* turning to, hanging out with more when he came back? Any friends you can think of who might be able to tell us more about his life in the past few years?"

Her gaze grew vacant. Distant. As if she'd withdrawn into her own world. A world where her son was still an innocent child saying his first words or walking across a stage to accept his high school diploma. Had he confided to her the horrors he'd seen in Afghanistan? Did Mrs. Randolph, through her blurry tears, picture Cody as she looked at Noah?

"Mrs. Randolph?"

"He was always such a good boy. He made straight A's in school, you know. Never put a single toe out of line."

"I know, Mrs. Randolph," Hutchins said, patting her shoulder.

She continued to stare at her plate, her eyes glassing over. Her tears dribbled onto the table, the napkin forgotten.

"Was he hanging around with anyone?" Hutchins' voice jarred her back to reality.

She shook her head. The black marks of her running mascara streaked her cheeks and nose, but she made no effort to wipe them away. "No. Like I said, he mostly kept to himself. But..."

Hutchins sat up a little straighter. "But what, Mrs. Randolph?"

"Well, one day he came over to dinner and had to leave early because he was meeting some girl. I can't remember her name."

"Someone he was dating?" McKenzie asked.

"I couldn't be sure. He told me he was meeting her, but we didn't talk much about it other than that. Now that you mention it, though, the way he said the name sounded more like a co-worker or something. I think I'd remember if I'd had the feeling she was a romantic interest."

Hutchins nodded, but his gaze darted to McKenzie's for the briefest of seconds. "Any chance you can think of that name, Mrs. Randolph? It might be helpful."

McKenzie held her breath. If only they could catch a break.

"Oh, I don't know. I think it might've been Kim, or Kimberly something or other. Lawlins? No, that's not right. Landon? No, that's not it either." Cody's mother continued trying out names. After a few minutes, she snapped her fingers. "It's Lawson. Kimberly Lawson."

Hutchins squeezed his partner's mother's shoulder and stood. "Thanks, Mrs. Randolph."

She stood and pecked him on the cheek, shaking her head in weary silence. Both McKenzie and Hutchins thanked her again for her help and the pie as she showed them out.

Mrs. Randolph no sooner shut the door behind them than McKenzie had her cell phone out.

"Who are you calling?" Hutchins asked, heading to the SUV.

"Information, of course," McKenzie said. "I think we need to have a talk with Kimberly Lawson."

CHAPTER SIXTEEN

Day 3: Afternoon (PST)
Los Angeles, California

"YOU'RE SURE SHE works here?" Hutchins asked as they climbed out of the rental car. He slammed the door. The SUV groaned as if to remind him to be gentle.

"Yes, she works here," McKenzie replied. "Shall we?"

The two were outside one the main office buildings of GRM Studios, which towered over the street taller than the film giant's signature elephant. The SEAL tilted his head back, staring. "When exactly did you become the leader of this op?"

McKenzie's lips twisted into a smile. "Just trying to be helpful, *Noah*."

"Hmph," he grunted, walking toward the set of double doors. McKenzie followed him toward the front desk.

"What's Kim's position here? A secretary or something?" he mumbled.

"Guess again," McKenzie said. She smiled at the receptionist. "We're here to see Kimberly Lawson."

"Of course." The woman picked up the handset of her phone. "Have a seat. The vice president will be with you shortly."

"Vice president?" Hutchins repeated so that only McKenzie could hear him. They parked in a pair of chairs near a burbling fountain. He nodded with approval. "Not bad. How did we manage an appointment with the vice president of GRM ?"

"Yeah. Vice president. She's done all right for herself," McKenzie said. Geez. She sounded more like an old high school classmate than someone here to investigate Kimberly Lawson's connection to an assassin. Still, McKenzie couldn't help but admire the movie executive's achievements. Being the vice president of a studio like GRM was an enormous accomplishment McKenzie would kill to match.

It wasn't the money of such a high-end job that was attractive. To think of her work on the front page and read by thousands would be the most rewarding. Up until now, she'd covered the tiniest stories relegated to places in the newspaper most people never reached during their morning coffee. She imagined herself as an editor of the *Herald*, Morton Gaines having handed his job over to her when he decided to retire and go sun his overlarge body on a beach somewhere far away...

"Hey. Mac." Hutchins snapped his fingers in front of her. "One more time. How do we have this convenient appointment, again?"

McKenzie smiled. "I'm not the highest reporter on the totem pole, but I do have one or two connections."

She didn't tell Hutchins that her "connection" happened to be Pierce hacking into e-mails at GRM to find Kimberly Lawson's three o'clock appointment and changing the names. From there, all it took was one phone call to the office of the three o'clock—a Ms. Tessa Parker. Posing as a GRM administrative assistant, McKenzie had explained that she'd accidentally double-booked the appointment block. Was there any way Ms. Parker could reschedule?

"Ms. Lawson will see you now," the real receptionist's voice broke McKenzie's train of thought.

As the elevator doors slid closed, Hutchins paced around the tiny box. "Do we have any idea what we're doing here?" he asked.

"Not the slightest."

They stepped off the elevator at the third floor and followed the corridor to the end of the hall. At the dead-end a polished mahogany office door boasted a gold name plate. *Kimberly Lawson, Vice President.*

"It's open," came the answer following McKenzie's knock.

The woman flipping through a stack of papers at the desk

looked to be in her early thirties. Her golden blonde locks were pulled into a sleek ponytail, and glasses perched on her thin nose. She looked more like a cheerleader for the Dallas Cowboys than an executive.

She didn't even glance up. "What can I do for you?"

Hutchins spoke first. "I'm Fredericks. This is my associate, Kelly. We're investigating the death of Cody Randolph."

"You Feds or something?" she asked, still perusing a paper.

Regardless of whether or not she looked at them, McKenzie detected the slightest note of anxiety in the way Kimberly's breaths quickened, her chest rising and falling rhythmically. The SEAL might be great at interrogating prisoners, but putting this woman on her guard was the opposite of what they needed. "No. Cody Randolph was a friend of ours. We're trying to find out what happened in the days before he—" McKenzie bit off the words *killed the vice president* and corrected, "—before he died."

So far, she had no reason to believe Cody Randolph *hadn't* killed the vice president. All evidence pointed to it, but she was with Hutchins. It was prudent for her to act as if she was on his side.

"And what makes you think you should be talking to me?" Kimberly asked. Her eyes remained trained on her work.

"His mother said you two had become close in the days leading up to the incident," Hutchins said.

McKenzie fought to keep her glance from darting toward Hutchins. "Close" was more than an exaggeration of what Mrs. Randolph had imparted.

Kimberly let out a single huff before a smirk painted her face. "I wouldn't call it close. I met Cody Randolph at a bar a couple of months ago. We were both there to meet others. We were both stood up. He bought me a drink, and we enjoyed each other's company. We hung out a few times, but it was no big deal."

Kimberly's words, however, didn't match her demeanor. She flipped sheets from the stack to the desk as she spoke. Never once did she meet Hutchins' or McKenzie's eyes.

"Do you have any idea who Cody was meeting that night?" Hutchins asked, his voice slow and steady.

"Nope."

McKenzie swallowed the urge to accuse the woman of being deliberately unhelpful. "Do you know *anything* about that meeting?"

"Look, the FBI, the CIA, the Secret Service—whoever the hell is in charge of this investigation—hasn't shown up to question me. *They* don't seem to give a damn who Cody was meeting the night I met him, so why should you?"

McKenzie sputtered. It was a worthy question, after all. There were far more skilled—more important—people investigating Cody Randolph. What made her and Hutchins think they could do any better?

Hutchins was the one to answer. "Because he was my partner. To them, he's a murderer. To me, he was a brother. I need to know."

Kimberly pursed her lips, seeming to debate whether or not to tell them anything more. She finally looked up at them, assessed Hutchins. "I think he might've called her Chris. Other than that, I can't be sure. I don't know if she was a friend, more than a friend, a business associate, anything. I don't have a last name, so don't ask me."

Kimberly flipped through her papers with her thumb, set the pile on its end to neaten the stack before idly thumbing through it again. They'd better wrap this up, and fast.

"When was the last time you saw him?" McKenzie asked.

Kimberly sighed and laid her glasses on the desk. "A couple of days before the shooting."

Neither Hutchins nor McKenzie stopped her to ask which shooting she was talking about—the vice president's or Cody's.

"I met him at In–n–Out Burger for lunch. He called me earlier that day, said he needed someone to talk to. He sounded stressed to the max, and I wondered if he'd been having nightmares again."

Lines rippled on Kimberly's forehead, a single sign that

betrayed her otherwise youthful appearance. She must've been closer to Randolph than she admitted if he'd confided in her about his nightmares and PTSD. That wasn't something a SEAL told every stranger he happened upon.

"Did you love him?" McKenzie asked, regretting it the same instant. She shifted, uncomfortable on her feet. "I mean, were you involved romantically?"

For the first time, Kimberly's eyes found McKenzie's. "No," she said with a finality that asserted the interview had come to an end.

CHAPTER SEVENTEEN

"SHE'S HIDING SOMETHING," McKenzie said the second they left the office building.

Hutchins shook his head. "She could be overwhelmed that these random people—" he gestured from McKenzie to himself "—showed up asking so many questions. She's only just been connected to the biggest crime of the century. I told you, Mac. I can tell liars."

"I didn't say she was lying. I said she was *hiding* something. Did you see how she wouldn't even look at us? You may've interrogated the entire population of Guantanamo Bay, but I've interviewed a lot of people, too, Hutchins. It's always the ones telling half-truths that won't look you in the eye."

"Okay, Sherlock," Hutchins said as he threw his hands into the air. "What do you think it could be?"

"I don't know yet," McKenzie said. "Call it a gut feeling."

They'd reached the SUV. McKenzie climbed in and slammed the door as Hutchins turned the key in the ignition.

"Let me know when this gut feeling gives you some specifics. For now, we need to concentrate on profitable routes, like tracking down this Chris character."

"How do you plan to do that? We have a first name, and that might not even be her first name. Chris is probably short for Christine or Christina or Kristen. You act like my hunch is so terrible, but the name 'Chris' isn't a whole lot better. How do you intend to find this girl in the proverbial haystack of California?"

"I don't know," Hutchins said, his voice a low growl as he made a right hand turn a little too sharply. The SUV bounced over a curb. "You're the investigative journalist. Investigate."

Filthy comments threatened to spew from McKenzie's mouth. "Okay, okay," she said. Calm would beget calm. "Don't get us killed. There's enough of that already." The second the sentence tumbled from her lips, McKenzie wished she could pull it back.

Hutchins' face clouded as if he'd been slapped.

"I didn't mean to——"

"Don't worry about it."

They rode in silence until Hutchins spotted a motel on the left hand side of the road. He eased the SUV into a parking spot and shut off the engine. Without a word to McKenzie, he removed his bag from the back hatch and trudged toward the lobby doors.

Oh, well. I'll let him stew for a few minutes and try to apologize again later.

McKenzie hopped out of the SUV and dug her phone out of her purse. She flipped it open and pressed one on her speed dial. Pierce answered on the second ring.

"What can I do ya for?"

"I need some help," McKenzie whispered. Even though she was alone in the parking lot, it felt as if even saying the words aloud would alert Hutchins to her treachery.

"So what else is new?"

"Oh, shut up, Pierce. I need you to do some digging for me."

"Grave, gold, or otherwise?"

"Will you quit being such a wiseass? We talked to that Kimberly Lawson woman you set up the meeting with today. My instinct says there's more to her than she's letting on. Can you find some dirt?"

"I specialize in all things sordid," Pierce replied with confidence.

"Great," McKenzie said, her pulse climbing at the thought of having an ally. Pierce could find out in a few keystrokes what it would take McKenzie days to learn. "Call me as soon as you can," she said.

"Will do," Pierce replied, and she heard the phone click as he hung up.

Spirits lifted, McKenzie raised the hatch to remove her ugly pink suitcase from the back.

Thank God for progress. Now, to make things right with Hutchins.

CHAPTER EIGHTEEN

Day 3: Evening (EST)
The White House

NOT LONG AFTER her meeting with General Helms, Elaine was back en route to the Situation Room, her blood pumping through her veins like a marching band sounding the call before a home game. When she arrived, the usual players were already assembled around the table. Ronald Garrety stood near the head. She motioned for them to sit.

"Tell me the latest," she said to her National Security Advisor.

Garrety leaned forward. "A video about the terrorist explosion surfaced online. Al-Musari has claimed responsibility. He also claims he didn't know Americans were on board until after the fact, but as you can imagine, the presence of Americans turned a base hit into a grand slam for him."

Elaine glanced to one of the flat monitors on the wall where footage of the infamous terrorist's online diatribe was streaming on CNN. The man had been proven responsible for many attacks on people in the Middle East who promoted Western ideas—many of them involving women in politics. He was suspected of dozens more.

"I guess the big question is do we know his location?" Elaine said. Al-Musari was born in Syria, but he'd long since been in hiding. Reports of his whereabouts ranged from the Middle East to claims he was in Canada, the Caribbean, or even that he'd entered the U.S.

Garrety nodded. "Pakistan. He's holed up in the Central

Makran Range somewhere. Pakistan is noncommittal as far as supporting or denouncing his policies, but they've made clear they're providing him refuge. It's also worth noting that when President Wasem was only an aide to the last president, Al-Musari had an arrangement with Wasem that provided Al-Musari land to train insurgents—conveniently overlooked by the government—in exchange for money and backing during Wasem's presidential campaign."

"I see," Elaine replied. "Do we have a statement from Pakistan regarding the current incident?"

The National Security Advisor opened a folder in front of him and skimmed a sheet. "They've offered condolences for the loss of our citizens, but nothing further. When asked specifically about Al-Musari, his whereabouts, and the government's position on his public declaration of guilt, they did nothing but equivocate."

Elaine clicked her tongue. "Lack of answer is an answer."

General agreement buzzed around the table with the exception of her Chief of Staff. Bert Royal sat to her right, his arms crossed and his mouth shut.

She turned away from him. "What are our options?"

The Secretary of Defense outlined a plan for an air strike on a small military base in the mountain range where the terrorist was suspected to be hiding. Elaine looked back to Garrety for his reaction.

"It's a scaled response, appropriate, and low risk. Our fighters will be in and out before anyone knows they were there. I think it's our best tactical option."

Bert Royal stiffened next to her. "We're about to cause an international incident over a mistake," he mumbled.

Elaine shook her head. "A country is harboring a terrorist who just murdered fifty innocent Americans to get to one woman."

Bert squeezed his fists, then flattened his palms on his lap. "Ikram Totah has nothing to do with us."

A dry laugh escaped Elaine's lips. "You're right, Bert. Ikram

86

Totah doesn't have a damn thing to do with us. That's my point. They wanted Totah, and in the process didn't mind killing a few Americans, too. This time it's fifty people, but next time maybe it's a hundred or a thousand. We can't put a Band-Aid on it and hope it doesn't bleed out."

Bert folded his hands together on the table. Elaine supposed it was the best he could do in the middle of such an important meeting short of sitting on them.

Garrety spoke up. "Madame President?"

Elaine gave a curt nod. "Attack."

"Yes, Madame President."

CHAPTER NINETEEN

Day 3: Late Afternoon (PST)
Los Angeles, California

"HUTCHINS?" MCKENZIE TAPPED on the door with her knuckles as she walked into the motel room, dragging her suitcase behind her. Hutchins' luggage lay open on the lone bed atop a bedspread that could be considered the eighth deadly sin. The SEAL wasn't in sight.

A moment after McKenzie set her stuff down, Hutchins walked out of the bathroom. Naked except for the towel around his waist, his body was cut with the kind of hard lines of muscle McKenzie thought were reserved for men on the covers of romance novels. She inhaled the smell of the motel's cheap soap, but the droplets trickling from his brown hair onto his bare chest made the industrial bar soap smell almost luxurious. His chest was smooth, and she couldn't help but imagine the steel of his arms holding her to it.

He didn't acknowledge her as he dropped the towel and pulled on a pair of blue boxers. McKenzie looked away.

"You should at least warn a girl," she said, trying to act blasé. Sure, she might need to share a room with him for her own safety, but who would protect her from *him*?

Again, he said nothing.

"Fine," McKenzie said. She toted her plaid pajama bottoms and a t-shirt into the bathroom along with her toothbrush.

When she came out, the bed was empty. Hutchins was lying on his side on a spare blanket on the floor. She smiled a little. Despite the earlier towel incident, he was still a gentleman. Kind of.

McKenzie climbed between the stiff sheets. God, she hated motel rooms. Whether it was the stale air or the dim lighting, they never felt clean. She tried not to think about how many people had slept in the bed before her as she shifted to find a comfortable position.

How much worse it must be for Hutchins, on the unyielding floor, his nose inches from a carpet so grungy that only God knew the last time it had been steam cleaned. "You didn't have to sleep on the ground, you know," she whispered under her breath.

"At least it's not a two foot ledge," he replied.

It was true. The motel wasn't well-ventilated, but as far as she knew, they weren't in any immediate danger of falling off a cliff or being blown apart by rogue militants.

"I'm sorry I said what I did about not getting us killed. It was careless," she whispered. "I know it must be hard."

"You don't know anything about what's hard for me."

The statement stung, and McKenzie's stomach knotted. He was right.

McKenzie closed her eyes, imagining Hutchins running from a spray of bullets in a war zone. The harder she tried, the closer tears came. She envisioned the ugliest picture she could muster, and yet, as she looked down at Hutchins on the floor, even that image was hollow. She'd seen movies and television footage, but what it was really like to be in hostile territory, she had no clue.

"Tell me," she said, her voice choking with unshed tears. She meant it. For the first time, she wondered who Hutchins was.

Silence. "Hutchins...I really want to know."

Hutchins was quiet for so long McKenzie thought he wouldn't answer.

"Enough with the 'Hutchins' stuff. My name is Noah."

"Noah," she whispered.

He nodded. Then, he sucked in a breath. "The night we were attacked by the militia group," he said, "I got shaken awake by gunshots exploding everywhere around me. It sounded like the Fourth of July. I'd been sleeping next to a buddy. He had a hole in his stomach the size of my fist. It didn't stop him. I watched him squeeze off rounds at the people firing at us. He was dying, dammit, and he still kept firing. He never stopped trying to give us a chance."

Noah paused, lost in a place he couldn't escape.

McKenzie gripped the covers tighter to her neck. She'd complained about so many things in her life, but she'd never seen anything like what he described. Painful guilt clamped around her stomach. She clenched her eyes tight, but a tear squeezed through.

"Someone threw a hand grenade, and then one teammate's arm was lying right next to another SEAL's body. This guy—this *friend*— had been shot in the head, and all I could think about was how I was a groomsman at his wedding. I gave a toast and told him what a lucky bastard he was for tying down such a fabulous girl. Not so lucky, I guess. The guy who lost his arm wasn't crawling around looking for it. He was using the arm that hadn't been blown to kingdom come to tie a tourniquet around his partner's leg. It wasn't any use, though. Bone splintered out of the guy's thigh. He was losing so much blood. Pretty soon, his eyes rolled back into his head. His partner screamed at him to come back. To not fucking die on him."

Stop. Please, stop.

McKenzie blinked away tears. God, she wanted to jump out of the bed to hug him. Hold him.

"We fought as best we could. Cody and I were the only ones who hadn't been shot. Not even a scratch between us. Our team kept yelling at us to get the hell out of there. To save ourselves. We fell back to regroup. We thought we could run in and pull them out one at a time. We made it to the beach and out of the range of fire and were about to cop a plan to help our team. That's when the whole freaking camp exploded, and we knew we were alone."

McKenzie's throat constricted. It was as if she'd swallowed a tennis ball and her voice couldn't fit past it.

"My turn to ask questions," Noah said. "Why did you really

come with me? I know you don't think Cody's innocent."

"I don't know how to answer that," she said.

"How about honestly."

McKenzie closed her eyes again, ashamed to utter something so petty. "There's this girl in my office. Jessie. You know the type. Tall, blonde. Aggressive. As long as I can remember, we've competed for stories. No matter what I do, she's one step ahead of me. She's the one who somehow found out there was a former SEAL involved, although she didn't have a name. I still don't know how she did it. When you came to my office, I thought this was my chance to scoop her." She paused, afraid to finish. She swallowed hard. "You know, the inside story on the SEAL who killed the vice president."

"He was my best friend."

McKenzie climbed out of the bed and sat on the floor next to him. She curled her toes ever so slightly under the pillow cushioning his head. He really believed this man couldn't have killed anyone.

Noah stared at the ceiling. "You still think he did it, don't you?"

"I don't know what I believe," McKenzie said. Regardless of the evidence, Noah had walked in hell with Cody when neither had known whether they'd be alive the next minute or not. When you're always two inches away from death, it only made sense to tell the person next to you your heart. After all, if you didn't, you might never have the chance to tell anyone.

Against her better judgment, McKenzie reached out and let her fingertips brush the stubble on his chin with her palm. "We'll make sure everyone knows he was a good man."

Noah stared up at her. She caught her own reflection in his icy blue eyes. The rush of affection for this man she barely knew took her off guard. Flames rose inside her. She leaned toward the pillow, her pulse thundering.

The sound of her cell phone skittering across the nightstand shattered the moment. She instinctively leapt off the floor and snatched it up.

Colby Marshall

"Impeccable timing," Noah groaned.

"Sorry."

McKenzie clambered into the bathroom, shut the door, and collapsed against it. She flipped her phone open, noting Pierce's cell number in the call window. "Hit me with it," she said, not even offering a hello.

"Well, you were right. Something's off about this Kimberly Lawson broad," Pierce said.

McKenzie could picture Pierce's smirk on the other end of the line. "Well?"

"Call me Santa Claus, doll. She may be an exec, but she has a past. You won't believe your ears."

"Look, Pierce. I'm exhausted, jet-lagged, and need about four hours of sleep before I can properly deal with B.S. again. You're wonderful, perfect, brilliant, and every other compliment your already over-inflated ego needs to hear. Can we cut to the chase?"

"Some people are so touchy," he said. "Okay. Kimberly Lawson not only belongs to a radical feminist group, the Redstockings, but she's also affiliated with their uber secret underling society known as the Shen. The history of the Redstockings is an open file. Your primo women's lib movement took root in the seventies but still has members today. You've probably heard of some of 'em. Does the name Margaret Thatcher ring a bell? History books are full of 'em. They were the original Ya Ya Sisterhood, if you will."

Pierce paused. McKenzie thought she heard him crunch a bite of something in between his teeth. "The Shen are a whole different story. Their past is murky at best. Technically, no one has ever proved they *exist*. There've been rumors over the years of a more extreme group of Redstockings prone to severe measures. Get this—investigations into the existence of the Shen have usually occurred surrounding *bombings* and *murders*."

McKenzie yanked a loose thread from her pajama pants. "And Kimberly Lawson is involved somehow?" she whispered.

"Well, like I said, there's no proof of the organization.

92

Everything they do, they cover well enough that it can't be linked back to them. But Kimberly Lawson's name came up in an investigation into some threats made to the California governor a few years back. A bill came to his desk that would restrict abortion rights. The bill passed through the California legislature, but the governor didn't sign it, despite the fact that he'd publicly *backed* the bill. Word trickled through the pipes that he'd been bought or bribed, and there was a quiet inquiry. Nothing came of it, but there's a record."

"Interesting," McKenzie breathed. "Still, it's a huge jump from threats to the governor to a presidential—"

"Another thing," Pierce said. McKenzie could tell he'd saved this last bit of information on purpose. "My sources say Kimberly Lawson has a private bank account in the Cayman Islands under the alias Rianne Darwin. A bank account that became millions of dollars poorer the week of the assassinations."

"What?" McKenzie clapped her hand over her mouth as she remembered Noah in the next room. Then in a whisper, she said, "And how do you know this?"

Pierce chuckled. "You did say I was brilliant before, right?" He laughed again. "Once I had the alias, it wasn't difficult. I am the king of computer hacking, after all. Piece of delicious red velvet cake."

McKenzie shook her head as she shifted her weight side to side, the equivalent of pacing in the motel bathroom. Hacking into Kimberly Lawson's bank accounts had to have been more trouble than Pierce was making it out to be. She didn't even want to think about how he'd obtained the alias. She'd take it. "I'll buy you a piece of that cake the next time I see you. In fact, I'll make the cake from scratch. You're awesome."

The door swung open, and McKenzie's hand wrenched forward as the phone was snatched out of it. Noah jabbed the end call button.

"What the hell?" she yelled, her cheeks heating.

He tossed the phone toward her, which by some miracle, she caught. "Keep your calls with your boyfriend short."

McKenzie raised her eyebrows. "Jealous?"

Noah turned his back on her. "Tired."

"You just hung up on my friend because you want to sleep? Right, Noah. Right. You know, you should control your damn temper."

Noah whirled to face her, grabbing her wrist. She clenched her hand tighter around the phone. "If I'd lost my temper, believe me, you'd know it by now." He dropped her arm. "They make phones with GPS, now, Mac. Write it down."

"Mine's too ancient for that," she huffed under her breath. She swept past him and climbed back in between the sheets, clutching the phone to her underneath the covers. She pressed the side button and peeked under the sheet at the open face that still registered Pierce's call. In only nine minutes and five seconds, her world had turned from upside down to just plain crazy.

And terrifying.

If Pierce was right, this story could rocket her into journalistic history. A violent ultra-feminist group, a huge amount of money paid from an offshore bank account, and the president and vice president shot *simultaneously*. The puzzle pieces eased closer together.

She gripped the phone tighter. What was the one glass ceiling the women's lib movement had yet to crack?

The president and vice president may have been assassinated to achieve one unattainable goal: to catapult the Speaker of the House—who happened to be a woman—into the Presidency of the United States.

CHAPTER TWENTY

Day 3: Evening (EST)
Washington, D.C.

THE MAN STRODE through the airport, another tourist or entrepreneur hurrying to catch his flight. His fellow passengers would never guess they'd just brushed shoulders with the man who killed the president.

Not until he'd eased through security did he breathe a sigh of relief. Guys in his line of work—talented guys—had been nabbed on stupid mistakes as tiny as a pocket knife in their carry-on bags.

Then again, he was better than all of them. He was the best.

After boarding the London bound plane, he settled in with a magazine to try to relax. His cell vibrated.

"Yeah," he answered. There was no name on the screen. Nothing to screw him up if the phone fell into the wrong hands. He recognized the number, one he knew by heart.

The urgent words on the other end made him swear. The woman beside him gasped, indignant. He slung his backpack over his shoulder and shoved past her, knocking her book from her lap into the aisle.

"Excuse you," she murmured.

Stupid bitch. You don't know how lucky you are I'm leaving this plane right now.

He elbowed past people storing their luggage in the overhead bins who lingered in the aisle as they argued over who got the window seat. When he reached the door of the plane, the flight attendant gave him a questioning look.

"I think I left my cell phone at the gate," he lied.

"We're closing up soon," she replied. "Better make it fast."

"You bet."

He sped through the terminal, annoyed. Twenty extra seconds standing on the moving sidewalk to swap out wallets, then he hugged the left side of the walkway moving past the slowpokes. He hung a right toward the ticket counter.

"I need your next flight to Los Angeles."

Damn. He'd just flown *in* from there, and now he was on his way back out.

"Yes, sir," she said. "I can have you out of here in the next hour."

"Fantastic." He tucked his boarding pass away and found a coffee shop. After ordering a black coffee with two shots of espresso, he sat back at a table with a magazine.

Noah Hutchins, you always were a pain in my ass.

The scalding liquid left his lips numb, his tongue seared with a bitterness to match his frustration at the image of Hutchins yelling in his face. He'd take good care of him, all right.

That, and Kimberly Lawson needed to be paid a visit.

Screw all. He hated needing other people. It was why he'd despised working in the military. Even on ops requiring the fewest people and the most headshots, they typically assigned him a spotter. The second man was a liability, because you couldn't predict his movements a hundred percent. If shit went down, the spotter was dead weight.

Unfortunately, Lucas couldn't do everything himself. He'd have to seek outside help whether he wanted to or not.

He picked up his phone and made the call to the man known as The Crocodile. He knew The Crocodile very well, but The Crocodile would never know he was the one calling.

In other words, The Crocodile was very much like him.

"I need a task completed," his garbled voice said through the distorter.

"Do you have a price point?" The Crocodile didn't ask who was calling to arrange the hit or the reasons for wanting someone dead. In fact, the word "kill" never even entered the conversation.

Of course, Lucas knew it wouldn't. After all, The Crocodile also dealt in death. The money was all that mattered.

He gave a name and an amount. They haggled for a moment, but the deal didn't take long. With the tap a few buttons on his laptop, Lucas watched dollars drain from his account into the one indicated by the assassin he'd hired. In a world where executions went by the million, this particular job had cost him a diminutive amount. And worth every cent. Damned reporters always sticking their pretty little noses in other people's business. This one wouldn't be asking any more stupid questions. Bye, bye, Miss Marple.

Now, the only chore left was to remove the complication of Noah Hutchins. Where the SEAL was concerned, Lucas trusted no one but himself to complete the job.

CHAPTER TWENTY ONE

Day 4: Early Morning (PST)
Los Angeles, CA

THE SUN WASN'T up yet, but Noah's body was hardwired to wake up at the same time every morning. No way around it. The girl was still asleep, soft mews drifting from her every few minutes in addition to the puffs of her breathing through parted lips. The covers hugged the curve of her ass perfectly, her body's form outlined by the thin bedspread.

Noah swallowed hard. The luxury of these moments to stare without inhibition would've been a lot more delicious if he wasn't such a damned awful human being for bringing her.

Having Mac around had been convenient at the bank. Few people were callous enough to interrogate a grieving sister too closely. Who'd suspect her of retrieving a gun? And she'd proved to be more useful than he'd originally thought. He'd never have been able to track down Kimberly Lawson on his own. However, the next stage of the operation was the one to which she was vital.

Too bad she didn't know it yet.

And now, things were so damn complicated. They'd almost fucking kissed last night. This was why they didn't let women in the SEALs. Too damn distracting.

Still, no need to clue her in just yet on the real reasons he was being such a cooperative little boy scout. Telling her she'd be a handy diversion to throw under the bus if he was being tailed probably wasn't the best way to keep her on board.

Christ in a party dress. This'll be interesting.

* * *

When McKenzie woke up, for a split-second she was able to pretend it was all a dream: the trip, the fight...the moment they'd almost kissed. Then, the bathroom door opened.

"Morning," Noah said with his toothbrush sticking out the corner of his mouth. He was already dressed in jeans and a brown pullover, but the chiseled form of his biceps showed even in a sweater.

"Morning," McKenzie answered.

Do not stare. You will not stare.

She started to push back the covers, then grabbed them tightly. Last night she'd tossed and turned, battling the blankets. She wasn't used to sleeping in clothes and had realized she'd never fall asleep unless she shed her pajama pants. And her underwear. She'd been sure she'd have plenty of time to retrieve them before Noah woke.

Without being too conspicuous, she leaned over to trail her fingers to frisk the floor for the panties.

"Looking for these?" Noah asked, smirking. He hooked her satin purple underwear on his pinkie finger and plucked them from the zipper of his suitcase.

McKenzie snatched them out of his hand. "Thanks," she mumbled.

Noah turned his back to give her some privacy as she pulled the underwear on under the covers.

"So, I think our first order of business today should be looking for this Chris chick," he said.

McKenzie shrugged. "It's a nice thought, but we know nothing about her aside from that she was meeting Cody at a bar one night. Any ideas how we go about locating her?"

"We're going to Cody's hotel room."

"What?"

"I have a hunch. We'll leave it at that," Noah replied. "You act like I told you we're about to storm the Pentagon."

"You might as well have. It's a crime scene. The FBI is

investigating the killing of the leader of the free world. I doubt they're shirking security."

"I think you're underestimating the company you're keeping." Noah's chin lifted, the smirk on his lips widening. "The FBI is good, but the SEALs are better."

Day 4: Morning (PST)
Los Angeles, CA

Noah parked the rental SUV a block away from the Five Points Hotel where Cody Randolph had been found dead.

McKenzie's legs pumped double time to keep up Noah's pace. On Noah's suggestion, she'd worn her tightest t-shirt and jeans along with her high heeled boots. Attractive, but not made for keeping up with Noah's long stride. At least she got a good view of the way his jeans molded his butt with every step.

They made a sharp curve around the building toward the main entrance. This would never work.

"Any last minute advice?" she asked.

"Don't get arrested."

"Gee."

They entered the main high-rise building. So far, so good.

"Remember, meet on the sixteenth floor. Luck," Noah said.

McKenzie branched off toward the elevators, Noah the other direction. The doors slid open just as she watched him duck into a stairwell. Somehow, it seemed too easy to head toward the floor where a suspected assassin was killed. Then again, short of closing the place down entirely, there was no way to make the elevators skip a level.

Either way, she had no idea what to expect when she reached that floor. Noah was convinced it would be virtually empty by now, but in her head, it was crawling with FBI, local police, CSI, and every other law enforcement official imaginable. After all, the floor had been cleared of other occupants following the shooting.

But it *had* been a few days. Like Noah said, surely the worthy evidence had been bagged, tagged, and whisked away for analysis.

A girl could hope.

The elevator climbed, and McKenzie's heart thumped harder with every floor the digital counter registered.

Game face.

The doors opened on the fourth floor to reveal a relatively empty hallway, save for a uniformed cop outside what she assumed was Cody Randolph's hotel room door.

Only one.

Of the few scenarios they'd talked about, one clicked into place.

Here goes nothing.

The cop approached the elevator as the doors opened. "This floor's off limits, ma'am. You'll need to turn around—"

Deep breaths.

"Oh, gosh. I'm so embarrassed. I thought I was at seven."

The cop punched the down button on the elevator but smiled. "No harm, no foul. Have a nice day."

The doors slid back open, and McKenzie took a step into the elevator.

Now, before you lose your nerve.

With all the acting chops she had, she crumpled to the floor. God willing, it was convincing enough. She lay still, trying not to breathe.

"Ma'am? Ma'am."

Footsteps. The cop kneeling beside her, taking her pulse.

She fluttered her eyelashes. "What...happened?"

The elevator doors closed.

Bingo.

"Oh, shit," the cop said. He jumped up and jabbed at the button, but they were already on their way down. Resigned to his fate, he turned back to her. "You okay, Miss?"

She blinked some more, pushed herself to her elbows. "Oh, gees. I'm so sorry. Second embarrassing moment of the day."

"Is there someone I can call for you?"

Sucker.

"Oh, no thank you. I didn't have enough lunch today,

apparently."

"Diabetic?"

"Pregnant."

The cop twitched uncomfortably. As she and Noah had decided, "female problems" were the least likely to draw suspicion and more questions.

"Oh. Well, um, congratulations," he muttered.

The doors opened again, and he extended a hand to her to help her off the floor. She obliged, clambering to her feet. "Thanks. I'm so sorry."

Hold him a few more seconds.

"Don't mention it," he replied, his words fast and clipped. He put his hands under her elbows to steady her as she stood like a wobbly baby deer, the slightest, hesitant pressure on her to move forward out of the elevator.

McKenzie took tiny steps toward the door, teetered from side to side a little. As they exited, the cop stopped right past the elevator door, caught between his desire to get back to his post and his fear of dropping a pregnant woman on her ass. Then, he steered her toward the benches in the lobby.

"Thank you for your help. God, I'm so, so sorry."

He eased her onto a bench. "Do me a favor and call your...husband? Boyfriend?" He sputtered a moment, then said, "You in town alone? I should get someone to help you to your room—"

"Oh, no need. I'm fine. Just need a minute to catch my breath."

And I don't need you to know I don't have a room.

"If you're sure."

No, I'm not, but...

"Yes. Thank you. I'm so sorry. I feel like such a klutz."

"All right then," he answered, staring at her like she might explode at any minute. He backed away a few steps, watching intently. When she didn't spontaneously combust, he turned and headed back toward the elevator.

Come on, Noah.

* * *

Noah used his feet like suction cups, alternating them one at the time against the metal inside the trash chute to inch his way up. He'd started on the floor beneath the one where Cody had been found. Easier to go up than down, right?

Yeah, right.

Nothing to grip, his palms pressed flat against the walls at his sides. Each push propelled him only a miniscule amount, but eventually, the opening was in sight.

Using only a pinky, he tested the chute door. No noise, thank Jesus' white pedigreed poodle.

A little more, slow and steady. Jerking movements caused squeaks. Smooth was key.

The alcove the trash chute opened into was identical to the one he'd entered on the floor below. Ice and vending machines, conveniently hidden from the main hall. His only worry would be if someone happened to be walking by, but today, fate was on his side.

With one final push, he snaked out of the chute head first.

Tuck and roll.

His skull thumped as he rolled onto the tile, but all in all, a fine dismount. In another second he was on his feet.

Noah pulled his cell from his pocket. Might not be good for much without a battery, but it had a black screen with a glare. He held it steady in front of him to check the hallway behind. No one.

His footsteps fell heel to toe, his mind fogging at the edges yet perfectly focused at the same time. While waiting for Mac to distract the guard, he'd thought about that quiet that would overtake him as soon as he started moving. It was a quiet SEALs all learned. Guys could look at pictures of their families before leaving for an op, then blank them from their thoughts while they dodged gunfire. It was the only way to snap an infidel's neck and come home to your girlfriend for dinner.

Now, he moved through the hotel suite. Not much time.

Come on, Cody. Give me something.

The place had been dusted, most everything bagged and tagged or removed.

The occasional thump on the ceiling kept him abreast of hotel guests above him, but all was silent on this floor. The bed had been stripped, the pillows strewn across the bare mattress. *Damn.*

Noah crept to the closet and cracked it. On the top shelf were extra pillows, their cases still intact. He pulled down the first one, checked. Nothing. The same with the second. *Damn.*

A quick check of the bathroom revealed nothing hidden in the toilet tank. He stepped carefully, trying to ignore the dried brown crust smeared on the floor that was his best friend's blood. The chest of drawers back in the bedroom was mostly empty. Nightstand standard. Phone, book about the hotel. No Bible. Interesting.

He moved to the far corner of the room, the only spot where he could take in the entire space with nothing at his back, no blind spots. Desk, chair, television.

So, this is what you saw, you sonofabitch. What did you do?

Noah took a fleeting look at the window, noted the tiniest crack between the industrial curtain and the wall. The pull shade fell to about an inch above the carpet.

Next to Noah's right foot, the carpet indented.

Chair.

Cody would've seen this room exactly this way. He'd do anything he did in here at the place where his back would be only to a wall. If this indentation was what Noah thought, he'd done it in that chair.

And yet, the chair sat in front of the desk. Same as in any other hotel room.

Maybe the Feds moved it, but why would they change a crime scene? Rookie mistake? Could be. But probably not.

Cody wouldn't have moved it. He was as trained as Noah and a hundred times more paranoid. Call it gut, but Noah knew it.

Noah cased the room again.

Something. Anything.

Then, there it was. A folded card on the nightstand with instructions for guests to leave towels on the floor if they wished for them to be washed. Newspapers had specifically said no one had serviced the room the day of Cody's death, but investigators who didn't know Cody might not notice the neat alignment of the chair in front of the desk, as if it had never been used by Cody.

You can't believe everything you read.

Noah slipped out of the room and into the stairwell without event. McKenzie had apparently done the job. He took the stairs two at a time toward the sixteenth floor.

"Even if someone went in, how do we know who? Wouldn't the FBI have seen it on security footage?" McKenzie asked.

McKenzie climbed the stairs behind Noah, puffing to keep up. He was already on the flight above her.

Next time, I'm asking for a head start.

"You think they monitor every single hall of a hotel?" Noah replied.

"Okay, let's assume they don't, and this mysterious cleaning person exists. The one who started to straighten up the room but then stopped. Cops would've noticed the missing sheets. Did they assume the killer took them away for some reason?" McKenzie paused for a quick breath before resuming the climb. "How do you suggest we find this person? Why wouldn't they have come forward?"

"You'd think. But they didn't. Trust me on this. Wouldn't be hard to find out who it was. All you'd have to do would be follow around a member of the housekeeping staff a few minutes, wait for them to go in a room, then hit up the utility closet while they're out of sight. You check the chart for staff assignments, and boom! We've nabbed our housekeeper."

Sounded easy enough. "All right. So, your plan is to start at the top and make our way down?"

Noah jerked his head. "Nope, the nineteenth and Palma are my plan. She cleaned that day."

"You already found her," McKenzie said through heavy breaths.

"You sound surprised."

"Try skeptical."

"We'll see."

They reached the nineteenth, and Noah held the door. McKenzie cut under his arm. A quick glance down the hall showed no sign of any housekeeper, Palma or otherwise. They forked to the right toward the next set of rooms.

A cleaning cart stood in the hallway, the whir of a vacuum humming nearby. McKenzie cocked her head toward room 1915.

They'd agreed she'd approach first. A lone female was definitely less scary for another female.

McKenzie tapped her knuckles on the door but pushed the ajar door open and entered before a response. Inside, a dark young woman maneuvered an old, bagged vacuum across the carpet. She straightened when she saw McKenzie, clicked off the vacuum.

"Help you, ma'am?"

"Are you Palma?"

The woman nodded, but she pulled the vacuum closer like a security blanket.

"Palma, I need to ask you a few questions."

Palma's knuckles whitened around the vacuum's handle. "I told policeman everything I know."

The broken English rang with fear. Timid or lying?

In McKenzie's interview experience, when someone had something to hide, they brought it up before you asked question number one. This had to have been on Palma's mind.

She thinks I'm a cop.

No interview experience was required to know someone like Palma probably grew up around a lot of people who didn't trust cops. In big cities like L.A. and New York, unless you were from certain neighborhoods predominantly occupied by the white upper class, you didn't.

I never did.

"Palma, I'm not with the police. I'm…" The words "a reporter" died on her lips. "I'm trying to help a friend who knew the man killed here."

Palma's eyes rounded, big as saucers. "No, no, no. Please not bad people…"

McKenzie held up her hands and shook her head hard. "No, nothing like that. Palma, I know you told the police you walked in, saw the body, and screamed, but we know you were cleaning in there."

The Latina shook her head. She looked over McKenzie's shoulder, face wild. "I tell you I not know anything. I tell you I told all I know."

The door behind McKenzie clicked shut. Noah.

"Palma, we're not here to hurt you, but we know you went into that room. I'm not planning to tell a soul about you or anything you did in there, but I have to know what else you saw in there. What you might've seen. Trash you took out, laundry. Anything," Noah said, his voice steady.

Both of Palma's hands wrung the vacuum handle, her face contorted into a grimace. "I not know anything else."

The whine—so high-pitched, so wavering—said she knew a *lot* more.

"Palma, trust me. I have nothing to gain by turning you in to the police—"

"But we *will* tip them off if you don't talk to us, and fast," Noah cut in.

McKenzie glared at him, but his focus remained on the housekeeper. Palma let the vacuum handle thud to the floor as she backed away from them. Her knees buckled, and she collapsed onto the bed, head in her hands.

"I leave work early that day. Baby sick. I not here. No one know."

"You weren't *here*?" McKenzie repeated.

Palma shook her head, still not looking at either of them. "No. I say I was, but only before I know what all trouble I am in no matter what I say. I have no time off to take for baby. None. I leave, I no get pay. Can't tell I leave. Get fired."

"If you were gone, Palma, how did your work get done?"

The turnaround time in hotels for room-cleaning was steep, and from what Noah said, Palma had several floors assigned to her that day. No way no one noticed she was gone.

"Please, promise me you not tell anyone. I no want...we in so much trouble..." Palma sniffed, wiped her nose on her shirt sleeve.

"We aren't out to get anyone in trouble, Palma. We need information. That's all. I swear, I won't breathe your name to anyone else."

"Or anyone else's name," Noah added. "Anyone else who might be involved."

At this, Palma glanced up, mascara dripping down her cheeks. The tears dribbled down her nose and chin onto her blue cotton uniform.

"My cousin Rita. She clean, too. She cover for me that day."

Rita shook harder than a twig in a torrent when she arrived at the room. Palma had called her up, and she'd come. Though Palma had spoken in Spanish, McKenzie knew enough to know she'd told her cousin not to bring anyone with her.

Rita stood next to Palma, her stockier frame firm in its grounding. She placed a hand on Palma's shoulder, and Palma sobbed louder.

"Rita, you went in the room where the man was shot, didn't you?"

Although she quaked like a Parkinson's patient, unlike the sobbing Palma, Rita's face was stone. She glanced at Palma, who buried her head in her hands and cried harder.

"I did."

"Rita, what did you do in that room?" Noah asked.

She shook her head back and forth. "I not know he was dead when I go in. Swear to it."

"We believe you," McKenzie whispered.

"Tell us what you did in the room," Noah repeated.

Rita looked at her feet, then back at them. "I take off sheets, pillowcases. Empty trash bin in main room. Then, I see. I see what happen." She shuddered.

Hotel rooms weren't the cleanest places on earth. Fibers or hair found from Rita could've been from any day she'd cleaned. The FBI had probably found one or two from every person on staff in the hotel. They'd have thought nothing of it after interviewing Rita and Palma, who both—at least openly—had no reason to lie.

"What did you do with the trash? The bedding?"

Rita closed her eyes, and her chest rose and fell sharply a few times. She opened them again. "I take them away. I think if I put in laundry, trashcan, someone will find them. Know I was in room. I couldn't put them back on bed. Not with the man on the floor. I no need to be in trouble, just like cousin. If I am involved in this, my husband, he—" A visible tremble ran over her body. "He have to go away."

Illegal immigration in the family. Perfect reason for a cousin you covered for to cover for you.

"Where'd you take them?" Noah said, his voice coaxing.

Rita stared back at him, one part defiant, another part sizing him up.

Please don't have thrown them away. We'll never find anything.

"Where, Rita?" Noah demanded again.

She squared her shoulders. "I took to another room and hid them while I wait for Palma to come back and say she is one who finds the man on the floor." She shrugged. "Police think killer takes things. No one ever ask about them. Until you."

Rita's key opened the door to a room on the second floor unoccupied for days due to a nasty plumbing problem. She led him and McKenzie to the closet.

On the top shelf sat the "fresh" set of sheets, extra pillows in cases.

I'll be damned.

Noah reached for the pillows instinctively. He'd looked for

them in Cody's room out of habit, though he'd known they'd have been checked by the FBI and picked clean if they had anything in them. But here, he was almost sure of his hunch.

He unrolled the pillow case and retrieved what he knew he'd find there. His adrenaline mostly drowned McKenzie's gasp.

Jackpot.

He yanked the second pillow from the top of the closet. Its case was rolled at the edge, too. He unfurled it, this time unsure what he'd find. An item dropped into his hand.

Holy God with ringside seats at Madison Square Garden. What the...

If there was anything he'd expected to find in Cody's possession, it wouldn't have been this.

"We need to leave," he said. "Now."

As soon as the vehicle was in sight, Noah spoke fast.

"In, in, in."

He jumped into the driver's seat in front of McKenzie, revved the engine. She sprinted to the SUV, gut taking over. Her door was only partly open when the SUV jammed into gear. She hefted her frame inside and slammed the door.

The tires screeched as Noah peeled away from the curb.

"What's wrong?" McKenzie asked, her heart pounding.

"Somebody's following us."

CHAPTER TWENTY TWO

MᴄKᴇɴᴢɪᴇ FUMBLED FOR her seatbelt as the car lurched underneath her. Noah ignored the stop sign and made a hard, solid right. McKenzie mumbled vague pleas under her breath to whatever deity might be listening.

The SUV sped along the street. Noah's gaze shifted back and forth between the rearview mirror and the side mirrors. "I don't see him anywhere."

As soon as he spoke, a black sedan pulled out from behind another car a few yards back, its tires screaming as it nearly rammed their bumper.

"Holy shit!" Noah said, slamming his foot onto the accelerator.

McKenzie could only glimpse flashes of passing cars as Noah weaved in and out of traffic. Horns blared, and drivers flipped them off as they passed. Noah could challenge the most talented NASCAR driver, but the sedan matched them lane change for lane change. In seconds, it clung to their bumper again.

"Hang on," Noah said, his voice steady as ever. He jerked the steering wheel hard to the right, spiraling the SUV into an alley.

McKenzie braced as the SUV tilted onto its left. Her body banged into the console, her seatbelt cutting into her lap. She gripped the overhead handle with sweaty palms and uttered a continuous stream of curse words.

"Did we lose them?" she asked.

Before Noah had a chance to answer the question, the sedan jarred them again.

"Mac, see if you can tell what he looks like." Noah floored the gas. There was no traffic to dodge. The alley was a straight shot.

McKenzie glanced back at the driver, but all she saw was a rainstorm of glass as the rear window of the SUV shattered. "Shit!" she screamed, ducking. "They're shooting—"

A stab of pain ran through her neck as Noah grabbed the back of her head and shoved it toward the console. She wheezed, shifting underneath his grip to suck a breath of air.

"Stay calm," he muttered.

She wasn't sure if he was talking to her or to himself.

Through the one eye not pressed into the console she saw the gunshot blast straight through the jagged glass that used to be the rear window. She couldn't see where it went, but from the clatter above her, she knew it had blown apart the front windshield.

Noah sank lower in the driver's seat, his eyes riveted on the road. He hunched over to make himself the smallest possible target for the spray of bullets. Slivers of glass fell around his face like snow, some sticking to his cheeks and arms.

McKenzie winced as a bullet zinged past her left ear. It slammed the dashboard and sent broken plastic over the front seat. Her ears rang with the sound. Every time she took a breath, a single thought sped through her head: *Is this my last one?*

The gunfire stopped, and Noah's grasp eased. McKenzie risked a peek up, a scared turtle peeking out of its shell. The alleyway opened up ahead, where it spilled into a divided highway. Cars sped both ways in a blur.

McKenzie squealed Noah's name in warning.

"It's either the traffic or the shooter. I pick the traffic," he bellowed as the SUV neared the entrance to the roadway. The sedan screeched to a halt. The driver must've seen the impending onslaught as well.

McKenzie closed her eyes just before they shot into oncoming traffic, but she couldn't stop herself from peering between her fingers. They narrowly missed a semi rumbling from their left. The SUV's front tires crashed into the divider, but their speed carried them up and over the concrete separator. McKenzie's body bounced out of the seat. Her head rammed the roof. She grappled for the hand hold over the passenger door while she watched cars collide in an effort to miss them.

Noah fought the steering wheel as the SUV careened toward the guard rail, the only thing standing between them and a ten foot drop. He pulled the SUV level with the rail. The piercing scrape of the hubcaps against the metal caused every muscle in McKenzie's body to clench.

Noah gunned the engine to keep a beat-up pickup truck from hitting them in the rear. Police cars wailed in the distance, but Noah didn't deign to pull over.

"You okay?" he asked.

McKenzie swallowed and nodded. "What are we going to do?"

"Well, we're not stopping to give them our insurance information, if that's what you mean," he said, shaking his head. "Being fugitives from a hit and run is the least of our worries."

"Why'd he stop?" McKenzie wondered out loud.

Noah shook his head again. "Fear of commitment?"

They rode for a few minutes catching their breath before McKenzie remembered the incident prior to the car chase.

Crazy how a little gunfire interrupts your train of thought.

"So, you didn't explain the stuff in the pillowcases," she said. At Noah's silence, she blew out a frustrated breath. "I just got *shot at* with you, Noah. I think I've earned the right to know what we got out of it."

Noah's jaw set in a tight line. He reached into his pocket and produced a small square memo book, the kind with the black and white marble design on the outside. Its corners were ragged, the cover faded.

"And that is?" McKenzie asked.

"Cody kept one of these all the time, even when we were behind enemy lines. Some guys look at pictures of their families. Cody wrote stuff." Noah grunted, though his face lifted with something like pride. "I'm probably the only person who'd know to look for it."

McKenzie stared at him. When he didn't continue, she

gestured her hand in a motion that said, "Please continue."

"He always kept it rolled up into the corner of his pillowcase on the base or on a carrier. I figured he did the same around here. Lucky guess, I suppose."

McKenzie smiled.

"Don't get too excited. Could be another dead end."

"Have you looked at it at all?"

"You've been with me the whole time, Mac. I haven't exactly had a lot of spare moments," he replied.

McKenzie eyed the notebook. Whatever was in that book may or may not lead them to someone who may or may not connect Cody to the assassination. McKenzie hadn't had the heart yet to tell Noah what Pierce told her about Kimberly Lawson's connection to the Shen. Cody just *happening* to be an ex-sniper who just *happened* to have a tie to Lawson would be the coincidence of a lifetime. Never mind that Kimberly Lawson had an offshore bank account with disappearing chunks of money.

"You said you got your first lead on Cody from your uncle the cop, right? You know, I don't think it's a bad idea to talk to him again," he said. "Even if we can find a lead on Chris, she might not be linked to this whole mess. She could've stood him up at the bar that night because their first date was as much fun as Amish porn," Noah said.

That, or Kimberly Lawson made Chris up entirely to throw us off the scent.

"I'll give him a call," McKenzie replied.

She whipped out her phone and dialed her uncle's cell.

He wasted no time with pleasantries. "McKenzie, I thought I told you to leave me out of this."

"Uncle Sal, I know I shouldn't ask you for anything else, but this guy—" she glanced sideways at Noah, who tried to pretend he wasn't listening, "—he says he knows his partner wouldn't have done this." McKenzie took a long pause, mustering the courage to spit out her next words.

Desperate times.

"You of all people should know what it's like to have a

brother-in-arms like that."

Uncle Sal didn't answer, but McKenzie knew he was picturing his own partner, who'd been killed during a drug bust five years earlier. Afterward, there'd been an inquiry into the circumstances leading up to the shooting. Some said Uncle Sal's partner was involved in the drug ring and had been getting kickbacks for turning a blind eye when he arrived first at the scene of drug-related crimes. Her uncle had stood firm and told anyone who'd listen that his partner wouldn't have had anything to do with something so heinous.

"Please," she said.

After a long moment of silence, Uncle Sal spoke. "You can come by in the morning, but I can't promise you anything."

"Thanks, Uncle Sal," she said. "I owe you."

"More than you know," he said, and he hung up.

"Subtle," Noah commented as she flipped her phone shut.

McKenzie rolled her neck in a slow circle. "Yeah, well, some matters call for the practiced hand of a professional."

The corner of Noah's mouth turned up ever so slightly, then his lips settled back into a rigid line.

"Is it a rule that you can't smile?" she asked.

His jaw twitched again. "More like raw talent."

"All right then," she said. He didn't have to be friendly if he didn't want to be. That was fine by her. This was nothing but a story.

She shifted away from him. Her gaze drifted out the window toward the buildings flitting past. A solid lead on Chris was a must, but she also wanted to talk to Kimberly Lawson again.

Only this time, she was going alone.

CHAPTER TWENTY THREE

Day 4: Evening (EST)
Washington, D.C.

"THANK YOU ALL for coming."

Despite sweating like a marathon runner in mid-July, the steady, clear ring of her own voice surprised Elaine. The reporters sat forward, pens poised, and the clicks of camera shutters tapped around her.

"Ladies and gentlemen, this morning our fighters attacked a small military base in the mountains of central Pakistan. While the need for military action is regrettable in any situation, we must not let such deliberate acts of violence as the bombing of the *Laramie* go unchecked. This includes decrying any and all who support those who seek to harm the United States and its citizens."

A murmur rippled through the room. Through the din Elaine caught the phrase, "diplomatic resolution." She cleared her throat.

"Today, fifty families mourn the loss of someone they loved. It's a sad day for us as a nation to know that fifty families no longer have a mother or a son, a grandparent or a fiancé." She turned her face in the direction from where she'd heard the words. "As far as diplomatic efforts prior to the weapons strike, I must make it clear that while we will make it the utmost priority to find and bring to justice the terrorists responsible for the attack, those who would harbor our enemies have thus declared themselves our foes. Be it man or country, those who have had any part in this vicious act will be held accountable. I would also like to assure the American people that while the crisis overseas is weighing heavily on our hearts, we are continuing to search for answers here at home in regard to the ongoing investigation into the deaths of President Seymour and Vice President Tifton."

Before she had a chance to return to her prepared speech, another voice from the crowd called over all the others.

"Isn't it true that a knife wound suggests suspected assassin Cody Randolph's murderer is also connected to the United States Navy SEALs?"

Elaine's attention darted to the voice in the second row. The blonde reporter from the *Herald*, the same girl who'd known Randolph was a SEAL.

"As you well know, I cannot—and *will not*—comment on the specifics of an ongoing investigation. Suffice it to say we are pursuing any and all profitable routes of inquiry. I thank you all for your time."

"Madame President, I apologize," Press Secretary Orellana whispered, falling in stride with Elaine as she stepped away from the podium. "We should've had you better prepped—"

"No, you should've made for damn sure that girl wasn't allowed in the Press Room again. Who is this little tart, and where is she finding her information?" Elaine snapped.

"Jessie Cartwright," Orellana stammered, "from the *Herald*. I have no idea how she slipped through the cracks. She wasn't supposed to be on the list—"

"Well, she obviously *was*. Find out which aide didn't make the right phone call and make sure he's relegated to dusting the desks of people who can actually do their jobs. Then, see that *someone* takes her name off that list. I shouldn't have to deal with this every single time I'm behind that podium. After that, figure out where the hell she's digging up everything she knows. There's clearly a leak on some level, *somewhere*, besides the moron who forgot to remove her name from the Press Corps. He isn't high up enough to know the shit that reporter does."

Elaine's chest clenched. On second thought, Andrea Orellana was probably the last person she should ask to track down information on Jessie Cartwright. This twit had already dropped the ball more than once where Jessie Cartwright was concerned, first by not prepping Elaine for questions and now letting the reporter come within a mile of the latest press conference. "Then again," she said, "maybe we *should* ask that aide. If good news travels this fast, he can probably tell us where to find both the president's assassin *and* Al-Musari."

With that, Elaine hurried off to her next appointment, leaving the stunned press secretary to stare at her back.

CHAPTER TWENTY FOUR

Day 4: Evening (PST)
Los Angeles, California

AFTER AN HOUR of driving around, Noah pulled the SUV into a driveway in a nice little neighborhood in Bel Air. The brick split-level was set back from the street, shielded by a pair of trees in the front yard. He eased into the garage and hopped out.

"Do we know them?" McKenzie ventured.

"We do now."

He removed something small and black from his pocket. It was about the size of a lighter, but when he flipped it open, it looked more like a Swiss Army Knife.

"What's that?"

"Leatherman," he replied. He flicked a skinny file with a hooked end from the center and inserted it into the bolt lock of the door.

"You trained to pick locks in the SEALs, too?"

The lock clicked, and Noah withdrew the file. "Tenth grade, my best friend's parents' lake house, actually. But yeah, sometimes even SEALs need to go in soft."

McKenzie tiptoed behind Noah through the front door. They seemed to be in the kitchen, though she couldn't be sure in the dark. "What if they come home?"

"Won't."

"How the hell do you know that?"

"I called Ms. Chloe earlier," he replied. Then, at her indignant huff, Noah said, "Newspapers. Either this house is recycling for the whole neighborhood, or they're on an extended vacation."

The lights flipped on. McKenzie squinted as her eyes adjusted. She stood next to a tall, skinny breakfast table for two, a vase with a single fake rose in the middle. On the refrigerator were crayon drawings of stick figures and sunshines, a clip bearing receipts, and a magnetic calendar. From the look of the picture in a frame on the counter, the couple appeared to be in their early thirties. Two red headed toddlers in matching polka-dotted jumpers sat in either of their laps.

"Happy little home," Noah said. He plucked open the refrigerator door and grabbed a jug of orange juice from the bottom shelf.

"Noah!"

"What? You think they're going to measure out the ounces of juice to make sure the refrigerator contents are intact?" He unscrewed the cap and chugged a few gulps.

When she didn't answer, he held the jug out to her. "Thirsty?"

She stared at him incredulously. Had he lost every bit of his sanity? Did the shootout make him forget reality?

He raised his eyebrows. "Fine by me."

The jug went back into the refrigerator. Noah turned his back to McKenzie and wandered through the hallway as if he'd lived in the home for years. "You want the top bunk or bottom?"

Heat crept up her neck and spine as she followed him. These people could come home at any second. What could she say then? Maybe she could manage to explain being in a bank with a gun from a safety deposit box or being in an assassin's hotel based on her job, but even her healthy imagination wouldn't be able to talk her way out of this one.

She rounded the corner to find Noah collapsed on the king-sized bed, his face buried in one of the pillows.

"If we get caught…"

"Relax," he said, tossing a throw pillow at her. "They'll never know we were here."

McKenzie's cheeks heated, her anger bubbling. "What

exactly happened to Mr. I-Have-A-Plan-Need-To-Know-Basis?"

Noah grinned. "I traded him in for Mr. Doesn't-Give-a-Fuck-Does-What-He-Wants."

"Are you drunk?"

The SEAL rolled lazily on the satin comforter. "They keep strong OJ in this house."

The bases of her palms pressed into her eyes, her fingers tangling into her hair. This was not happening. Someone so in control couldn't snap that easily. "We can't stay here," she moaned.

"Sure we can. It's cozy, and they have nice sheets." He swung his legs off the edge of the bed. "I bet they even buy the expensive bubble bath. None of that two ninety-nine shit at the supermarket. I'm gonna go take a shower and check."

"Noah! You can't just use their stuff!" she called after him. Shit. She couldn't be the voice of reason to a guy more than twice her size who was trained to kill people. If he'd gone crazy, what was to say he wasn't about to snap and kill *her?*

"It's a shower, Mac. I'm not re-wallpapering," he said in the doorway of the bathroom. His hands pushed against the doorframe, making him seem even larger.

McKenzie drew herself up to full height and stood only a few inches from him. "What is wrong with you?" she yelled. Her eyes brimmed with angry tears.

Noah bent forward through the doorframe, his nose inches away from McKenzie's face. His eyes had suddenly clouded over; whatever had been rushing through him moments before sucked out as if she'd pulled the plug on a drain.

His face hovered in front of her. They were both so silent that for a moment, McKenzie could feel their chests rise and fall almost in tandem. She closed her eyes and breathed him in, leaning in, inviting. God, her lips wanted to taste his.

They didn't. Instead, his lips brushed her eyelids as he said, "There's nothing wrong with me. Now get out, unless you want to come in here with me."

CHAPTER TWENTY FIVE

Day 4
Central Makran Mountain Range, Pakistan

IN THE DIM room, people gathered around the table. Al-Musari sat at the head, hands clasped in front of him. "We have had success," he proclaimed. "But do not become complacent just because we have managed to rid ourselves of Totah. Rest assured, there are plenty left who will stand up to take her place. We must continue to cut away one evil head at a time."

Angry agreements were muttered amongst the assembled men. Uhlig swallowed the lump in his throat. This was not the place for him to speak his heart.

"That said," Al-Musari continued, "Our next step is to find Lima Olmstead."

Uhlig's head snapped to attention, as did several others. The man seated to his right spoke up, "Isn't she—"

"Yes," Al-Musari confirmed.

The ball bounced across the hot August pavement. Uhlig chased after it. He could hear his brother on his heels, feet scuffling to get there first.

His mother stopped it with her toe, then reached down and scooped it up. She looked up from the book she'd been reading, a ray of late afternoon sun glinting on her shiny black hair. "Whose turn is it?"

Both had answered at once. "Mine."

She laughed, and her hand not holding the ball fingered her necklace. "Okay, then. Who deserves it?"

Robbie, however, had been distracted by her hand. "What's that, Mama?" he asked as he reached out to touch the necklace.

Uhlig had rolled his eyes. Here they went again. Robbie was still young enough that the story was new to him every time, but Uhlig had heard it plenty.

His mother's patience with it hadn't worn, though. She unclasped the gold chain and held it out for Robbie to admire. "Ancient people didn't have letters and words the same as ours," she explained. "In Egypt, they used this symbol because it's a circle. Go ahead, Robbie. Show me where the circle ends."

She watched as Robbie traced along the gold shape with his finger. Uhlig groaned. "You're being really stupid, Robbie—"

"Shh," his mother hissed. "Let him find it for himself."

After a long couple of minutes, Robbie looked up from the symbol and into his mother's face. "It doesn't have an end."

She smiled the same smile she had back when Uhlig used to ask about the symbol. "Very good. It doesn't."

"So what's it for?"

"Maybe Fabian will tell you," she said, looking to him.

Up until now, Fabian Uhlig had wanted nothing to do with talking about that symbol. But now, his mother waited expectantly. He had to. This was something he could do.

"The Egyptians used pictures called hieroglyphs instead of letters like we have," he said. The drawings on the walls filled his mind. "They also had different gods than we do. One of the goddesses was called Mu. The symbol they used for her was a vulture. Mu's vulture symbol was on the crowns of all the queens. Even Cleopatra."

"That circle don't look like a bird," Robbie said slowly. He looked at it again as if trying to decide. He shook his head. "Not a bird."

"Doesn't look like a bird, Robbie. And, no, it's not a bird. But a lot of times in those hieroglyphs, the bird was drawn carrying this symbol. It doesn't have a beginning or an end, so it symbolizes eternity. It's called a shen, which means 'encircle.' Its meaning is why it ended up on the crowns, too. It hovered over the heads of the queens, giving them eternal protection," their mother replied.

Robbie stared at the roped gold, thoughtful. "Does it protect you, too, Mama?"

She sighed, her eyes not on Robbie, but on Uhlig. "I hope so, baby. I hope so."

Now, Al-Musari tapped a long bony finger on the table. "Lima Olmstead is a problem that I daresay will not go away. No, she's not in the public eye. Nevertheless, she knows too many people, has too many contacts, too much money. Her children can better spend that money buying an ornate casket."

Uhlig expressed his concurrence along with the others, though his stomach rebelled against him. It was the same angst that washed over him any time a job of this sort was mentioned. Every new opportunity brought more and more frustration. He was beginning to realize, of course, it might never end.

"We will use Xavier."

Night had fallen, but the air had not cooled. It pressed in too close, making it hard to sleep. The knock on the door and the raised voices of his mother's visitors had drawn him from his bed.

Uhlig crouched at the top of the stairs just behind the wall where he couldn't be seen. He could crawl to the bedroom, try to alert the neighbors. These men weren't friends. He knew it because they'd been here before.

One of the men was lumpy like his grandfather's bowling bag, and the other was the size of most other men Uhlig had seen. Granted, there hadn't been many men around. His father had left when Robbie was a baby. Uhlig could hardly remember what he looked like anymore.

The exchange below heated. His mother shook her head furiously and pointed to the door. The garbled voice of one of the men argued. His mother stepped forward and slapped her palm into her other hand to emphasize whatever point she was making.

Suddenly, the larger man reared back. Uhlig heard a sickening crack as the back of his hand connected to his mother's cheek. He sucked a hard breath through his nose. She'd told him to never cry out. Never let them know he was here.

The lumpy man dragged his mother to her feet and leveled his face with hers. The words were too soft for Uhlig to make them out, but as the man continued to talk, his mother kept shaking her head, blood leaking down her face.

"Call them off! I know you are the contact!" the man bellowed.

His mother stared at him, a wild look in her eyes. "I won't."

Uhlig heard stirring behind him. He didn't think. He grabbed Robbie and pinned him to the ground, hand over his mouth. His lips found Robbie's ear. "Quiet. We're playing a game with Mama. She said she'd make us both ice cream sundaes if we could be so quiet she couldn't tell we were here."

He never looked at his brother, though. Uhlig's gaze was transfixed on the scene in the den below. The lumpy man nodded to the other. "So be it," he said.

In one horrifying motion, the second man stepped behind his mother and shoved a plastic bag over her head. Uhlig held tight to his brother's mouth as he watched his mother's nostrils suck the plastic to her face. She clawed at the bag for what seemed like forever until finally, her limbs went slack.

He pressed his lips to Robbie's ear again, the lie quick and easy off his tongue. "It's okay, Robbie. Mama is only playing a game."

Uhlig raised his hand, almost child-like. "I would like to volunteer for this task, Your Eminence. To assist in the elimination of the problem Lima Olmstead presents."

Al-Musari nodded his approval, but Uhlig expected no different. He'd worked hard over the years, building this reputation. This was his specialty.

"Very well, Uhlig. Go to Xavier. Tell him what we need."

CHAPTER TWENTY SIX

Day 4: Evening (PST)
Los Angeles, California

MCKENZIE CRACKED THE bathroom door. Shampoo-scented clouds of steam rolled out. Would the owners of the temporarily-purloined bungalow notice a few stray brown hairs against the gleaming white tub?

"Son of a bitch," Noah muttered, shaking his head. "Why are you doing this?"

He stood in front of the bathroom counter with only a towel around his waist. He grabbed the hand towel from the bar and roughed his head.

Funny. She'd almost grown accustomed to seeing him half-naked every other day. Almost.

McKenzie pushed the door open a little further. "Are you okay?"

"Yeah."

When he'd filled her in on his plan before breaking into Cody Randolph's hotel room, he'd looked like a mischievous little boy. Just a stealth-trained soldier having a little fun out of retirement. Now he looked worn, a t-shirt thrown into the wash one too many times.

McKenzie reached out and traced a stripe down his arm with her hand, the line she was crossing. He closed his heavy eyelids.

"Talk to me," she said. Christ, she made it sound as if he confided in her regularly. What had he become to her? Could this even be called friendship?

I only came to leech a story out of you.

"It's nothing," he said. "The gunfire. It just reminded me."

His words trailed off. He squeezed his eyes tighter as if forcing the memory away. He didn't have to say any more.

"Is there anything I can do?" she asked, though she knew the answer.

His eyes found hers in the foggy bathroom mirror. "You shouldn't be here."

"I know." She stared into the mirror at the drops of water still glistening on his chest. "I know I only came because of the story—"

"That's not what I meant." He pushed her hand away from him. "I know why you came. You have no idea why I let you."

"What?" McKenzie stepped back, injured.

Noah hung his head and shook it like a dog. "Nothing. Never mind."

He looked so sad, tired.

To hell with it.

Holy jump-roping Jesus. Before he could stop her, she pressed her palms against his chest, leaned forward, and kissed him. Hard. There was no preventing his arms from wrapping around the small of her back and drawing her in to devour her mouth. He couldn't help himself. God, her body felt so small against his. Round, soft, and so damned female. He drew in a deep, appreciative breath, reveling in the scent that was uniquely Mac.

He drank hungrily from her lips. She squirmed under the strength of his grip, her head tilted up to him, wanting more. He dipped his tongue into her mouth, found hers. Sweet. Wet. His body hummed in response, immediately hard and heavy. *Goddamn.*

Her back arched underneath his palm. He let go of her, took a step back, and raised his hands as if he'd been caught pilfering something forbidden. His breaths were shallow, ragged, his length stiff under the towel. "Walk away, Mac."

She stood rooted to the spot, stung. "What if I don't want to?"

"You do. Walk away."

Fists curled into balls. Back straight. Attack posture.

"Don't," he commanded.

The argument inside her seemed to deflate. "I won't," she said. She turned and left the bathroom.

He collapsed against the wall for support, her scent still swirling in the air around him. He beat his head twice against the wall.

Control. Control is vital. You fucking idiot.

When he entered the bedroom, she lay between the sheets. Her auburn hair spilled over the pillow underneath her, her stare glued to the forty-two inch TV mounted on the wall. How could a woman look so sexy in a ratty t-shirt?

"You won't believe this," she mumbled without looking at him.

The words of the newscasters had already caught his attention. They were discussing a news conference earlier in the day when the new president had explained ordering an attack on a Pakistani air base.

"Retaliation for a bombing," Mac said, filling in the parts he'd missed. "One that killed Ikram Totah. And forty-seven Americans. And others."

If only there were a prescribed number of assassinations allowed per year. God. If only the blankets didn't mold to her body like that. He grabbed the other pillow from beside her. He could keep an eye on her from the living room. "Gonna sleep on the couch."

Finally, her head wrenched toward him. "Don't you want to know what happened?"

"Sure," he replied. "Let me know when you find out."

McKenzie watched from the bedroom until she saw Noah's breathing even out. *Don't think about his abs or the strength of his biceps holding you or how his tongue darted into your mouth. Kiss or no kiss, you have things to do. Oh, and his ass. Don't think about his ass.*

She grabbed her clothes and dressed, cringing at the rustle her shirt made sliding over her head, the swish of the zipper on her jeans. The keys to the SUV would be nearly impossible to retrieve without waking him. Besides, she wasn't sure how to get where she needed to go. Her sense of direction was about as stellar as Morton Gaines' knowledge of health foods.

She closed herself in the bathroom and dialed information. They connected her to a cab company.

"Address?"

Damn it.

She'd seen mail on the kitchen table. "Um, hold on a minute."

The phone clinked against the counter as she set it down, but she couldn't worry about that so much as what would happen if she took it with her. The guy on the other line might yell, or her phone could make some bizarre beeping noise while she crept past Noah.

She tiptoed across the living room, retrieved last month's power bill from the kitchen table, and returned without him stirring at all. Safely back inside the bathroom, she read the street address to the cab operator. "I'll wait outside. Don't honk."

Twenty minutes later, McKenzie climbed into the cab and shut the door behind her. "202 Dover Court."

"Beverly Hills, isn't it?" the driver asked.

"Yep."

Headlights flashed briefly in the cab's rearview mirror as they pulled away from the curb. Someone heading out for the late shift at work or an after hours party, maybe. Grateful the cabbie wasn't the talkative kind, she settled back in the seat and mentally lined up her questions.

This time, she'd get answers from Kimberly Lawson no matter what.

CHAPTER TWENTY SEVEN

Day 4: Late Night (PST)
Los Angeles, California

THE LIGHTS WERE off in the two adjoining townhomes. No cars were in either of their driveways. McKenzie walked up to the middle door, knocked twice, and stepped back. She expected to hear footfalls, but nothing happened. Funny. There *was* a car in this driveway.

She knocked again, this time harder. Maybe Kimberly was in the shower. She *could* be asleep, despite the lights peeking through the blinds upstairs.

McKenzie leaned forward, trying to see movement through the window in the door. Maybe Kimberly stood in the shadows, waiting for her to go away. Maybe she was the kind who didn't open her door to someone knocking in the middle of the night. McKenzie put her hands on either side of the pane and stood on her toes to peer in closer. To her surprise, the pressure of her hands pushed the door open.

The hair on McKenzie's neck stood at attention. In the middle of Beverly Hills, a woman living alone wouldn't leave her door *unlocked*, much less open a crack. McKenzie stepped into the townhouse and listened, halfway expecting to hear the low buzz of a television or the spray of a running shower. Nothing.

She rounded a corner. In the small kitchen, a pan of baked lasagna lay uncovered on the counter. McKenzie backed away into the living room across the hall. This room was dark, too, a TV tray with a dirty plate sitting next to a can of diet Coke.

McKenzie's palms beaded with sweat. She rubbed them

against her pants in a vain attempt to dry them.

It's okay, McKenzie. No reason to get upset. It's only an empty house.

Why hadn't she brought Noah? What kind of moron with a former SEAL at her disposal would go out alone in the middle of the night while trying to find out who assassinated the *president?* She should be committed.

McKenzie imagined the smell of her own fear wafting around her in circles as she came to a staircase.

I don't even have a weapon. I should've looked for a fireplace poker or something.

She shook the thought from her head and ignored her gut telling her not to go up. Instead, she began her ascent, her fists clenched so tight on the railing she lost the feeling in her fingers.

The door of the room on the right stood open. The edge of a double bed jutted from the wall. She took a deep breath.

I'm going to be okay. Everything will be all right.

That mantra continued on replay in her mind as she walked into the room.

Blood rushed to her racing heart, making her lightheaded. Kimberly Lawson lay on the carpet underneath the window, her body crumpled in a heap like a deflated blow-up doll.

So much blood pooled around the blonde movie executive that McKenzie couldn't tell where it was coming from. Not that it mattered. She couldn't look away from Kimberly's wide-open eyes. The girl's countenance was frozen toward some terror McKenzie couldn't see. Her stare rooted McKenzie where she stood.

If I don't move, this won't be real.

Thoughts kaleidoscoped as the blood returned in a rush to McKenzie's brain. What if the killer was still inside the townhouse? Her eyes darted around the room. She backed toward the door, afraid to turn around lest the killer jump from his hiding spot in the bathroom or under the bed.

Her feet backpedaled faster. She spotted the edge of the doorframe from the corner of her eye just before she rammed into something.

Solid. Tall.

Breathing.

She whirled around and swung her knee upward toward what she hoped was an unprotected groin. A steady palm met her leg, forcing it back toward the ground.

"Whoa, now," Noah said.

McKenzie's panic melted like snow in July. She threw her arms around him, shaking. "Holy shit," she said, gulping air, her heart still pounding. "You scared me to death."

Immediately, she regretted her choice of words.

He hugged her to his chest. "Shh. It's okay."

She tensed in his arms. "Wait. What are you doing here?"

Just like that, relief turned back into terror. What *was* he doing here? It was just him, her, and a dead girl in the room, and McKenzie knew *she* hadn't killed Kimberly Lawson.

"Calm down," he said, backing away a few inches as if to show her he wasn't threatening. "You didn't actually think you could leave the house without me knowing, did you? I told you, Mac. I'm trained in SpecWar skills. We've already established you have the stealth of a rhinoceros. You never had a chance. After today's excitement I couldn't be too careful, so I followed you. Guess I was right."

For the first time, he turned from McKenzie to Kimberly's body. Noah knelt next to the woman. He touched nothing, but he studied the corpse with x-ray precision.

"I'll be right back," McKenzie said, backing out the door. While Noah did whatever he was doing, McKenzie could search the house for anything that might answer her questions. Plus, if she had to look at the dead woman another second, chances were good she'd end up leaving a pile of "evidence" in the middle of the floor. Her stomach couldn't be trusted.

"Don't touch anything," Noah warned.

Wandering down the hall, McKenzie scanned the open rooms until she found a small space to the right that looked like an office. Desk, computer, armchair. She reached for the top desk drawer but recoiled. *Don't touch anything.*

She glanced around for something to use to open the drawer. Every minute was precious. In the next two seconds, she'd peeled her shirt off, wrapped it around the wrought iron handle, and pulled open the drawer. A few envelopes, pens, loose stationary. Nothing of importance.

The computer was the most obvious answer. Oh, God. She really shouldn't. She *really* shouldn't.

But she had to.

Hurry, McKenzie.

She opened two more desk drawers before she finally found what she needed. She sat down in the desk chair, stuck the flash drive into the USB port, and opened Kimberly Lawson's documents, grateful there was no password. If she was connected to the Shen—and the assassinations—something on here might prove it.

The computer contained so many documents and files she had no idea which to copy to the flash drive. Surely someone involved in a secret, no-one-even-knows-it-exists organization wouldn't just save files pertaining to said association without encrypting them. Where the hell was Pierce when she needed him?

Then, her heart skipped a beat.

Oh, please be what I think this is.

Her hands dove underneath the desk. She removed the tray where the keyboard sat, pulling it completely off the tracks, and rested it on the floor.

Pierce's desk had a panel underneath the desk top he called his "trap door." It was where he kept things he wanted no one to know about, like his collection of 1950's pin-up calendars. Identical to a regular desk top at first glance, on closer inspection, one could tell there was something a bit off about the way it sat a hair too close to the knees, the depth underneath not quite matching the size of the board in the front.

If McKenzie wasn't mistaken, she'd seen that same slight difference in Kimberly's desk. She squatted on the floor and peeked under the desk. Sure enough, there was a square panel that looked like it had been cut into the desk top, a thin slice of board settled underneath it. She used the t-shirt to pry up the corner. Then a second corner.

Yes!

She slid out the piece of plywood. She could've cried at the sight that met her. There, wedged into the false panel, was an external hard drive.

Once she'd hastily put the pieces of the hidden space back in place—and put her shirt back on—McKenzie returned to the bedroom with the hard drive tucked in her coat pocket.

Noah was still examining the body.

"Do we call the police?" McKenzie asked.

"I'm already suspected in the assassination of the president," Noah said. "Somehow adding this murder scene to my resume doesn't seem conducive to clearing Cody's name. *Or* mine."

"You've been using a fake name," she reminded him.

"Even better. Add fraud to the list."

McKenzie nodded. "So what do we do?"

"The first thing we do is get the hell out of here."

CHAPTER TWENTY EIGHT

AS SOON AS they were safely in the SUV, McKenzie looked to Noah. "Do you have a plan?"

Noah glanced at her out of the corner of his eye. He pulled away from the curb. "First, we get out of here and pray none of the neighbors were taking Fido for a late night stroll. We have no excuse for being outside a murdered woman's house. Then, we'll call in an anonymous tip. After that, I have to figure out what to do next with what I know."

McKenzie felt her eyes go wide. "What do you know?"

"First, why don't you tell me why you snuck out in the dead of night to go see Kimberly Lawson?"

McKenzie looked at her toes, twisted her hands in her lap. She should've told him all along, but she'd hoped she wouldn't have to. When had she started feeling the need to protect him?

"I found out something about her," McKenzie said, licking her lips as she tried to figure out the best way to word it. "I had my friend Pierce do some checking into her."

"And?"

"Kimberly Lawson is tied to an underground ultra-feminist group called the Shen," she replied. "*Was* tied, I mean."

"Never heard of it," Noah said.

"Most people haven't," McKenzie said. "There's another feminist group called the Redstockings that isn't a big secret. I'd never heard of them either until I started researching Kimberly Lawson, but they've been around since the seventies. The Shen are a more secret group within the Redstockings. The official Redstockings don't admit the Shen exist. Hell, some of the Redstockings may not *know* they exist. The Shen are a little more serious about accomplishing goals, if you know what I mean."

"Okay. Bra burners. Stocking burners. Shen. What the hell does this—does *Kimberly Lawson*—have to do with Cody and the assassinations?"

How to say this without getting his defenses up?

"Kimberly Lawson was suspected as being a negotiator of sorts for the group, I think. Anyway, Pierce found out about an offshore bank account of hers in the Cayman Islands. This bank account transferred tens of millions of dollars to another account right before the assassinations."

Noah's face went blank for a moment, then his eyes fell. "Shit. She hired them, didn't she? The assassins."

"Looks like it," McKenzie said, not pointing out that she was pretty sure "them" included Noah's ex-partner.

"And now she's dead," he said. "Perfect."

McKenzie debated a few seconds before removing the hard drive from her coat. "Then there's this."

"Aw, honey, if you needed a hard drive, we could've stopped at a Best Buy."

She stuck the drive back in her coat and folded her arms across her chest. "You could be thankful. I might've found us a lead."

"I could, but that would require too much optimism. Shit. What I can't figure out is why Cody would've had anything to do with him."

"To do with who?"

Noah's eyes shifted toward McKenzie, distrustful. "Look, no matter what's happened between us, you're still a reporter."

McKenzie stared at him, mouth gaping. "We got shot at, broke into someone's house, kissed, then found a dead woman in her home and *ran*, Noah. Do you still honestly think I'm *only* here for a story?"

"You tell me."

McKenzie closed her eyes, not sure how to answer. Yes, she still wanted an article, but everything had changed. She kept seeing Kimberly Lawson's frozen stare. Cody's mother's tear-streaked face. She wanted the truth for them. For Noah.

And then there was the kiss…

"I won't write anything until you say it's okay."

Noah's gaze flitted back and forth from the road to her as if he was trying to read her thoughts. "I know who killed Kimberly Lawson."

She wasn't sure what was louder: the rush of the air through the bullet-riddled windshield or the thoughts whooshing through her head as she tried to comprehend this new development. "How could you possibly—"

"Let's just say you're not the only one who hasn't been entirely forthcoming."

"Meaning?"

"The knife I found in the pillowcase from Cody's hotel room? It's a SEAL specialty knife. A Mad Dog ATAK. I thought it was weird Cody had one. I've only known one guy my whole career with one of those, and it wasn't Cody. That particular make of knife was manufactured in the early nineties, but less than fifty of the things were issued before it was discontinued. The blades were custom made, which caused all sorts of problems with deliveries and mix-ups. The guy I knew with one had an uncle who was a former SEAL. The uncle died, and the ATAK was handed down to him. This guy was—" Noah blew out a slow breath as if he was choosing his words with care, "—an old teammate of mine."

Noah's emphasis on the past tense didn't escape her. "Was?" she asked.

"Yeah. We were in a village in Pakistan to apprehend and interrogate a suspected terrorist. One night, we found this *SEAL*," he said through clenched teeth, "with a woman." He paused. "He'd raped her."

McKenzie pressed her lips together, gritting her teeth.

Noah shook his head. "The screaming woke us all. She'd have had the whole village awake. I didn't see it happen myself, but Cody and a couple other guys ran in to see what the commotion was. This guy pulled out his knife and stabbed her. Just killed her right there."

Tears burned the corners of McKenzie's eyes. How did things like this happen? Talk about a story she could never write. It proved her point about SEALs being trained killers, but it turned out Noah wasn't like that at all. Not the way this other guy was. She could never open Noah up to the kind of attacks he'd face if the public knew he'd come within a fifty mile radius of something like this.

"Most of us—SEALs, I mean—we're violent when we're required to be. SEALs have to have a degree of controlled aggression. You'd be eaten alive doing what we did without it. But that's the thing. You have to be in command of it. This guy had no control. He liked the power that came with our brand of work. He was brutal without cause, which is the reason they kicked him off the team."

Noah drew a deep breath. "Of course, the events surrounding his dismissal were kept quiet, but when I saw how Kimberly Lawson was killed, I knew it was him. She died from a hard thrust into the femoral artery that was sliced downward for a quick bleed out. That was his signature maneuver. We never talked about why. You don't really talk about things like your kill style on a team. Too personal."

McKenzie didn't know what to say. Somehow, words would only cheapen the horrifying image in her mind.

Almost as an afterthought, Noah added, "It's how he killed that woman in Pakistan."

McKenzie digested the statement. The enormity of it all surrounded her, suffocating her.

Noah jammed the SUV into park beside a pay phone on the sidewalk.

"So basically what you're telling me is," she said so low it was almost inaudible, "we know who killed the president."

"Basically," Noah replied.

CHAPTER TWENTY NINE

"WE HAVE TO move fast. They'll think I was the killer phoning in my own murder," Noah said, climbing back into the SUV after jogging away from the phone booth. He'd just given a 911 dispatcher Kimberly Lawson's address.

As they peeled out of the parking lot, a horrible thought struck McKenzie. "What if we left fibers or hairs or something?"

"One bridge at a time," Noah said. "For now, back to Chris."

The dreaded name had come up again.

"Noah, I hate to say this, but do you actually think we should keep looking? I mean, we've more or less found out Cody *did* pull the trigger on the vice president. Don't you think we should leave it at that?"

Noah shook his head hard, clicking his tongue. "That's just it. Cody may have done it, but now more than ever I need to know why. It makes no sense for him to have been involved with that guy. He wasn't the type to do this for money."

McKenzie kept quiet. Maybe when Noah knew him, worked beside him, Cody Randolph would've helped a troop of Girl Scouts rescue a kitten from up a tree, but he'd obviously turned into the opposite of the SEAL he'd been in the military. Even his mother admitted he'd suffered from PTSD. Maybe he'd snapped.

Whether or not the memories of watching his friends die tipped Cody over the edge, McKenzie remained convinced the Shen hired him to shoot the vice president. What better way to achieve their ultra-feminist goals than to clear the path for a woman to become President of the United States? The evidence was overwhelming. Why couldn't Noah see that?

Then again, sometimes it could be very hard to see

something right in front of your face.

"Will knowing Cody's reasons change anything?" she asked.

Noah shrugged. "I have no idea. But I need to know."

Once they were reasonably far away from Kimberly Lawson's townhouse, they stopped at an all-night diner on the side of the highway.

McKenzie dumped sugar into her coffee while Noah used the restroom. When he returned, she nodded to his pants pocket. "The notebook?"

He lifted her laptop case toward her. "First things first. Let's have a look at that hard drive."

"I'm sure it's protected," McKenzie replied as she slid her computer out of the case. Still, curiosity bubbled in her stomach. If they could access information on the drive, maybe they'd know better where to go next besides this crummy joint in East Timbuktu.

Her laptop took forever to boot up, and she crossed and uncrossed her legs at least a dozen times while she waited. Her hands shook as she plugged in the portable drive from Kimberly Lawson's drawer.

McKenzie clicked an icon to open a folder to view the files. A password prompt popped up on the screen. Not unexpected, but at the same time, McKenzie's spirits sank like she'd just discovered she'd be splitting her lottery winnings with eighty other people. The chances of her guessing the right code were about the same as the chances of them finding someone named Chris who happened to be the person who stood Cody up on the night he and Kimberly met.

"Notebook it is," Noah replied. He passed the composition book across the table.

"Have you looked through it?" she asked, opening it to the first page.

"Can't," he replied. "Doesn't feel right."

She skimmed the pages one at a time. Cody's letters were so minute and squeezed together on most pages, deciphering anything useful was a task in itself. One page contained a list of comedy movies he'd seen, ranking them on a scale of one to a hundred based on how hard he'd laughed. A few notes were more personal. McKenzie skipped right over some of them as soon as she realized the nature of a particular thought. After all, she wouldn't want anyone reading *her* mind after she was dead.

Suddenly, McKenzie's stomach turned a somersault. On one of the last pages, Cody had scrawled a name and address. Finally, the name of someone Cody knew, even if it wasn't Chris. "Noah, look at this."

Noah read the page out loud. "Brian, 531 Fletcher Circle."

"What are we waiting for?" McKenzie replied, already packing up her computer.

"In case you haven't noticed, Mac, it's three o'clock in the morning. I doubt this Brian guy would appreciate us knocking on his door right now."

McKenzie sighed. "You're probably right." She let the laptop case fall back into the seat before collapsing against the back of the booth again. "That is, if the address is a home address. It could be a company."

"Touché," Noah said. "We need to find somewhere with Wi-Fi. I doubt Aunt Bea running this joint has ever heard of a computer, much less internet access for her customers. Plus, we need to get rid of that damned SUV. Hard to be inconspicuous when you're driving with a shot-out back windshield."

"Where do we go?"

Noah reached for McKenzie's cell phone. "I have an idea."

CHAPTER THIRTY

NOAH WATCHED OUT the window of their booth for the gold Crown Vic, all the while taking note of the shitload of ways this could go wrong. He was more than capable of nipping problems he knew existed. The surprises were the things that could get them killed.

On a hostage evacuation once, Noah and his team had gone in hard. The breacher applied a charge and blew in the door of the underground bunker with surgical precision so as not to injure the person they went in to retrieve. Then, the targets decided for themselves to turn over their captive the hard way: they picked up their guns. The team neutralized all of them within seconds of entry. They'd been heavy a hostage and ready to rock when out of nowhere, a twelve-year-old kid with an M16 blew one of Noah's teammates off his feet.

Headlights streamed through the restaurant's mini-blinds. Noah tossed a twenty on the table to cover their tab. "Come on."

The car parked on the other side of the lot from the SUV as instructed. Its lights went off, and the door opened.

Mrs. Randolph stepped out of the car and rubbed her arms as if it were the middle of winter.

As Noah and McKenzie approached, her control reached its end. "Oh, Noah," she cried. She flung her arms around his middle. He tensed but forced himself to relax.

You need her on your side.

"Thank you for coming," he said. "You didn't tell anyone where you were going, right?"

She shook her head fiercely, eyes burning with purpose. "No. I got in the car and left right when you called. Didn't talk to anyone."

He nodded and patted her back. "Good. You have a cab coming?"

"Yes," she replied. Her hand brushed the jagged scrape on his chin where one of the many shards of glass had pelted him during the car chase. "Noah. Your face."

Once upon a time, he would've felt her touch and been comforted. Now, he gently pushed her hand away. "It's nothing."

She blinked tears away. "Don't tell me it's nothing. I saw why you needed me to come." Her gaze fluttered in the SUV's direction. "What's going on, Noah?"

"Mrs. Randolph, I appreciate you helping us more than you'll ever know, and I know Cody would, too," he said. Ignoring her flinch at her son's name was tough, but it was even more difficult to keep from glancing at Mac when he said his next words. "But what I'm doing has to be on a need to know basis. Not just to keep my movements secret, but to keep you safe, too."

At this, Mrs. Randolph squeezed Noah's hand and pressed her car keys into his palm. "Don't give it another thought," she said in earnest. "You do what you have to."

Embrace the suck.

God, how many times had he had to tell himself that in the past? How many more times could he do it?

"Mrs. Randolph, did you do the other thing I asked you to do?"

Again, she nodded. After digging around in her purse for a moment, Cody's mother produced a wadded up receipt. She'd jotted the number on the back. "I got on the internet and searched the address you gave me. It looks like it's a house *and* a business. Varnes Custom Firearms."

Noah blanked his eyes and didn't react. Proper response.

"Okay. I'll check into it."

A taxi turned into the diner parking lot.

Not a second too soon. Think.

Her hand still clutched his. He squeezed her hand the same way she had his only moments before. "I need you to forget we talked."

The woman's eyes held his, and for a split-second, Noah could've sworn he saw Cody flash in them. "You can trust me," she whispered.

He crooked his neck toward the cab. "I know. Now, go on."

She squeezed his fingers one last time, then trotted toward the taxi. If he had the time, he'd kick his own ass right now. Here he was with a damned *New York Herald* reporter he'd brought along because he was unwilling to involve his *own* mother in this ordeal. Trying to be a good partner, yet screwing over the one person Cody would probably tell him to watch out for. This is what happened when you lost focus—or didn't have enough to begin with.

As she climbed into the cab, Mrs. Randolph glanced back over her shoulder. No questions. She'd just come. *Christ, Cody.*

"Let's go," Noah said. "We need to go find out how we got into this festering pile of shit."

Noah veered off the highway onto an access road. Once he seemed satisfied they were out of sight of the interstate, he slammed the gear shift of Mrs. Randolph's Crown Vic into park. "Get some sleep. We're back on the road at zero-seven hundred."

McKenzie balled herself up in the seat and relaxed her head against the cool glass of the window. She couldn't help but think of Kimberly Lawson crumpled on her own bedroom floor. "I don't think I'll ever sleep again after tonight."

You're being stupid, McKenzie. The woman hired assassins to kill government leaders. Why do you care about her?

"Can't we get another motel room?" she asked.

Noah reclined the driver's seat. "Everyone knows moving targets are harder to hit."

"You're worried about him," McKenzie said. "The SEAL, I mean."

"*Ex*-SEAL. And yeah, now that I know who it is, I can't help but be concerned."

McKenzie heard fear in Noah's voice she hadn't noticed until now. "What aren't you telling me?"

Noah sat back up. "You're less conducive to sleep than warzone gunfire, you know that?"

He ran his hands down his face as if to wake himself up. He shook his head hard like a dog. "His name's Lucas Crawford. He killed the freakin' president." He took a breath. "I was the one who got him kicked off the team."

A stone dropped into McKenzie's stomach. So, this wasn't paranoia. This guy had a reason to hate Noah. "What—"

"Cody told me he'd seen Crawford with that woman in Pakistan. As hard as I tried, I couldn't drop it. A loose cannon like that is a danger to his team. If you don't have trust within the team, you're as good as dead. I had to turn him in."

The reporter in McKenzie wanted to ask more questions, but Noah held up a hand. "There's something else I should probably tell you, now that we're being frank."

If the first revelation was that the madman who'd killed the leader of the free world had a vendetta against the man she was sleeping next to, she hated to think what the next would be.

Noah leaned back and shut his eyes again. "Varnes Firearms. Brian Varnes. I know the guy. He was on our SEAL team, too. Now shut up so I can sleep."

CHAPTER THIRTY ONE

Day 5: Morning (PST)
Bakersfield, California

"SO WERE YOU and this Brian on good terms?" McKenzie ventured. Seeing as how they were on the way to Varnes Firearms, best to know what she was heading into.

"Oh, yeah. Varnes is a really good guy. With the exception of Lucas the team was like brothers. Brian was tight with Cody in particular. For a while, Brian was Cody's spotter in the field. I kind of doubt he had anything to do with *this* crap, though."

Noah was probably right. For all they knew, Cody jotted that address down months before any of this craziness began.

The further they followed the directions McKenzie had found online for Varnes Firearms, the more the area looked like a farm in Texas instead of near Los Angeles. They passed fields full of cows and little ponds brimming with ducks before turning onto a dirt driveway. McKenzie had an idea she was about to meet a card-carrying NRA member with a God Bless America belt buckle.

A tiny brunette answered the door. McKenzie noted the wedding ring on her finger.

"We're here to see Brian," Noah said.

"Oh, he works on the guns back in the shed. I won't let him in the house with those things. They scare the living daylights out of me. You can head on back."

"Thanks," Noah said.

They went through the fence and toward the "shed," as Brian's wife had called it, though it was a barn if McKenzie'd ever seen one. Noah rapped his knuckles on the door.

"Come in," said a voice, but it wasn't one with the country twang McKenzie expected.

Neither was the man on the other side of the door.

Brian Varnes sat polishing some kind of handgun with a dirty cloth. His mahogany hair was close-cropped in a crew cut, and a sleeve of tattoos sprawled across his arm from underneath his grease-covered T-shirt. One of the tattoos was a trident, a symbol McKenzie now knew to be associated with the Navy SEALs.

"How can I help you?" he asked, turning his eyes up. They widened. "Noah?"

"Long time no see," Noah said. His face broke into a smile.

Brian set the gun down and stood. He embraced Noah. "How the heck are you?"

"Been better," Noah said as he patted Brian on the back.

McKenzie cleared her throat.

"Oh, sorry, Mac. Brian, this is Mac. She's a..." Noah's speech stumbled, "a friend of mine."

"Well, any friend of Noah's," Brian said, stretching out a hand to shake McKenzie's. "What brings you to my neck of the woods?"

"Cody," Noah said.

"I figured this was about him. To be honest, I'm a little surprised no one else has come looking for me about that, but then again, no one else probably knows..." He looked thoughtful for a moment. "Come to think of it, what made you guys come looking for me?"

Noah reached into his pocket and pulled out Cody's black and white composition book. "We found your address in here."

Brian turned the book over in his hands. "Cody never let this thing out of his sight. Always had his Wheel Book and his own book. Should I ask how you got this, or is it better if I don't know?"

"Probably better for you if you don't know," Noah replied.

"Point taken," Brian said, flipping through the book without asking further questions.

McKenzie wasn't about to let Brian off that easily. "Brian, you said nobody else knew. What were you talking about?"

Brian rolled his head in a slow circle, popping his neck. "A few months back, Cody asked me if he could borrow some money. A *lot* of money. He wouldn't tell me what it was for, but I asked him if he was in trouble."

Brian paced. "He said he was being blackmailed. He wouldn't tell me anything else except he needed to try and pay them off."

"What could Cody have done that someone could use to blackmail him?" Noah asked.

"Beats me," Brian said. "You know as well as I do that he was a good guy and a damn fine SEAL. As far as I can tell, he didn't even touch a gun after we came home. I can't imagine who could want to hurt him."

"Did you give him the money?" McKenzie asked.

Brian nodded. "I did. A few weeks later, he brought it back. Hadn't spent a penny of it. He thanked me but said he couldn't use it. That was the last time I ever saw him."

Noah squinted, seeming to toss the facts in his mind. "After the vice president was assassinated and you found out Cody was a suspect, why didn't you tell the cops about this?"

"I don't believe Cody did this any more than you do, Noah. Telling the FBI he had something in his past worth blackmailing would only make him look guiltier. He was dead either way. No need to help make a case against him. Not to mention, I don't want to be mixed up with it myself. You know what kind of shit we're dealing with here. My family and I would never have any peace again. If I learned one thing in the SEALs, it's that my gut instinct almost always does me justice."

McKenzie's brain was in knots. So much evidence pointed to Cody being the killer. Yet somehow, no one who knew him seemed willing to believe it was a possibility. What's more, Cody was being blackmailed. If the extortion occurred within months of the assassinations, it would be an impossible coincidence for them to be unconnected. But how?

"Have you ever heard of a woman named Kimberly Lawson?" Noah asked.

"Lawson?" Brian looked at the ceiling like a list of all his contacts was printed there. "Nah. No Lawson I can think of. Is she military?"

"No, she wasn't," Noah said. He glanced at the digital clock on Brian's table. "We'd better move on. Last thing you need is for us to hang around here too long."

"You don't know of a woman Cody knew or might've dated named Chris, Christina, Christen, or anything like that, do you?" McKenzie ventured.

Brian shook his head. "Doesn't ring a bell."

McKenzie kicked the sawdust on the ground as Brian bumped Noah's fist.

"Be careful, man," Brian said. "If I can do anything to help, let me know."

"Will do," Noah replied.

As McKenzie and Noah left, Brian hollered, "Hooyah!"

"Hooyah!" Noah yelled back, closing the barn door behind him.

CHAPTER THIRTY TWO

Day 5: Early Afternoon (CST)
Mexico City

IT HAD TAKEN an entire day for him to travel here, but once Uhlig had Xavier's house in his sight, the long days and years leading up to this moment evaporated. Right now, there was nothing but this.

As he stood waiting for the man to answer the door, he couldn't help but marvel at what his life had been. So many failures. One time after the other, he'd missed chances. Not this time.

The door creaked open. "Who are you?"

Uhlig raised his palm to the man, displaying the small mark tattooed on his wrist. "He has sent me."

Everything with Xavier had to be done in person by messenger. Even in this day of technological advancement, the killer wouldn't carry a cell phone or a computer. He was good, but also paranoid about being tracked.

It was the very reason it had taken Uhlig this long.

"Come in," came the response.

Uhlig followed the back of Xavier's balding head through a maze of hallways until they were in a room with nothing but two wooden chairs. It felt more like a dungeon than a home. No pictures, no other furniture.

Fitting.

Following Xavier's lead, Uhlig sat. The man stared, waiting for Uhlig to state his business. He drummed his fingers on the chair.

Uhlig studied him. The nose, skinny and short, barely a dot

on the face. Those eyes, shaped like Christmas baubles. Just like the photograph.

"You aren't an easy man to find," Uhlig stated. He was well aware he was trying Xavier's patience, but probably no one in the world cared less.

Xavier's lips cinched. "Those who need to find me do."

Uhlig nodded his agreement. "That is true."

When Uhlig didn't continue, Xavier threw his arms out. "Well? What have you come here for?"

At this, Uhlig leaned forward, still examining the man in front of him. "Don't rush me," he said. His voice had lowered an octave, as if some strange creature inside him was taking over. "You have taken my whole life. I can take these few minutes."

Xavier leaned back, his eyes narrowing. "What the hell do you mean by this? What is the job you've come here for?"

Uhlig cocked his head. "You don't recognize me, do you?"

For a moment, the words hung in the stale air, threatening. In the next instant, Xavier jumped up, moved for the gun at his ankle.

The short barrel of the SIG across from his forehead stilled him. Xavier eased back into the chair.

"Who are you?" he breathed.

With the hand not holding the gun, Uhlig produced stainless steel wire ties in a practiced motion. "We'll get to that. Hands where I can see them."

Xavier didn't move. He was either contemplating a break for the gun or another way to try to take Uhlig down.

Uhlig dug the barrel of the pistol into Xavier's skull. "Hands," he repeated.

The man held his palms high, his face unreadable.

Uhlig extended a tie toward him. "First, your feet."

Xavier threw his head back and laughed. "Right, you imbecile. I bind my own feet, let you bind my hands. Give up any chance I have? You going to shoot me if I don't?"

"Have it your way."

Uhlig shifted the SIG three inches and blew a hole into

Xavier's right shoulder. The man cried out in pain. His mouth gaped.

"Should've tied your feet," Uhlig said, shifting the gun again. He fired three times in rapid succession. Left shoulder, left knee cap. Right knee cap. "It's all right, though. I'm flexible."

Xavier slid out of the chair onto the wooden floor, moans of agony rattling from his throat. Uhlig shrugged. Al-Musari may have him hunted down and killed for this when he eventually found out, but seeing the man in this state was worth every possible scenario Uhlig had entertained. And he'd thought of most of them.

Even though Xavier's body was a pulpy mess, Uhlig took a moment to snug the steel ties around his wrists and ankles anyway. Helpless to stop him, Xavier squeezed his eyes shut as he gasped.

When Uhlig finished, he removed a small bottle from his pocket. He flipped the top up and squirted the liquid on Xavier. The man squirmed, shaking his head.

Uhlig picked up a shard from where one of the bullets had splintered the chair leg. He pressed it into Xavier's open lips. "You might want to bite down. I imagine this will be painful."

Xavier screamed through the wood in his teeth and rolled over on the floor. When he realized he could go nowhere, his head fell hard against the ground. Angry tears dripped from his eyes, his face purple and covered with sweat.

It was a shame to leave, but other things had to be done today. Uhlig reached the door and looked back to take in the sight one last time. He'd recognize that lumpy man anywhere. After all, his image had been burned into Uhlig's brain ever since he was twelve.

Uhlig struck the match. The flame danced in front of the man he'd hated for so long. Purpose drowned out the doomed man's frantic yells. Uhlig could hear only the words he'd heard all those years ago.

"So be it," Uhlig whispered. He threw the fire and walked away.

CHAPTER THIRTY THREE

Day 5: Afternoon (PST)
Los Angeles, California

"YOUR UNCLE KNOWS we're coming, right?" Noah asked as he put the Crown Vic into park.

The scheme had to have come right out of Wile E. Coyote's playbook. They'd done so much to evade the cops, yet here they were, at the police station. "He does. I'm not sure how much help he'll be, though."

"Better than nothing," Noah said.

"Just let me do the talking."

"Funny," Noah replied, "You're good at that."

McKenzie shot him a look then turned to the female officer working the front desk. "We're here to see Detective Becker. I'm his niece."

"Follow me," she said.

They followed the receptionist through a hallway full of signs bearing phrases like, "Felons with Guns Do Time." *Cheery little place.*

They came to a corner office. "Detective Becker, this girl says you're expecting her," the officer said.

Uncle Sal interjected. "Yes, Pilar. Thank you."

"No problem."

After the officer left, Uncle Sal sat up from where he'd been leaning back with his feet propped on the desk. He closed a file folder and tossed it aside.

"Bumble Bee," he said, a grin spreading over his lips. He came around the desk to give her a hug.

It'd been so long since she'd last seen him. She didn't

remember his face having so many lines, but she did remember his eyes, bright and inquisitive as a sparrow. "Hi, Uncle Sal. This is my friend. The one I told you about."

"I'm glad you came to see me. I'm not sure what I can do to help, but tell me what you need. We'll go from there."

The explanation about Noah's partner must've struck a chord.

McKenzie searched for words.

I have to tell Uncle Sal we're looking for someone named Chris without telling him she stood up Cody Randolph. The night he happened to meet Kimberly Lawson. Who happened to be connected to a radical feminist group that may or may not have hired Cody to assassinate the vice president.

They had no clue what they were looking for, but if Cody was the journaling type, chances were he'd jotted things down elsewhere, too. The FBI had probably already taken anything worth looking for, and yet, Noah knew Cody better than anyone. *Damn.*

Noah cut McKenzie off before she had the chance to answer. "You see, sir, Cody had this girlfriend named Chris, but I don't know her number. I don't even know her last name. I never met her, but he was my best friend and my partner. I just want to make sure she's all right." Then he added, "I know Cody would want me to do that for him."

Her uncle bit his lip. "I could lose my job," he said, more to himself than to them.

He considered Noah for a long moment then looked at McKenzie. "Most of the hotel room evidence has already been handed over to the FBI, but they haven't moved it all to Quantico yet. The stuff they've deemed less important will probably catch dust here for months. Find what you need and get out. Don't *take* anything. You were never here."

Uncle Sal opened a cabinet and removed a box of latex gloves. He handed them both a pair. "You don't want your prints within five counties of Randolph's stuff."

They wandered down the hall and toward the evidence

room. Her uncle motioned them into an alcove while he keyed in his code. They ducked inside.

"Good luck," he said as he closed them in.

As soon as he'd shut the door, McKenzie regretted not asking him for specific directions. Row after row of shelves were stacked to the ceiling, piled high with evidence bags, files, confiscated computers and radios. The room had to be organized somehow, but there was so much crammed into it McKenzie wondered how anyone ever found anything. Without coordinates of where to search, it could take the two of them all day.

It wasn't long before they knew they wouldn't have anywhere near that much time.

"I'll be right back, Chuck," a voice hollered out the doorway.

They weren't alone.

McKenzie dropped to the ground behind a shelf. Noah squatted beside her.

A few seconds passed before she realized Noah was speaking to her, his voice was so soft. "Don't respond. Just do what I say. Stomach. Now. If you have to use your knees, make sure to lift your feet. Keep your ass tucked down."

Crawling along the floors, snakes on their bellies, McKenzie tried to hear where the new man's footsteps fell so they could avoid him. She read the shelves' labels as best she could from the ground.

When they were sandwiched in between the third and fourth row, McKenzie caught sight of a shelf marker with Cody Randolph's name. She tapped Noah and gestured towards it. He nodded. She adjusted her gloves. Noah would be the better one to do this. After all, his fingers were used to working with sensitive explosives and picking locks, so this would be nothing. However, the way they were positioned on the floor, they'd make far more noise trying to switch places to get Noah closer to the shelf. She was the logical choice.

She stood, climbed onto the first shelf to reach the higher spot where the box sat.

She sifted through pile in the box while Noah kept watch on

the man's feet. After she'd gone through half the stack, she finally saw a tiny brown book. Carefully, she touched it with her fingertips. Squeezing her arm to the other side of the shelf, she used her index finger to nudge the book toward her. The hardback novel on top of it shook slightly, so she slowed down. The brown book's end peeked out. Just a bit more...

Finally, enough of the book's spine stuck out that she could grab it. She eased the book inch by inch from underneath the heavier volume, cushioning the top book with her left hand to avoid it clunking down once the little brown book was free.

Yes. She finally had it in her hand. Her palms sweated underneath the gloves. She flipped the book open, and her heart kicked into overdrive as her elbow scraped a nearby container. It tumbled toward the floor. She thrust her hand out to catch it, but it was too late. The crash sounded as loud as a cough in a library.

"Who's there?" the man shouted.

McKenzie held her breath. Maybe the clerk would think he imagined it.

No such luck. Footsteps thudded. McKenzie heard the door fly open. She looked toward Noah, who crouched on the floor, ready to spring to action.

"Call backup. Someone's in the evidence room."

There was nothing else for it. Both Noah and McKenzie shot up from their hiding place, the brown notebook still in McKenzie's hand. They sped down the rows toward the open door. Before the evidence clerk had a chance to react, Noah punched him in the jaw. The clerk fell backward, and the two of them jumped over his prone form.

Confused looks plastered the faces of everyone in the waiting area as the pair whisked through the lobby. Cops behind the desk jostled to get out from behind the partition, but McKenzie and Noah were already running out the door and into the parking lot.

In their wake, McKenzie could hear police yelling, "Stop right there!"

Noah hopped in the driver's seat beside her, cranking Mrs. Randolph's gold car. He slammed the accelerator, and the Crown

Vic spun backwards out of the parking lot. McKenzie's arm seared with pain as her shoulder jammed hard into the passenger's side door.

"Sorry," Noah mumbled. He threw the Crown Vic into gear without braking. The car growled its objection as it shifted.

A gunshot cracked the air.

"What the hell?" McKenzie yelled. It was like they were back in the alley outside Cody's hotel.

"Trying to shoot out the tires," Noah said.

They were too far out of range, though. McKenzie chanced a glance back and saw the police station growing smaller until it was out of sight.

"Whew," McKenzie said. "That was close. It doesn't look like they're trying to follow us."

"I wouldn't celebrate yet," Noah said. "They're cops. Besides the fact that they'll interrogate your uncle, I'd be willing to bet one of them took down our plate numbers."

CHAPTER THIRTY FOUR

Day 5: Late Night (EST)
The White House

"SOMEONE BROKE INTO the California evidence room housing everything from Cody Randolph's hotel room," General Helms said as soon as the door to the Oval Office closed behind him. "A car registered to Randolph's mother fled the scene, but the descriptions of the two perps match the descriptions of Hutchins and the reporter."

"Wait," Elaine said. "Randolph's *mother?* Why isn't she under surveillance? Did they take anything? And why the hell is the evidence in a *police station* and not with the Los Angeles FBI field office?" She leaned forward, hands fisted on top of the desk.

"We're not sure if they made off with anything yet. Clerks are wading through the inventory as we speak. As for the evidence housing, we had concerns about a departmental leak at the L.A. FBI lockup. We're in the process of transferring all the evidence back to Quantico."

"Right," Elaine seethed. "That little jailhouse couldn't *possibly* be less secure than the FBI evidence room. You have to be kidding me!"

Elaine pushed back from the desk. Helms sat in silence as she paced the blue carpet. "We're in one of the most advanced countries in the world, and evidence in an assassination investigation is floating around in a minimum security jail. Are we *inviting* tampering? Do we *want* the media to destroy us?" She didn't wait for an answer. "Have the L.A. police brought Hutchins in yet? Why aren't *we* bringing him in?"

General Helms once again adopted the smug look he was prone to anytime he spoke to Elaine. "We've told the L.A. police to back off. Noah Hutchins has an alibi for the night in question, but we don't think his presence in L.A. is innocent. Even if he didn't shoot the president, he might lead us to the person who did."

CHAPTER THIRTY FIVE

Day 5: Evening (PST)
Los Angeles, California

"WE HAVE TO ditch this car," Noah said a few miles down the road. He made a left into a shopping center packed with cars.

"I'm sure Mrs. Randolph will be thrilled," McKenzie said.

"We can call her and tell her where to pick it up, but it'd probably be best to let her tell them we stole it. That way, she's not culpable, and she can collect insurance," he replied as they hopped out.

"Okay, so how are we planning to get around without a car?" McKenzie asked, rolling the hideous pink suitcase behind her. She squinted in the direction of the setting sun to see where Noah was going.

He was already wandering toward a man hefting bags into a beat-up old Chevy, which groaned underneath the weight of a carton of sodas. "Excuse me, sir. Would you be interested in selling that truck?"

The man looked at Noah as if he'd asked him to donate a kidney. "Why in God's name would you want to buy my truck in the middle of a strip mall parking lot?"

"My wife and I are traveling, and our car broke down up the highway," Noah said.

The man glanced at Noah's bare ring finger. "Right," he said.

McKenzie was sure he was about to turn them down, but he said, "How much?"

Noah raised an eyebrow but drew a roll of bills out of his wallet. "I don't have a lot. A couple thousand is the best I can do."

The man didn't look impressed. "I know she ain't much to look at, but she's worth more than that."

McKenzie slid a ring off her right hand. She tried not to think about Nana as she extended her great grandmother's diamond toward the man. "It's real. One and a half carats."

The man eyed the gem, skeptical. "Real diamond, you say?" The old timer held the ring up to his face and scrunched his nose. "I'll take it."

They exchanged the money and the ring for the car keys. McKenzie and Noah loaded their stuff into the truck.

"We could've bought a used car at a dealership and not had to hock my grandmother's ring," McKenzie grumbled.

"Paper trails, Mac. We don't want paper trails."

"Right. Why leave paper trails when you can bust up police stations?"

Just then, McKenzie's phone rang. She fished in her purse and flipped it open on the third ring. As she listened to the firm voice chew her out from the earpiece, she hoped the volume wasn't up loud enough for Noah to hear everything on the other end.

"I know that, sir, but I'm not quite ready to—"

The voice cut her off. All she could do was listen.

Again, she tried to explain. "I *know*, but I need to clarify some things before I put it into print. I need a few more days—"

McKenzie swore under her breath. She couldn't afford to lose this article. "Yes, sir. I'll have it in."

Noah ripped the phone out of her hand. In one quick motion, he popped off the back and snapped the battery pack out. "Traceable. Stupid and traceable. Your editor, I'm guessing?"

"Yeah," she said, guilt causing her blood to run hot.

He tossed the phone and its battery into the floorboard. "Mac, you can't write that article yet. You'll scare off anyone who might be willing to give us answers. Cops will swarm in. We don't even know what's on the damned hard drive yet. Not to mention, you'll be cementing Cody's reputation."

McKenzie forced down the retort that Cody sealed his own

place in history long before now. "Noah, if I don't write this article, my job will be in the toilet."

"So what?" he said, fuming. "You have the biggest story in decades—maybe ever. Editors at other papers would sell their own children to pick it up."

She was quiet for a minute as she considered his words. Noah would never be able to comprehend all the mitigating factors. The longer she waited, the greater the likelihood someone else would break the story before she did.

"I have to write it, Noah."

"What the hell happened to not sending your editor anything until we talked about it? You said you'd write the truth about Cody. That was the whole point in bringing you along. I wanted people to know he wasn't what they say he is."

"You said yourself that isn't the only reason you brought me along," McKenzie shot back. Then, her voice softened. "Noah, the main thing is that Cody *is* what they say. We *know* he did it. We're not sure of all the details or the reason why, but we *know*."

Noah's face hardened. "After everything we've seen and been through together, I was sure that even if you didn't give a damn about *Cody*, you gave one about *me*."

Tears stung McKenzie's eyes. "I wish you could understand."

"Oh," Noah replied, his tone plucking a bitter note. "I understand perfectly."

After what felt like hours, they pulled into a motel off the interstate.

"I thought motels were out of the question now," McKenzie said warily.

Noah slammed the door of the old pickup so hard the truck squeaked under the blow. "Well, I need a good night's sleep, and this doesn't look like the kind of place that got five stars in *Luxury Hotel Monthly*. I'm pretty sure they'll take cash and look the other way. Besides, the cops will still be looking for the Crown Vic."

Once inside their room, McKenzie threw her suitcase on the bed and fired up her laptop to start the article.

"Somehow, I didn't actually believe you'd do it."

She smoothed her hands on her pants, willing herself to remain composed. "I think I'll write in the lobby," she said as she snapped the laptop closed again. "I can't concentrate here."

McKenzie slammed the door on her way out. He just didn't get it. She'd love to prove Cody wasn't a crazed killer, but there was more to it than that. The article couldn't wait any longer.

A card table and a fold-out metal chair were the best she could manage for a makeshift office in the dingy lobby. She opened the new document that would be the highlight of her career. And the end of her relationship with Noah.

As she pounded out the words, out of the corner of her eye she saw a man checking in at the desk. In spite of the fact that she'd been on the run, sleeping in cars, and her hair hadn't seen a brush or shampoo in days, he seemed to be glancing at her a lot. He had close-cropped hair—a crew cut.

Were we followed?

No, it was her imagination. All the excitement in the last few days had her on edge. Either that or he was the kind who thought anything in a skirt—especially in a fleabag motel—was fair game. Pig.

She shook the thought out of her head and concentrated on her article. All of her findings supported her feminist conspiracy theory. She wrote how a violent feminist group wanted to bypass voter referendums to create the first woman president, even if it took a double homicide to do it.

When she finished typing, reading, and re-reading the article, she saved the document. Waiting until morning to send it seemed like the best option.

I have to be sure.

McKenzie trudged up the cement stairs outside the motel. She passed the alcove housing the drink machine and paused for a second. Maybe she had change to buy a soda.

She realized she wasn't alone one second too late. As arms wrapped her body, her scream caught in her throat. Something cool touched the fleshy place right above her voice box. A knife.

Colby Marshall

"You know, some matters don't *need* to be prodded. You keep poking a stick in dark holes long enough, you're bound to scare up something nasty. Something that bites."

McKenzie tried to keep her breathing even so she wouldn't hyperventilate, but the knife pressed harder against her skin. "What do you want?" she whispered.

The man yanked back a handful of her hair to expose even more of her neck. McKenzie let out a tiny squeak.

"Tell Noah Hutchins to leave L.A. If he doesn't, next time I see you, I'll leave more than a bruise on your pretty throat."

He grabbed her neck, crushing her windpipe under his thumbs. She gasped for air. Her eyes bulged, throat burned.

Just when she was about to black out, her assailant let go. He shoved her face into the wall of the alcove and again grabbed a fistful of her hair. His hot breath brushed her ear. "Tell him."

McKenzie's body jarred into the wall as he released her. She squeezed her eyes tightly, both praying he was leaving and at the same time bracing for something worse. She waited, breathless, until footsteps sounded in the stairwell, then scrambled out of the alcove and ran to the room. It took three swipes of the stupid key card before the lock finally turned green and clicked open. She darted in, bolting the door behind her.

"Back so soon?" Noah asked, his back to her, eyes on the TV.

"Noah, he's here."

He whirled around, all anger forgotten. "Who? What happened to you?"

McKenzie glanced at herself in the mirror on the wall. Her hair was disheveled, and her throat bore bright red welts already turning purple. "The assassin," she said, knowing who the man must be. "Lucas."

Noah leapt to his feet, pulling out the Beretta she'd retrieved at the bank. He exploded out the door.

A minute later, he returned. He locked the door, cursing its flimsiness. "He's gone. Are you okay?"

She took a step toward him, then another and another until her head pressed against his chest. "I didn't see where he went.

164

I'm fine."

"Are you sure? Did you see his face?" Noah's words were quick. "Tell me you didn't see his face."

"I'm sure. No, I didn't see him. He was behind me the whole time. He told me to tell you to leave Los Angeles. He said if you didn't—" She gulped, afraid to repeat the rest. "He said he'll kill me. He must think I'm important to you."

Noah's eyes softened, his shoulders hunched. He looked at his feet, then back into McKenzie's eyes.

"You are."

He cupped the back of her neck, drawing her into him. She tilted her chin up, and her lips brushed his. Noah's mouth pressed harder and harder against hers, and with every second, McKenzie registered that she might've never seen him again. She reached for his belt buckle as he tugged at her shirt.

A knock at the door brought them crashing back to reality.

Noah held his finger to his lips and motioned for McKenzie to take cover behind the bed. He positioned himself beside the door, flush against the wall. He unlatched the bolt and leveled his Beretta.

The door fell open.

"No!" McKenzie screamed.

"What the hell is going on?" asked the man standing in the doorway.

In his usual flamboyant and perfectly timed manner, Pierce had come to her rescue.

CHAPTER THIRTY SIX

MCKENZIE LEAPT FROM behind the bed and threw her arms around Pierce. "It's okay, Noah. He's a friend."

"Apparently," Noah said, lowering the Beretta.

Pierce glanced at the gun for the first time. He jumped back. "Holy shit. Why were you guys about to shoot me?"

"We thought you were someone else," Noah replied as he clicked on the gun's safety.

McKenzie detected the slightest note of jealousy in his voice. She choked on a laugh. *Clarification needed.*

"Pierce is my roommate," she said. "My strictly *platonic* roommate. He's the one who found the information on Kimberly Lawson."

"I don't know if I should shake your hand or punch you in the nose." Noah extended his hand. "Thanks, buddy."

"Pierce, how the hell did you find us?" McKenzie asked.

"I put a tracking trojan on your laptop the night before you left," Pierce explained. "They don't pay me the big bucks in computer programming for nothin'."

"You could've called," McKenzie said even though her phone battery was out. Her heart rate spiked. Pierce would be able to crack Kimberly Lawson's hard drive. She knew it. "Actually, I want you to look at something."

His smile faded a touch. "I found out some stuff you need to know, too, but ladies first."

He didn't have to tell her twice. She rifled through the laptop case for the portable hard drive and handed it to Pierce. "It's encrypted. We really need to find out what's on the thing," she said.

* * *

This guy made Noah nervous, and that was saying something. It wasn't so much the high-priced shoes or the hundred dollar haircut as the fierce intelligence in his eyes.

He watched Mac's friend shut off her laptop and produce a small thumb drive from his pocket. Pierce inserted it and started the computer again. People with guns and knives, Noah could handle. You didn't see fuckers like this coming.

Words filled the black screen. After a few moments, some sort of prompt appeared. Pierce typed, and an operating system Noah had never seen popped up. *Sneaky son of a bitch.*

Pierce clicked an application. More writing filled the screen. The guy's fingers flew over the keyboard, typing strange commands Noah couldn't make out and wouldn't understand even if he could. After a minute, different white letters scrolled across the screen. Whatever this guy was, Noah was damn glad he was on *their* side.

"Voila," Pierce said, scribbling something on his palm.

"What?" Mac asked.

Good to know someone else is as confused as I am.

"Password," Pierce replied.

"Just like that?" Noah asked.

Pierce smirked. "Yeah. Note to self: if someone really wants to know what's on your computer, they probably can."

"Jesus eating a Cobb salad."

"And now," Pierce said, turning off the computer again, "we boot this puppy up…"

The three waited while the laptop rebooted. When Windows started again, Pierce's fingers ran over the keys. "…throw in the password, and wham, bam, thank you ma'am, we are…whoa! Kimberly Lawson."

Mac coughed. "Um, yeah. About that. It's hers."

A wicked grin broke across Pierce's face. "I gathered. Let's see what we have here."

* * *

McKenzie scanned text as Pierce cruised through the recently altered files. A couple documents about a senator from Kentucky, one about the governor of California, the obituary of someone named Marie Uhlig. Folders of pictures, archived video, music, and a slew of other titles swam in her vision. The names blurred together.

"No way we'll get through all this tonight. There's too much," he said. "Besides, if we try, I'll never get to tell you why I came. It's kind of important."

McKenzie nodded and rubbed her eyes. "I'll have to go back over anything I read tonight anyway. You should get some sleep, too, Pierce. You came a long way. I still don't understand why you didn't call first."

Pierce frowned. "This isn't an 'over the phone' sort of thing."

"What's this about, Pierce?"

"The last time I talked to you, you had nothing to go on. Jessie, however, was turning up all kinds of information no one else could get. Two nights ago, I hung around the office and went through her desk to see if I could get you a few leads. I found loads of notes on the assassinations and on Cody. And would you believe, in the middle of her notes on Cody, I found a name written in all capital letters? Chris."

"You're kidding," McKenzie gasped.

Now more than ever, McKenzie knew Chris had to be the key to Cody's connection to the Shen. "Oh, tell me you know how to find her."

"It's not a hard drive full of God-knows-what, but I have a phone number. That should be a start."

"Unless Jessie gets there first," McKenzie said, despondent. Jessie always sabotaged McKenzie's legitimate stories.

"McKenzie, you don't understand. That's the reason I came in person." Pierce's face turned grave, his eyes boring into her own. "McKenzie, Jessie's dead. She was murdered last night."

CHAPTER THIRTY SEVEN

WHILE THE TWO men were curled up to sleep on the floor, McKenzie sat on the bed, her laptop screen glowing in front of her. As she composed an e-mail and attached the file of the article she'd written, she tried not to imagine Jessie. The tall blonde with the annoying laugh had been her fiercest competitor, but she'd also been a colleague.

Pierce had told her a single gunshot wound to the head killed her. The police hadn't found fingerprints, and they didn't have any suspects. No way was her murder some random New York mugging. Jessie Cartwright died because she'd gone after the truth. The same truth McKenzie was still chasing.

This was the right move. She wouldn't end up like Jessie, a story in her head she was never allowed to tell.

With only Pierce's snoring to cover the sound of her own guilt, she hit send.

When she woke the next morning, Noah's cool attitude was already noticeable. She hadn't heard Noah leave or return, but sure enough, a copy of the *Herald* lay atop the corner table next to a box of donuts. Her story had made the front page. For one last day, so had Jessie. This time, no envy ate at McKenzie—just grief for a rival cut down pursuing a story.

McKenzie kept quiet. Mentioning the fiasco would only reignite Noah's temper.

"It's better if we show up rather than call and try to explain," Noah said to Pierce. "Now that people know the situation—" he shot a look in McKenzie's direction "—they might not be as eager to talk to us. Best if we just surprise this Chris girl in person."

Pierce sat on the bed with McKenzie's laptop. He typed the phone number into the white pages' reverse lookup function. "Bingo," he said as results appeared on the screen.

"You coming with us, Pierce?" McKenzie asked, taking a bite of a donut.

"Nah, I have to head back to New York. My day job hates it when I up and fly across the country without notice. I need to crawl back and smooth it over."

Pierce zipped his duffle bag and slung it over his shoulder.

McKenzie hugged him. "It means a lot to me that you'd come all this way."

"I'd do anything for you, Nancy Drew," he said. "In fact, you guys should take my rental. I'll drive that decrepit fart you bought. It'll take me to the airport fine. You're the ones who might need a trustier steed."

Pierce dug into his pockets and thrust his keys into McKenzie's palm.

Noah tossed him the keys to the truck. "Thanks, Man. We owe you one."

"Or two or three. I accept cash and all major credit cards." Pierce grinned. "I better move if I want to make my flight."

McKenzie closed the door behind Pierce and turned to Noah, who stood rigid, icy and distant. The smile he'd given Pierce had disappeared. She touched his shoulder, hoping an apology could carry through touch the way metal conducted electricity. "Listen, Noah, I—"

A boom resonated from outside the motel, shaking the building. A car alarm honked nearby.

"Oh, Jesus!" Noah leapt out of his chair and ripped open the door.

McKenzie couldn't see at first. Noah's frame blocked her view. When he stepped aside, however, she screamed. Below them in the parking lot was the spot where the Chevy they'd traded Pierce had been parked.

Now, the truck was nothing but a blazing inferno of smoke and flame.

CHAPTER THIRTY EIGHT

MCKENZIE CRUMBLED TO the floor like a demolished wall. The world rocked and spun. If she moved, she'd explode like the truck that had just taken Pierce from her.

Pierce was gone. The reality of it crashed over her. Her body racked with sobs. Something huge pressed on her chest, crushing it. He'd been there, always. Her best friend.

And it was all her fault. She'd let him take the Chevy. It was supposed to be her smoldering in that truck.

She wanted to sit and let grief take her, but Noah grabbed her hands and urged her to stand.

"Come on," he said. "We have to get out of here before the cops show up."

McKenzie clambered to her feet, light-headed. She stood frozen as Noah thrust her laptop case under her arm, then followed him with no more sense or feeling than a mechanical wind-up doll. He opened the door. The sight of blue lights met her eyes. Police were already swarming the wreckage.

"There has to be another way out. Come on," Noah said in a harsh whisper.

He ducked into the bathroom. He chucked her suitcase out the window. McKenzie heard it thud as it hit the cement of the alley below.

Noah hoisted himself through the window and onto the narrow ledge. He shinnied down the drain pipe and hopped the last few feet to the ground.

"You next," he called.

McKenzie mimicked Noah's motions as she heaved herself up through the window, tugging her laptop case through with her.

She looked at the drain pipe, unsure if it would stand the impact of another leap. It already wobbled in its socket.

"I'll check around here," a voice said, and McKenzie's heart fluttered. The cops were searching the building.

"Do it now," Noah commanded.

A surge of adrenaline sent McKenzie's body into overdrive, and she hurdled for the drain pipe. As she wrapped her arms around it, the force of her weight caused it to lurch underneath her. The pipe swung, and McKenzie's stomach rolled.

"Let go. I've got you," Noah said.

"I hear something down here," a cop called to another. Despite the concrete beneath her, she had to jump. *Trust.*

For a horrible second she was in the air, terrified the next sound she'd hear would be her body crunching against the pavement. Then, she landed with a soft puff in Noah's arms. He threw her to her feet, grabbed her bag, and they sprinted toward the parking lot.

Noah slowed as they reached the edge of the building. McKenzie followed suit. The parking area overflowed with police and emergency workers, yet the other two cops' footsteps thundered toward the alley.

"Don't look at anything except the rental car," Noah breathed into her ear. He shoved her in the small of her back. "Don't stop, no matter what happens. Three. Two. Run!"

Noah shot out of the alley. McKenzie was right on his heels, the rental car the finish line. Smoke burned her eyes. Sulfur flamed in her nostrils.

Focus on the car.

She heard a click as Noah unlocked the car with the remote entry key. Cops ran toward them. McKenzie's lungs burned, but she forced one foot in front of the other. *Ten more steps.*

Her fingers grappled with the door handle, which she couldn't see for the tears streaming down her face. "Shit!" she yelled as the door opened into her shin. She threw herself inside and slammed the door in the face of a cop only a few steps away.

As the rental flew out of the parking lot, McKenzie looked

back at the burning wreckage containing Pierce's body. She'd never forgive herself.

She'd never forgive *Lucas*. This wasn't about a story anymore. Now, it was personal.

CHAPTER THIRTY NINE

"BUCKLE UP AND hang on," Noah said as he glanced into the rearview mirror. "This could get interesting."

A police cruiser was gaining on them, blue lights flashing. Noah sliced in front of a Mustang. Its driver honked and cussed at them as they passed. The police cruiser matched their speed, its siren wailing like a battle cry.

Noah revved the engine. They rocketed straight through a red light, barely skimming through cars crossing the intersection. The sedan between them and the cruiser halted for the light. By the time the cop was around it, Noah had turned onto a side road and out of sight.

He pounded his fist on the steering wheel. "Now we have to ditch *another* car."

A slew of vehicles were parallel parked outside of the apartment buildings lining the street. Noah eased into a space between two cars.

This time, McKenzie didn't even ask. She followed Noah as he lugged her laptop case and the horrible pink suitcase to a gray Honda a few cars up. He dropped them beside the car, which had a window partially rolled down.

"Will you be careful with those?" she said, finally finding her voice.

He ignored her warning completely. "Mac, your hands are smaller than mine. Stick your arm through the crack and pull up the lock." Without waiting for a reply, he turned and headed back toward the rental.

No time to argue with him. The fact that the car's owner left the window open was a sure sign he or she would return soon.

What was a little grand theft auto when you'd already tampered with a crime scene, broken into a house, robbed a police station, and fled the scene of a car bombing?

She stretched her arm into the narrow space. The glass squeezed her bicep as she pushed harder and harder, trying to reach the top of the door. Finally, she plucked the lock, but her arm was stuck.

"A little help, please," she said, the edge of the window pinching into her flesh.

Now that the car was unlocked, Noah opened the door. "I promise I'll get you out as soon as the car is cranked."

"You don't have any keys," McKenzie whined. Her arm throbbed as if constricted by a snake.

"Really? I hadn't thought of that. Thanks."

"Asshole," she muttered, but he was already working inside the car.

Noah took off the steering wheel's cover and untangled two red wires, then whipped out a pen knife. When he'd stripped both wires, he twisted them into a tight coil. He stripped another wire, a brown one. McKenzie expected him to twine it with the red ones, but instead, he touched it to their ends.

The Honda revved to life. McKenzie pressed the power window button to release her arm. She flung her luggage in the car then ran around the other side, savoring the feeling of blood flowing back into her limb.

The seatbelt was priority number one when she hopped into the car. God only knew what kind of insanity *this* car would endure.

"You did get the directions out of the other car, right?" she asked after about ten minutes.

"Yes. I grabbed them while you were trapping your arm," Noah answered, veering onto the on ramp of the interstate.

"You mean while I was *unlocking* the car like you *told* me to?"

"Why don't you let your mouth have a break and rest some? You have plenty of time."

McKenzie's head snapped toward Noah, her brain tripping a fuse. "Cut me some slack, will you? I just saw my best friend get killed. You of all people should know what that's like."

Noah's mouth closed, a faraway look shadowing his eyes. She turned away and rested her head against the window pane.

Time. *She* had plenty of it. Pierce had none. Jessie had none. Unanswered questions swirled like a hurricane in her brain. Jessie was dead because she knew too much, but how had she known the things she did? They'd come all the way to California chasing lead after unproductive lead in the hope that luck would point them in the right direction. Yet, information seemed to *find* Jessie in New York City. If only she knew Jessie's source.

Now there was another problem. In writing the article, McKenzie had set up a whole new route of inquiry for the FBI and CIA to follow. They'd want to know *her* source when they found her and Noah. It would be tricky to stay out of jail for obstruction of justice and keep Noah safe at the same time.

Might be easier to fling myself off a cliff when this is over.

No. I can do this. This is what I wanted. The story of a lifetime. To beat Jessie. I can do this. I can do it for Pierce.

Day 6: Noon (PST)

The check of the brakes jolted McKenzie awake. "Where are we?"

"Almost there."

They were stopped at a red light in the middle of Sacramento. Buildings towered on either side of them. McKenzie had only visited the city once before, but even so, she recognized the area near L Street.

"According to the directions, our stop should be on the next road," Noah said as he made a right hand turn.

All of the sudden, McKenzie realized why the sights were so familiar to her.

The Capitol Building gleamed bright white in the noonday sun, its distinctive dome similar to the Capitol building in D.C. Noah was still scanning the numbers lining the street and didn't seem to notice the looming structure until he put the car into park.

McKenzie watched as comprehension dawned on his face.

"We're at the freakin' Capitol," he said.

"No kidding."

"Maybe she works here. She could be a page or a janitor or..." Noah's voice trailed off, a light sparking in his eyes.

"Or what?"

"Mac, who's the governor of California?"

"Um, Christopher Bartley. Why?"

Then, her head snapped to attention. "Oh, no. Noah, you don't think—"

"Yeah, I do," Noah said. "I think we've found Chris."

CHAPTER FORTY

MCKENZIE AND NOAH couldn't waltz into the Capitol and demand an audience with the governor, so instead they drove through town until they found a sandwich shop. They both ordered ham on wheat before talking through their next steps.

"I guess it would be too much to hope we could call his office and make an appointment?" McKenzie ventured.

"Yeah. Slightly. Do you know how many people try to see the governor every day? Besides, he won't come within five feet of us once he finds out who *you* are," Noah remarked.

"So, what do you suggest?"

"I don't know. Considering it's not plastered all over the news that the governor of California was somehow involved with the guy who killed the vice president, I'm guessing Governor Bartley hasn't volunteered the information."

McKenzie winced. For the first time, Noah had spoken as though he was sure of Cody's guilt.

"I think we'll have to play hardball. I—" Noah stopped short. He was glaring over McKenzie's shoulder. His mouth twitched at the corners.

McKenzie turned around. Her own picture stared back at her from the TV above the deli counter. "The FBI is looking for this man and woman, who are wanted for questioning in the investigation of the death of Vice President Tifton."

Time seemed to thicken as faces around the restaurant turned toward Noah and McKenzie. The chatter of the other deli patrons buzzed like a hoard of locusts in McKenzie's ears. All around her, people whipped out Droids. iPhone cameras snapped pictures. The waitress at the counter lifted the portable from the wall.

Noah grabbed McKenzie's hand, unfreezing her from the eerie slow-motion moment. "We have to move."

McKenzie was vaguely aware of yelling as she followed Noah out the door and jogged behind him toward the stolen Honda. She had no way out of this. Pierce was dead, and she was wanted by the FBI.

What the hell have I done?

Noah eased away from the curb and kept the car steady at the forty-five miles per hour limit for ten minutes. They didn't need to attract any more attention, but the fact that he wasn't whisking them from disaster at full speed amped McKenzie's nerves.

"The FBI is hunting us now, so the butcher, the baker, and the candlestick maker'll be more than willing to turn us in. We need to disguise ourselves," Noah said, making a left into a gas station.

The restrooms were on the outside of the building. Thankfully, the guy at the counter didn't even look up from his crossword as McKenzie and Noah disappeared inside.

A rusty toilet sat in the corner, a sink with a half-broken mirror on the adjacent wall. Toilet paper covered the floor along with water and maybe worse. The room reeked of urine. McKenzie forced down the urge to vomit.

"Breathe through your mouth," Noah commanded, already at work rubbing water and industrial soap from the wall dispenser on his head.

He produced a strange knife from his pocket like no blade McKenzie had seen before. She gasped as he pressed the sharp edge against his head to shave.

When his head was bare, he chopped through his beard. He ran the knife flush with his chin until his jaw was smooth.

He turned to McKenzie. "Pull your hair back."

She secured her reddish-brown locks with a rubber band from her purse. Air eddied around her neck as she heard the soft thump that was her ponytail being sliced off. She glanced in the mirror. The choppy bob left behind looked like it was cut by a hairdresser with a drinking problem.

"Wait here," Noah said, and he left the bathroom.

A minute later, he came back carrying a package of Solo cups and several bags of Skittles.

"Nothing like a good snack to pass the dull moments," she said, brows raised.

"Not exactly," he said, filling a cup with water. He ripped open bag after bag of Skittles and dumped them into the cup. The water turned an ugly shade of brown as the coating melted off the candy.

"Lean over the sink so we don't make you a *complete* mess," he said.

In a horrible moment of realization, McKenzie understood what he was planning. She bent over, half agonizing about what was coming, half in awe of Noah's inventiveness.

The cool mixture washed over her head. *Disgusting.*

Noah's fingers combed through her hair to help soak in the blend.

"I take it the police at the station finally ran our plates?" McKenzie asked.

"I'm surprised it's taken them this long, to tell you the truth. The motel manager probably identified us after Pierce—" His voice hit a strange, high octave as he said her friend's name.

McKenzie fought the tears that threatened. "We didn't use our real names at the motel."

"I know," Noah said. "I guess he described us, and they put it together from there."

"Maybe," McKenzie mumbled.

She couldn't make any sense of why they hadn't been plastered across the news as soon as they stole evidence back in Los Angeles. What kind of law enforcement agency doesn't pursue evidence theft, especially when it's connected with the death of the Vice President of the United States?

Noah twisted McKenzie's hair and wrung it out. "You can stand up now," he said.

McKenzie lifted her head, and water dribbled down her cheek. She barely recognized the stranger reflected in the cracked mirror in front of her. Forget drinking problem. This hairdresser was a toddler.

"McKenzie McClendon, the asylum escapee," she mused.

"Better that than McKenzie McClendon, *Herald* reporter, wanted by the FBI."

"By the end of all this I might be both," she said.

She fussed with her drenched scalp, trying to make herself somewhat presentable. Looking as if she'd almost drowned in the gas station bathroom wasn't conducive to staying under the radar, either. "Next brilliant plan?"

"Need your cell phone and battery. I'm calling Governor Bartley. It's time for a reprieve."

He unfolded a wrinkled piece of paper and pressed it flat with his palm. McKenzie flinched as she saw Pierce's untidy scrawl. She squinted to read the digits her friend had written before they'd known Chris was a well-known political figure.

"How're you planning to bypass the secretary?" McKenzie asked as Noah punched the glowing numbers on the phone.

"I have a thought. We had code names in the SEALs, but a lot of us used 'em at home, too," he said. "I just hope it works. Now, quiet."

McKenzie heard the muffled voice of someone answering on the other line.

"I'm calling for Governor Bartley," Noah replied.

The secretary must've asked the nature of his call, because after she spoke, Noah said, "This is a personal call."

He paused, maybe to summon his nerves. "This is Hawk."

McKenzie's lips pinched together. Any second Noah would have to start explaining himself again. Surely this secretary wouldn't put through a call to the governor of California that easily. God willing, whatever story Noah concocted on the spot would be good enough.

Even though the phone was to Noah's ear, McKenzie heard the secretary's reply.

"Yes, sir. I'll put you right through."

McKenzie clapped her hand over her mouth to shove down

the expletive that almost flew out. Governor Bartley must've received tons of calls using Cody's SEAL code name for his calls to be patched through without question.

They'd found Chris.

Noah relayed the call to speaker phone. They waited thirty breathless seconds until finally, the holding music ceased.

The "hello" sounded wary and confused. McKenzie wasn't surprised. The governor—along with everyone else in the country—could hardly have missed the news of Cody Randolph's death. He had to be scared shitless that someone knew about Hawk. Whatever he had to do with Cody, he'd kept it secret for a *reason*. Could there have been a conspiracy in the California government that required the expertise of a former Navy SEAL? Or worse—was the governor connected to the assassinations?

If so, how did that tie in with the Shen?

Noah didn't ask him any of the questions running through McKenzie's head, though. Instead, he rattled off an address.

Then he said, "We know about Cody Randolph. Come alone."

CHAPTER FORTY ONE

Day 6: Afternoon (EST)
Washington, D.C.

LIGHTS FLASHED AROUND Elaine as dozens of cameras captured her entering the cathedral where minutes later, President Seymour's state funeral would begin. Elaine had chosen to take part in the procession on foot, though her advisors had quarreled with her endlessly over the decision. Of course they were worried about the dangers after two sitting heads of the nation had been shot this week. At the end of the day, for Elaine, there was no choice to be made. Lyndon Johnson had done it for Kennedy, and she would do it now.

Inside the church, sniffles echoed off the towering walls, the only sounds aside from the organ music playing softly in the background. Elaine took her seat next to Bert Royal and turned to watch the doorway. At any moment, the former First Lady would enter just ahead of the pallbearers.

Elaine rose with the crowd as the former First Lady entered, head bowed, a tissue at her eyes. Earlier in the day, Elaine had taken a phone call from Hayley Seymour, who had assured her she wouldn't be offended if Elaine chose not to take part in the procession. Elaine had extended her personal condolences and told her she would see her there.

Next, a group of pristine military officers marched in carrying the black-lacquered casket where the former President of the United States rested. Elaine's chest constricted as if her lungs had shrunk to half capacity. No matter how prepared she thought she was for this moment, seeing that box was different from what she'd imagined.

She followed the progress of the officers until they set the casket down at the front. A ray of light from one of the deep-hued stained glass windows caught the side of Bert's face next to her. Elaine noticed for the first time he was crying.

Bert and President Seymour had been great friends, but until this moment, Elaine hadn't thought of Bert as much more than President Seymour's Chief of Staff. Here, however, the enormity of Bert's week, of his phone call to her in the early hours of the morning after the president was shot, suddenly made Elaine's breathing shallow.

For over an hour, the funeral proceeded. Elaine thoughtfully listened to the remarks made about her predecessor and tried to concentrate on nothing else. All of these tears and pain, and she sat in his place.

An honor and a curse at the same time.

At last, the priest stood to offer a final prayer. Elaine bowed her head with him.

But as he spoke, she heard a second, softer voice in her ear.

"Madame President, the U.S. Embassy in Pakistan has been bombed. Please proceed with us to your vehicle following the recessional out of the church."

She sucked in a breath and smoothed her hands over her ebony dress. Perfect timing, as ever.

"Amen," the priest concluded.

The recessional snaked out of the cathedral, its—and Elaine's—pace way too slow for her speeding heart. Daylight hit her eyes as she reached the doors. Secret Service whisked her toward the left of the building and away from the rest of the recessional, which continued forward.

She could feel the heads turning, heard one Secret Service agent over her shoulder speak into his radio.

"Glass on the move."

Day 6: Afternoon (CST)
San Antonio, Texas

The laundromat never had any customers. Nevertheless, the dark Ford Focus sat parked outside the building exactly where it was supposed to be. At three o'clock, several figures emerged. Two men ushered a willowy figure toward the car, sandwiching her between them. Her shiny black hair swayed gently beneath her shoulders in the wind as they reached the vehicle.

Lima Olmstead opened the car door and climbed into the backseat. One of the men settled beside her. The other closed them in and trotted around the Focus. He took the passenger's seat position.

The driver pulled away from the curb while Lima Olmstead whispered with the man in the backseat. "I knew it would take some time for the efforts to come to fruition, but I'd hoped we'd get wind of it before something else like this occurred." She shook her head. "Bhutto, Totah. How many more will we lose before the end?"

"There won't be an end," replied the man next to her. "This will go on forever, unfortunately."

The man in the back then leaned forward. "Gentry, this isn't the right way. We were supposed to turn back at the four way stop."

Uhlig eased the car onto the shoulder of the road as if heeding the instructions, but instead, he grabbed his SIG. "I'm aware."

Before the man in the front seat could register what was happening, Uhlig put a bullet into his forehead. Blood sprayed the passenger's side window.

The man in the backseat received a round through his heart before he could reach his gun. Uhlig trained the pistol on Lima Olmstead.

She froze halfway to her own weapon, her teeth flashing in anger. After a second's hesitation and a glance toward her own weapon, she folded her hands in her lap.

185

"What do you want from me?" There was no fear in her voice.

Uhlig's laugh came out dry and cruel. *What do I want?*

Time had been a lot kinder to this woman than it should've been. She had to be in her sixties by now, but barely a line marred her face, save for the tiny etches of crow's feet that branched from the corners of her eyes. Her nerve, to sit here so perfect, when she was sending others left and right to be maimed and die for her cause.

"I want nothing you can give me," he replied.

She spread her palms onto her knees, resigned. "Who sent you?"

Xavier was to be the man who came here to kill this woman, the woman who held one of the highest positions in the Shen. It had been ordered. The fact that Xavier was no longer available to complete the task had no bearing on whether or not it had to be done.

"No one."

Olmstead let out a nervous laugh. At first, Uhlig thought it seemed a strange reaction, given the circumstances, but then again, she had probably been expecting this for some time now. Maybe she didn't know how or when, but her death at an assassin's hands had always been certain.

"Come now," she said in her thick Spanish accent. "If you've come to shoot me, at least give me the satisfaction of knowing who won the prize."

Images filled Uhlig's mind. He could almost smell the urine from Robbie's wet pants that night as they watched the men drag their mother's body toward the bedroom. She'd devoted her life to the Shen, and what had it gotten her? A bag over her head and two orphaned children. All because of her stupid "cause". The men had laid her in the shower, ran water over her to wash away any traces of evidence left behind.

"You weren't the prize," he said truthfully, "more of a consequence."

"Perhaps I should've asked what I did—specifically—to

186

deserve this honor."

The fire in her eyes was familiar to him. It was the same passion that burned in his mother's eyes the night she refused to give in to the two thugs who came to their home.

Uhlig shook his head. "You can't have believed you'd orchestrate the rise of a female President of the United States and be allowed to continue. The Shen have enemies everywhere, all of whom now realize just how dangerous you are as the group's leader."

Lima Olmstead cocked her head and raised an eyebrow. "Interesting," she said.

In a burst of movement, Olmstead lurched for her gun. Reflex alone locked Uhlig's finger down on the trigger. The shot caught the woman in the chest.

Crimson poured from the wound. Lily white fingers splayed across it, resting there, almost in relief. Her breaths rattled as Uhlig watched the fight in her eyes vanish, the life draining from her.

Then, just before she took her last shuddering breath, she whispered something that Uhlig, for everything he'd seen and done, simply could not believe.

CHAPTER FORTY TWO

Day 6: Evening (PST)
Sacramento, California

"WE'RE MEETING HIM *here?* The governor of California?" McKenzie gestured vaguely to indicate the crowd around them in the mall. "Doesn't he have security tailing him at all times? We'll be caught."

"Slow down, Mac," Noah said. "Something tells me he'll ditch the security team for this. I doubt even they know he was associated with Cody."

McKenzie nodded. He made sense. "What time is it?"

"Ten after seven," Noah said.

Governor Bartley had agreed to meet them at seven fifteen. McKenzie glanced around as children holding their mothers' hands passed. Teenagers ambled by, yammering on their cell phones. No sign of anyone who looked important.

A few moments later, however, a man in a baseball cap made eye contact from the bench where he sat. He nodded at Noah. McKenzie was strongly reminded of the way mafia movies depicted informants.

She followed Noah toward the man, who stood as they approached.

"Are you the person who called me?" Governor Bartley asked.

Noah's gaze darted about the surrounding area.

"Don't worry," Governor Bartley said, "I don't want anyone to know I'm meeting you any more than you do."

McKenzie shifted nervously as Noah motioned toward the

food court to their left. "Let's have a seat and chat a while."

The strange little group sat at a table in the corner next to a Chinese take-out shop. "Did we have to meet somewhere this crowded?" the governor asked, his voice weak and shaky. His bony fingers drummed the table, his skin waxy over his gaunt face.

"It's better here. The louder it is, the less the chance somebody overhears," Noah answered. "Now, tell us about Cody."

Bartley's fists were balled, his foot tapping. "First, why don't you tell me who the hell you are."

So, the niceties are over. That didn't take long.

Noah's brow furrowed. McKenzie silently willed him to explain. The governor would be more apt to talk if he knew why they were here.

"You're not exactly in the position to make demands," Noah said.

Please, Noah. He thinks we're only here to blackmail him.

The governor leaned back, pressing his palms flat against his legs. "You're not cops. The cops aren't with you."

Noah grunted. "I'm not here to extort you. I was Cody's partner in the SEALs."

It didn't escape McKenzie that he hadn't mentioned who *she* was. In fact, the exchange reminded McKenzie of the first time they'd met up with Cody's mother; Noah hadn't acknowledged McKenzie's presence at all then, either.

"Ah." The governor sighed, the shadow of something like regret falling across his face. He stared at Noah for a moment, searching. Then, he turned to McKenzie. "And you are?"

"McKenzie McClendon," she answered, not anxious to reveal more.

Bartley gesticulated with his right hand, urging her to continue. "And what do you have to do with all this?"

McKenzie gulped. "I'm a reporter for the *New York Herald*."

"What?" Bartley shoved back from the table as if it was on fire. "No way. You'll blab whatever I say all over the damn country."

Noah put his hand on the governor's shoulder. "Sit."

Unsettled, Governor Bartley eased himself back into the chair. He scowled at Noah, who glared right back. "I know she's a reporter, but I can promise you that if you don't talk to us, you'll be talking to the FBI and the CIA soon. I know you don't want that. If you did, you'd have called them the second you found out Cody was killed."

"How do you know I haven't?" the governor asked.

"Because if you had, you wouldn't be here without security in your little ball cap, now would you?" Noah replied. "Plus, you'd have been all over the news by now."

Defeated, Governor Bartley stared down at the white Formica table. His eyes looked tired, dark bags underneath them. He twisted his hands in his lap.

"You said on the phone you know about Cody Randolph. So what do you want from me? You want money?"

McKenzie had figured the governor would think they were here to blackmail him, but until now, she hadn't thought about that Governor Bartley would assume they knew what his connection to Cody *was*.

"I already told you I'm not here for money. I'm here because Cody was my friend," Noah said. "Since there's no good way to ask this, I'll be blunt. Were you or weren't you involved with the assassinations?"

The governor's head jerked back in shock. Whatever he thought they knew about him, this was apparently not it.

"Are you asking if I'm responsible for some huge government conspiracy? Good Lord, no," he said, horrified.

"You didn't say you had nothing to do with it," Noah countered.

"I can't." Chris Bartley shook his head, close to tears. "I just can't. If she wrote about it, it would ruin me."

"Governor." McKenzie reached out, touching the man's hand. The look in his eyes gave him away. There was something more at root here than politics. She wasn't oblivious to another human's hurting, no matter how important—or possibly corrupt—he might be. "I promise you I'll keep this conversation confidential. You have my word."

McKenzie felt more than saw the look Noah shot her way. She thought of the promise to him she'd broken by writing the article about Cody. God, she had screwed up.

She shoved that worry aside. They needed to hear what Bartley knew about Cody. Barring a search through every last file on Kimberly Lawson's hard drive—a nearly impossible task while on the run from the FBI—he was their only other clue as to how Cody had been brought into the killings. "Did you hire Cody Randolph to hurt someone?"

Governor Chris Bartley looked into McKenzie's face, and grief echoed on his own. "You don't understand." A tear formed in the corner of his hazel eye. "Cody didn't work for me."

He took a great shuddering breath. "We were in love."

CHAPTER FORTY THREE

Day 6: Evening (PST)
Los Angeles, California

LUCAS CRAWFORD BELIEVED he'd done a clean enough job on the hit to escape without questions. He *would* have if that prick Noah Hutchins would've stayed out of it.

A good bomb called for a doze, so he'd taken a nap when he'd returned. He'd slept longer than he meant to, though, and now it was almost dark outside. Alarm clocks pissed him off. Usually his body was trained to do without them, but his schedule had been thrown by the adrenaline rush of rigging the truck.

He scrambled out of bed and began his systematic cleanup of the hotel room. A scrub down of the tables, floor, and base boards was necessary. *No such thing as too careful.*

Weapons went back into their cases and into a plain duffle bag. The fool back at the apartment had noticed the rifle case. Of course, Lucas had disposed of the old man, but he wouldn't make the mistake of using the shiny case alone again.

As he packed, he flipped on the TV to the evening news. The room was too quiet without some kind of white noise.

He almost choked on his own spit when he saw the pictures plastered on the screen under the tag, "Wanted by the FBI."

They described Noah Hutchins and the reporter, who he now knew to be named McKenzie McClendon. He bumped the volume up a few notches. He remembered how the smell of her fear had risen off of her like steam from a freshly rained-on pavement in July. Made him hard just thinking about it. She was a pretty thing. It would be such a shame to waste her.

Hutchins and McClendon were wanted for stealing evidence collected from Cody Randolph's hotel room. McClendon's uncle, a Detective Sal Becker, was now suspended from the LAPD pending investigation. The pair was also suspected in a car bombing outside a local motel.

Shit. They weren't in the damn car. *They're like fucking roaches.*

Pissed as hell, Lucas threw everything into his suitcase so haphazardly it wouldn't zip. He slammed his fists against it, forcing it closed. This was getting ridiculous. They needed to disappear. Now.

He checked over every inch of the room one more time to be sure he'd left nothing. He slung his bags over his shoulder and went across the street without stopping to pay the motel. He'd never checked in in the first place.

His head was about to explode the same way President Seymour's had. All that time to wire up the truck, and it blew to high hell without taking Hutchins with it. Unbelievable.

With the address he'd looked up already plugged into the rental's GPS, he sped off. This time, he'd leave nothing to chance. He'd walk straight up to them and put bullets into both their fucking skulls.

Well, he'd put one in Hutchins' head right away. He might keep the girl around a bit longer.

One thing was for sure: he'd find Noah Hutchins, and God help anyone who stood in his way.

Day 6: Evening (PST)
Los Angeles, California

Al-Musari had said only one man alive and still working could pull off the shot. Uhlig didn't know who he was, but he knew who'd know where to find him.

Shariphe Bruno had never dealt with Uhlig in person, but the two had talked on several occasions. The man dealt in black market arms and outfitted half the underworld with the most up

5Colby Marshall

to date weaponry the manufacturers—and more importantly, the United States military—had to offer. He should. After all, he used to work for them.

Now, Uhlig stood across room from Bruno in the basement of a Greek restaurant. There was nothing he could do anymore other than find whoever shot the president and kill the bastard himself. It wasn't that he gave a damn about the U.S. or its leader. As with Lima Olmstead, it was more of a consequence.

Bruno twisted a screwdriver into a new model gun he was working on. "If you could find him this easily, he'd have already been caught, in jail, and waiting for the gas chamber by now," he said. The scars were shiny on his black skin, gifts from men who'd taught him the price of not getting the ammunition they needed when they needed it.

Uhlig swigged the beer he'd been offered upon entering Bruno's workshop. Bruno was in a hard place, of course. He had to know he was screwed whether he identified the shooter or not. Uhlig's task was simply to make him realize not telling was the more immediate danger.

He slammed the bottle down on the work table. A dribble of condensation slid down its side. "I know you know how to find him, Shariphe."

The arms dealer set the gun he was fixing onto the work station and leaned toward Uhlig. "Are you sure you *want* to find him, Fabian?"

Uhlig picked up the gun between them and admired the craftsmanship, its perfect specs designed for someone ready to take down an enemy from afar.

"No," Uhlig replied. "I don't want to. I have to."

Day 6: Evening (PST)
Los Angeles, California

Lucas eased through the carport toward the back door of the split-level house. He removed a utility knife from his belt and inserted it into the lock.

194

No alarm. Come on. No alarm.

There wasn't.

Of course not. Stupid shit thinks he's protection enough, because he's a cop.

Lucas shifted through the house without noise, his feet falling from heel to toe to pad sound. He wasn't a SEAL anymore, but some things you didn't forget. He made mental notes as he moved. Points of exit. Phones within reach. Possible weapons.

At the living room door, he pressed his body against the frame and assessed the situation. The glow of the muted television bathed the face of the man asleep on the plaid sofa. His Glock lay on a table three feet away. *No place for a gun in your sweats, huh?*

The firearms case on the wall appeared to be locked. The glass could break in a skirmish, though. *Must contain as soon as possible.*

No one else was in the house. The man's wife had left him long ago. Pictures around the room showed off their little boy as a toddler: atop a horse, face messy after eating spaghetti, smiling beside his dad at a ballgame. The kid's older pictures were sparse, a sure sign he lived with his mother—and maybe a charming step family—except on weekends and Christmas.

Which, tonight, was a good thing for the kid.

Sal Becker didn't stir as Lucas crawled behind the couch. He touched the cold barrel of his Beretta to the guy's temple. "Don't move."

Sal's eyes flew open. His hand jumped in the direction of his gun.

"Don't move, or I'll blow your brains out."

Sal's eyes stretched wider. A gun against the temple did that to a man. His hand fluttered back to his chest. "Who are you?"

"Not important," said Lucas as he lifted Detective Becker's Glock. He stored it in his side holster, then stepped in front of Sal, gun still trained on his forehead.

"What do you want, you son of a bitch?" Beads of sweat dripped down Sal's face.

"Oh, come now, Sal," Lucas said, "play nice. If you don't, I won't, either."

Sal shook so much that Lucas wondered if the detective had ever been in real peril. Cops really were all talk, weren't they?

"Please tell me why you're here," Sal said through gritted teeth.

"That's a better," Lucas said with a sneer. He reached for the thick rope in his pocket but spotted a pair of handcuffs on the table where the detective had emptied his pockets. He cuffed Sal's hands in front of him. Once the detective's hands were no longer free, Lucas slipped knots into the rope to bind his feet. Such a good little sailor.

"Down to business," he said to Sal, disgusted at how drenched the man was in his own perspiration already. "Where's your niece?"

Becker didn't so much as blink. "I don't have a niece."

Lucas let out a sarcastic laugh. "Good try, Sal, but no dice. I already know you've helped sweet little McKenzie and her buddy the SEAL. It's all over the news. You know, you really shouldn't have done that. Cops are supposed to have ethics. I hear they're giving you a time-out while they look into it." Lucas clicked his tongue. "You're already in deep shit. I suggest you give me some straight answers and fast, or this could get even worse for you."

He plucked a knife from its sheath on his belt. He flipped it open and pointed it at Becker. "Talk."

Sal shook his head. "Honestly. I...I don't know where she is." Then, he took a deep breath and lifted his chin. "Even if I did, I wouldn't tell you."

"Aren't you the classic hero?" Lucas spat. "But we disagree on that point, I'm afraid. I think you know exactly where she is. I also think you're very wrong if you're under the impression you won't tell me. I've made bigger men than you confide in me, if you know what I mean."

He held Sal's hand up to him, pressed the blade hard into Sal's left palm, and sliced downward. A stream of scarlet trickled the length of Sal's arm and onto the beige carpet. The cop winced, his breathing heavy.

"Oops," Lucas simpered. "Slipped. By the way, are you right-handed or left-handed, Sal?"

Sal didn't answer. He closed his eyes tighter.

"Pretending you can't see me won't make me less real." Lucas chuckled. "Still not in a talking mood?" he asked, shaking his head. "I'll go with the odds and say you're right-handed. In that case, I'll start with your left so we can work our way up to more important things. Maybe you'll do yourself a favor and wise up."

He gripped the pointer finger of Sal's left hand. Becker twisted and writhed, trying to slither away. Lucas was stronger.

Sal puffed air loud and hard through his nose. He knew what was coming.

Lucas held his Emerson to the slippery knuckle of Sal's finger. "Where is she, Sal?"

"I don't know. I swear," Sal said, his voice rising in panic.

Lucas sliced down the way a scythe cuts grain. Sal muffled his agonizing scream by biting his bottom lip. Damn. The guy was tougher than he thought.

He produced a lighter from his pocket and held it to Sal's finger to cauterize the bleeding. The smell of sizzling flesh met Lucas' nostrils. The cop moaned. Tears streaked his face.

"I'll give you a second to rest, and then we'll try this again," Lucas said. He flipped the lighter in the air and caught it in one hand. "Let me tell you a secret, Sal. You listening? You're going to tell me what you know. There's an easy way and a hard way. The longer you hold out, the worse you'll make it."

The detective squirmed as he tried to edge off the sofa toward where the fireplace poker lay. Lucas laughed. "Do you think you're in shape for a fight, old man? With your hands cuffed? Let's try. This could be fun."

Sal collapsed back against the sofa. He grimaced, holding his mutilated left hand gently in his right.

"Shame," Lucas said, nodding to the blood oozing from the stump of Sal's finger. "Such pretty carpet."

Lucas held each finger in turn and asked the cop again and again. Every time, Sal denied having information. Every time he gave nothing, Lucas sliced another finger from his hand. Sal's gaze shifted around the room as if searching for some hidden strength.

The detective grew paler. His body vibrated. Still, he hadn't screamed. Lucas was floored. Men a lot tougher than this pansy excuse for a cop had hollered in agony during the same technique. It was almost a challenge.

"With any luck, you'll pass out by the time we get to the right hand," he said as he singed Sal's hand with the lighter once more.

When Sal was about to lose the thumb on his left hand, the cop spoke again. His voice was quiet as a SEAL's footfalls on the beach. Probably going into shock.

"Please," he sputtered, "I don't know anything."

Lucas reached into his pocket and extracted another tool. "In that case, I suggest you find out something. If you pass out, you'll be of no use to me anymore."

CHAPTER FORTY FOUR

Day 6: Evening (PST)
Sacramento, California

MCKENZIE AND NOAH bustled through the mall crowd. "Lucas somehow found out about Cody and the governor. He knew Cody would be the perfect accomplice. He had SEAL sniper experience *and* something in his life worth killing for," Noah whispered. "It all makes sense now. Cody wasn't doing it for himself. Outing one of the most conservative Republican figures in the country would be the scandal of the century. Cody couldn't let that happen, because he loved the guy."

Goosebumps prickled McKenzie's arms. Her intense concentration on Noah's words nearly caused her to bump into a woman pushing a stroller. "Excuse me," she mumbled, shuffling out of the way. "Okay," she said. "Kimberly Lawson and the Shen hired Lucas. He couldn't carry out simultaneous assassinations by himself. I get that. But how did he find out about Cody and the governor?"

Noah shook his head. "I don't know. We're still missing something, but—" He cut off mid-sentence, his hand seizing McKenzie's.

He needn't have stopped her, though. She'd heard the commotion behind them, as well.

The woman with the stroller stood where McKenzie had jarred her, screaming. "Help! It's that couple the FBI has all over the TV."

McKenzie took off running, following Noah. The two of them tore through the crowd. McKenzie almost knocked over an old man as her shoulder slammed him. Noah still had her hand, yanking her through the maze like a wild dog pulling his owner on his leash. An exit sign glowed in view, but a security guard stood in front of the door, Taser in hand.

Noah released McKenzie's hand. "Get out," he yelled as he moved toward the guard.

In the split-second the guard hesitated to use the Taser, Noah eradicated the option with a swift kick to the guy's wrist. The guard clutched his arm, moaning. The Taser skidded across the floor. The guard threw a punch, but Noah ducked it and moved behind him. He wrapped the man's neck in the crook of one elbow, pushing the guard's head toward it with the other hand. The guy grabbed at Noah's arms helplessly, trying to pull them off. The skin on his face blotched, and his eyes slid out of focus. The guard's knees collapsed as he melted to the floor.

"What are you waiting for? Go," Noah shouted.

McKenzie jolted back into reality. She sprinted out the door, Noah's footsteps just behind her.

Shit!

They'd exited two lots over from where the stolen Honda was parked.

Noah charged toward a woman loading bags into her minivan. Though he brandished no weapon, she let out a threatened squeak. She dropped the bag she was holding and stretched her arms in the air.

"I don't want to hurt you. Just give me your keys," Noah said.

The woman stuttered, fear shining in her eyes. "My...my son."

A small boy sat buckled in the backseat. He had to be about the same age as her cousin Levi.

The woman's whimper was sharp in McKenzie's ears as Noah opened the sliding door of the van. He pressed the release button on the kid's seatbelt.

"Out, son," Noah said. The boy slid out of the seat, crying.

The lady tossed Noah her keys as the little boy skidded into her arms. The kid buried his head in his mother's neck. She slid her fingers through his hair, holding him to her.

Noah caught the keys. "I'm so sorry," he mumbled.

McKenzie tore her eyes from the embrace and jumped into the minivan. Good thing she'd brought her laptop case into the mall with her along with the hard drive. The pink suitcase wasn't as much a loss as either of those would've been.

She almost didn't hear her cell phone ring over the sound that was Noah revving the van's engine. She'd completely forgotten to remove the battery again after Noah's call to the governor.

"What is it with your phone and getaways?" Noah shouted as the van bounced over a speed bump.

"Wouldn't be an issue if we weren't always getting away from something," McKenzie said. She fiddled with the belt to buckle herself in, but she had to answer the phone. Call it a gut feeling, but only a handful of people would be calling her. She picked up, trying not to drop the phone as the van bounded along.

Deep, raspy breaths met her ears. Her hand tightened on the phone.

What the hell?

"McKenzie." Although in many ways, the strained voice sounded like a stranger's, there was no mistaking that it was her uncle. The quality of his tone sent shivers rippling down McKenzie's legs.

"Uncle Sal?"

"McKenzie, where are you?" The words sounded as if they were uttered under water.

"Uncle Sal, are you okay?" she asked. Her heart skipped.

"Where are you?"

"I'm in Sacramento," she replied. Were those choked sobs crackling into the phone's speaker? "Why? Uncle Sal, what's wrong?"

"I need you to meet me," he said. "I have some new…information…about the killings…just for you." His words were thin. Deep gasps came in between them as if he was drowning in his own sentences.

Her heart was now trying to escape from her chest. She lowered her voice to a whisper. "Uncle Sal, are you alone?"

"McKenzie," he muttered. The phone line went dead.

Fear erupted from her as she hit the button to call back.

Damn it!

There was no answer. She knew there wouldn't be. "Noah, we have to do something. Something's wrong with Uncle Sal."

Her hands shook as she relayed the telephone conversation. Color washed out of Noah's face and left his lips drawn in a thin, tight line. He took a sidelong glance at McKenzie before spinning a U-turn in the middle of the road.

"Call 911," Noah directed as the van shot down the freeway. "Give Sal's address, tell them there's an emergency, then hang up and power the phone off. No time for details. Remember, if that phone has GPS, they could trace us."

McKenzie nodded and punched the numbers on the keypad, so familiar and yet so foreign at the same time. A voice weary from a day full of talking to panicked people answered. "911. What is your emergency?"

McKenzie rattled off Uncle Sal's home address, spelling the street name as she went. The operator asked another question, but McKenzie interrupted her. "Please hurry. He could be hurt."

Her heart galloped as she ended the call, powered off the phone, and popped the battery out again.

Hurry.

"Very good," Lucas said, taking the cell phone from Sal's ear. "But, I could've done without the sputtering. You'd think you were in pain."

Sal's hands dripped crimson, and a mixture of perspiration and tears poured from his face. He blinked the moisture away.

Lucas watched as Sal huffed and puffed, clenched his jaw as though willing himself composure.

Such a shame.

"Please," Sal begged. "I've done everything you've asked of

me. Please leave me."

God, I hate it when they turn pathetic.

"I appreciate your getting in touch for me." Lucas leveled the Beretta with Sal's forehead. "It was a big help."

He fired a single shot between Sal's eyes.

A small sound barely louder than the air conditioner whirring to life. He turned to face the bedroom hallway. There stood a small boy, bleary-eyed from recent sleep. He looked from his dead father to Lucas, terrified comprehension dawning on his face.

Lucas shook his head in disbelief. No wonder Sal had been so quiet and compliant while having his fingers sawed off. "This just keeps getting more complicated."

He fired the gun once more.

CHAPTER FORTY FIVE

Day 6: Late Night (EST)
The White House

IN PAST YEARS, the Situation Room of the White House had been known to the Secret Service as "The Cement Mixer." Elaine used to think it was because this was the place where officials solidified tough choices to solve messy situations. However, the more Elaine visited the complex of conference rooms, the more she became sure its name reflected that it was where, if you were still for even a moment, you would get stuck.

As Elaine listened to the fast-paced discussion, the funeral seemed decades away. They'd been pouring over tactical options for hours.

Now, National Security Advisor Ronald Garrety, still in the formal black suit and sedate gray tie he'd worn to the funeral, stood to relay new information. "The Pakistani government has claimed responsibility for the embassy bombing, citing it as a response to our strike of their army base. We knew this was a possibility."

"I'd hoped they'd give up Al-Musari before being stupid enough to attack us," Elaine replied.

"Sometimes the so-so kids turn against the bully on the playground," Garrety shrugged. "Sometimes they don't."

Elaine nodded. A migraine stewed behind her eyes, and waves of nausea crashed over her. She longed to remove the pins that held her hair in the prim updo she'd worn for the funeral, if only to relieve some of the ache in her head. "Remind me again. How many are dead?"

"Emergency response teams are still extricating bodies from the wreckage. Based on how many people we think were in the embassy at the time, probably around seventy or eighty. Most were U.S. citizens."

Elaine massaged her temples in short circles.

Damn. Only two weeks into the presidency, and I already have the makings of a full-fledged war on my hands.

"I can't see a way around it," she mumbled to Garrety as others talked amongst themselves.

"It hasn't even been a week since the president and vice president were killed. Conspiracy buffs will have a field day."

"I realize that, but the presidency is multifaceted. It can't have only one objective at a time. I can't control that."

Garrety shifted in his seat. "As much as I hate to say it, you're right. It wasn't on our soil, but they were our people. I can't say I see another option that will work long-term."

Elaine nodded, turning to Bert. Terror churned in her gut. "Have a declaration drafted and to Congress by morning. We cautioned them once with the air strike. We're done with warnings."

She pushed back from the table, and the advisors did so as well. "Good evening, ladies and gentlemen," she said. Then, she exited the room.

As she sped through the hallways, her feet ached inside her heels. The collar of her black dress, now wrinkled from hours in the cramped Situation Room, felt as if it were a noose around her neck cutting off her oxygen. She'd downed several cups of coffee to stay awake, and yet she was still close to falling asleep on her feet.

Bert Royal called out from behind her. "Madame President, a word if you please."

"Of course, Bert. Walk with me."

"Madame President, please consider scaling back our response. With all due respect, the last thing we want or need is the appearance that we've rushed into an unpopular war."

"Do *you* think we're rushing into it, Bert?" Elaine shot back.

"Yes and no," he replied, his face reddening. The cleft in his chin twitched. "I'm aware we must act, but a declaration of war is a bit like using an AK-47 to kill a chipmunk, isn't it?"

Elaine tapped her foot on the hardwood floor as she met Bert's eyes. "Yes. A particularly annoying chipmunk that keeps showing up where it's not wanted."

"You remember what happened the last time an administration started a war the majority of American voters disagreed with, right?"

"I do," she replied. "I also recall that said conflict didn't arise from a response to someone blowing up random American boats and embassies."

They'd come to the door of Elaine's private study. "Bert, you're the Chief of Staff. I appreciate all you do in that capacity, but leave the strategizing to me," she said before she slammed the door in his face.

CHAPTER FORTY SIX

Day 7: Early Morning (PST)
Los Angeles, California

FIVE HOURS AFTER the scramble from the mall and the unnerving phone call from Uncle Sal, Noah and Mac were back in Los Angeles. Mac had tried several times to call her uncle, but as expected, he didn't answer. Noah tried to reassure her that help could've already come and taken him to the hospital. Doubtful, but possible. 911 had been called, and they would act if they arrived and he was incapacitated.

McKenzie seemed most worried about her cousin, Levi. Hopefully the boy had been at his mother's house and wasn't alone with his injured or ill father.

As they approached Sal's house, the darkness of the windows was ominous. Noah passed the driveway and parked in the cul-de-sac down the road. If someone was there, he'd have the element of surprise. Maybe.

Light on upstairs, none on the lower level. No footprints in the dirt or grass leading to the house, nothing out of the ordinary. Didn't mean anything, of course. Noah was well aware who he was dealing with.

Of the points of entry, the garage door looked like the best tactical bet. He'd prefer to enter through the back window, which would be more unexpected, but without the right equipment and the added weight of the reporter, the door was more practical. From the way the windows were set outside the house, it looked like they'd have at least a few seconds upon entry before being seen by anyone inside.

Noah tried the door. Unlocked. Kimberly Lawson's apartment flashed in his mind.

Never a good sign.

He stepped into the shadows of the house, vaguely aware of the increase in Mac's breathing rate behind him. His finger wrapped the trigger of the Beretta at his side.

Ready. Steady. Assess and contain.

Gun first around the corner, Noah pivoted to look into the living room.

Christ.

"McKenzie, wait. Don't come in here."

The dread in his voice only served to force McKenzie's feet forward. No matter how bad it was, she had to know. She crossed the barrier into the living room. Her head spun as if she'd just ridden the teacups at Disney World.

Uncle Sal lay dead on the floor, the cylinder of a bullet hole seared in his head. She dry heaved as she saw his fingers strewn around his body. His left hand was nothing but bloody stumps.

"If you need to puke, do it," Noah said. "Holding it in won't help."

"Yeah," she said, but talking was a bad idea.

McKenzie retched and ran for the bathroom, but as she passed the couch, another sight caught her eyes. "Oh, no. Oh, no, no, no!" Her chest constricted. No air.

"What?" Noah said as he came around the sofa.

McKenzie met Noah's eyes, then guided his gaze toward the little boy on the floor, a single bullet wound in his chest. A dark stain ran down his front. His blue eyes were still wide with the fear of the last thing they'd seen.

"Levi," she whispered. Tears flooded her cheeks. She gulped. "That old witch kept Uncle Sal from Levi as much as possible. She always said being with Sal wasn't safe for him." She took another long rattling breath. "He was only seven."

Though she knew she shouldn't, McKenzie squatted next to Levi's body, put her hand to his tiny face. She expected Noah to stop her, to yell at her not to contaminate the crime scene. He didn't.

She ran her fingers over Levi's eyes to close them. His lids felt rubbery underneath her fingertips. Another tear trickled down her nose. Now, he looked like he could've fallen asleep in the middle of the hallway.

"We can't stay," Noah said as he pulled upward on McKenzie's hand.

She obeyed his hand's steadiness even though she didn't want to peel her eyes from Levi. The last time she'd seen him was his third birthday. She could still see the grin on his face as he bounced around the kitchen on a stick-horse. He'd asked the guests if they wanted to pet "Lightnin' Man."

The sight of Levi, his Spider-Man pajamas coated in blood, had driven away her previous nausea, drowned it in a bottomless well of grief. So many people she loved, gone, their lives extinguished as if they were of no more consequence than an ant crushed beneath someone's heel. She had to get out of this nightmare of a house. Now. Luckily, Noah was already leading her that way.

At the doorway, a figure stepped out of the shadows.

Brian Varnes held a customized handgun, matte black as if it had absorbed all the light around it, complete with laser sight and a silencer.

McKenzie's whole world narrowed to the lethal black hole at the end of the gun.

Noah snapped his own weapon to bear on his old teammate. "What the hell are you doing here?"

Brian, however, lowered his weapon. The red eye of the laser dotted the floor. "Put it down, Noah. I'm not here to shoot you. I thought you might be him." He looked twenty years older than when McKenzie had seen him in the barn behind his house a few days ago.

"Well, why *are* you here then?" McKenzie's voice dripped with accusation.

"Lucas found me. Yeah, I know it was Lucas," Brian

answered their confused stares. "He didn't tell me it was him, but I'm not a damn fool. His smartass remarks identified him better than if he'd sent me an autographed picture. Some voices you don't forget."

He turned to McKenzie. "Ask Noah. SEAL teams can't hide much from each other. I've never forgotten a teammate's style."

McKenzie nodded. Noah said something similar the night he pegged Lucas as Kimberly Lawson's killer; he'd recognized Lucas' signature.

Brian went on. "He called me and said for me to come to this address in case you showed up. I figure he realized he couldn't wait here for you himself when the firemen showed up to check out an emergency call. First responders are one thing, but the cops would've been less easy to fool. Police aren't exactly your best pals when you've shot the president."

Brian shook his head in a cocktail of amazement and disgust. "I guess it was you folks who called in the tip?" He looked to Noah for confirmation.

When Noah jerked his head in agreement, Brian continued. "He pretended to be Sal when they came. Told 'em everything was okay. He warned me if the police came, I'd best do the same. Threatened to snap my kids' necks if I didn't."

"So you're going to give us up?" McKenzie asked, picturing Brian's wife's face back at the cabin. It was just like Cody Randolph's relationship with the governor. Varnes would protect the people he loved.

"Of course not," Brian said. "I'm a *real* SEAL. We *know* about honor."

"Lucas is batshit crazy, Man," Noah said. "You and your family better hide out for a while. He'll come after you."

"I know he will," Brian said. "Which is why I'm really sorry I have to do this."

With that, Brian aimed his Beretta at Noah and fired.

CHAPTER FORTY SEVEN

"SHIT, DUDE!" NOAH hollered and clutched his left arm. Brian had just skimmed a bullet by him. It zinged his bicep, leaving a spongy mound of torn skin. "You could've at least warned me."

"Would've been worse if you anticipated it," Brian said, lowering his weapon.

McKenzie alone was confused about this bizarre turn of events. She halted from where she'd leapt for the only weapon she saw in the room. She held the fireplace poker at her side. "What the hell—"

"Necessary," Brian said. "Had to make it look like I tried to hold you guys up. Now come on, Noah. Give me a couple good whacks."

Noah's left arm hung limp by his side, so he threw a hard right upper cut into Brian's jaw. Brian didn't fight back. He stood there, waiting to take more. Noah hit him again. An angry red welt blossomed on Brian's face. His eye would be black in a few minutes. Noah threw one last punch, his fist cracking into Brian's left cheek.

"Hardly consolation for you shooting me," Noah said through gritted teeth.

"Will someone *please* tell me what the hell is happening?" McKenzie pleaded.

"Don't think we've forgotten you," Brian said. "Noah, you can do that later."

Noah gave a slight nod.

"Excuse me?" McKenzie said. She locked eyes with Noah. If the two of them enjoyed this sort of thing, fine, but no way was a

SEAL painting a showy canvas of bruises on *her*.

"It has to look like we fought. Brian's family is in jeopardy either way, but if Lucas thinks Brian screwed him over, he'll make it a *point* to find and kill his family."

"And this way, it's more of a fifty-fifty *chance?*" McKenzie asked.

"More like this way, he'd only kill them if he happened to run into 'em at a bar mitzvah," Noah muttered.

"So shooting someone in the arm is just standard procedure?" McKenzie's eyes were wide. The two of them belonged in an asylum.

"It's not as bad as it looks," Noah replied. "A few stitches will put it right."

"Oh, I see. Good thing we can just waltz into a hospital and have them do that little thing for you. Are you nuts? The FBI, the CIA, and half the free world are looking for us. No one will notice a suspect in an assassination investigation saunter into the emergency room with a bullet wound."

"Of course we can't go to an emergency room," Noah said. "But I'm sure we can find a needle and thread around here somewhere."

"A needle and thread? Do I look like a damn doctor? I can't sew a button on my own pants, Noah, much less stitch skin back together." McKenzie said. "Besides, isn't that unsanitary?"

Neither of the two men seemed upset, which pissed her off. They stood in the middle of the smoldering dead bodies of her family, completely calm, like two kids playing cowboys and Indians.

"It's not safe to stay here," Brian said. "I would say come stay at my place, but that's obviously not a good idea. Not going back, myself. Meeting my lady and kids and getting the heck out of dodge. I do know somewhere you can hide out, though."

He found a piece of paper on Uncle Sal's coffee table and scribbled some directions. He handed Noah a set of keys. "It's my parents' old place. We rent it out during the summer season as a beach house, but no one's there this time of year. It's under a realty company, so I don't think anyone would connect it to me."

"Sure you don't need it?" Noah asked.

Varnes waved him off. "Nah. I've had a contingency plan for this sort of thing for a while."

McKenzie's mind flashed to the fake IDs in the locker at the airport, the gun at the bank. Of course Varnes had a second life all planned and ready to go. Why wouldn't he?

Noah accepted the paper. The two of them, broken and bloodied, embraced. "I'd say thanks, but I don't think you can say that to someone who just shot you," Noah said.

"All in a day's work, my friend," Brian said, patting Noah's back with his balled fist. "Be careful. I know you know what you're doing, but try to remember that *he* does, too."

Day 7: Early Morning (PST)
Los Angeles, CA

Uhlig drove through Los Angeles straight toward the airport. He wasn't boarding another plane today, though. Not yet.

He rapped his knuckles on an office door inside a building close to the airfield. Great thing, airports. They ran twenty-four seven.

"Enter," came the voice from the other side.

Uhlig opened the door to see a stocky Indian woman at the desk, her shiny black hair tousled in waves around her thick jowls. "Can I help you?"

"Ms. Jarriel?" he asked to be sure, though the woman looked exactly as Shariphe Bruno, the arms dealer, had described.

"Yes," she answered cheerily, offering her meaty hand. "Have I had the pleasure?"

Uhlig shook her hand and introduced himself. "Shariphe Bruno said you might be able to help me."

A shadow crossed her face, and the pleasant demeanor she'd displayed earlier clouded. Her pupils constricted ever so slightly.

In an instant, however, she looked up, her smile back. "Ah, yes. Shariphe. Never steers me wrong."

Uhlig took out the piece of paper where he'd scrawled the names the arms dealer had given him. All aliases possibly being used by the shooter, the man he had to locate now. It was the only way.

"I need access to the passenger manifests. Any and all flights these men were on the past year, I have to see."

The woman took the paper and read. She pursed her lips. "Daunting."

He cocked his head. "Not for a woman of your purported talents. The sooner the better."

Her eyes met his before she looked away, blinking rapidly. Good. She'd understood the unspoken threat.

"Give me an hour," she replied. "I'll have everything you need."

Uhlig nodded. "Perfect."

CHAPTER FORTY EIGHT

Day 7: Early Morning (PST)
Los Angeles, California

MCKENZIE FLIPPED ON the lights of the beach house. The smell of the salty sea air caught in her nostrils. If she hadn't been so concerned about finding something in the house other than Noah's own shirt to stanch the bleeding of his arm, she might've been content to sit in the rocker on the front porch. She could listen to the waves and just breathe. And grieve.

"God at a greyhound race. It's like I'm in the Middle East all over again," Noah said, his voice a pot boiling over with pain. "The sounds of the beach, and I'm shot to shit."

He pulled the bloody t-shirt away from his arm and glanced at the wound. "Well, maybe 'shot to shit' is overdoing it."

"Relax a minute while I look for bandages."

She headed down a hallway, which smelled as stale as a dusty museum. No one had been here in a long time. A bathroom off to the side was decorated in an ugly floral pattern. God willing, it would have something she could use, even though she wasn't really sure what that would be. It wasn't like she treated gunshot wounds on a daily basis. Or ever, for that matter.

Under the sink, a wooden container sat behind a bottle of cleaner. The letters etched into the pine said, "Boo-Boo Box." She couldn't help the laugh that escaped her. In the midst of assassins and conspiracies, she would be treating Noah's gunshot wound with a "Boo-Boo Box."

A bar of shell-shaped soap lay next to the sink. Might be antibacterial, might not, but it was better than nothing. She flipped the faucet on, but nothing happened. No running water. Great.

She bundled the supplies in her arms and carried them back to the living room, where Noah lay with his eyes closed. "You ready for this?" She wasn't sure if she was asking him or herself.

"What do I have to lose?" he asked.

"Don't ask me that at a time like this," McKenzie said.

While she unscrewed the cap from the bottle of rubbing alcohol in the first-aid kit, Noah removed his shirt. He pulled the bloody t-shirt from the wound. McKenzie dumped the contents of the bottle over it.

Noah groaned.

McKenzie could almost feel the alcohol searing her own arm as it flowed across the raw hole in Noah's. The skin bubbled a little, and she had to look away for a second. This was nerve racking enough without feeling like she was making it more painful.

"We should've checked the cupboard for scotch before we started this," Noah said.

"Nah," McKenzie said. "I wouldn't do as good of a job if I was drunk."

Noah grunted something that might've been an attempt at a laugh, but grimaced again just as quickly.

"I'm sorry," she mumbled. She blotted at the oozing mess with a few gauze pads before pressing one to his arm. "Hold that."

She doused her hands with alcohol and patted them on paper towels. Not exactly a hospital scrub-up, but it was all she knew to do with what she had. The Boo-Boo Box was ill-equipped for sterility. When her hands were dry, she tipped the alcohol bottle over a needle from the sewing kit she'd found in the back bedroom and pulled out a spool of hot pink thread.

"Seriously?" he asked, eyeing the neon thread with contempt.

She shrugged and threaded the needle. "It's all there is."

"Perfect," he muttered.

Noah leaned his head back and closed his eyes. His arm jumped under McKenzie's fingers, but no sound escaped his lips.

He breathed through his nose like an angry rhinoceros, and McKenzie's hair blew into her face.

It wasn't as hard to mend skin as McKenzie thought it would be. The most difficult part was meeting the raw edges to sew them together, but the needle poked through easier than she'd anticipated.

After several long minutes of work, she was finished.

Noah's arm looked like a five-year-old's arts and crafts project. The sloppy stitches zigged and zagged, and the hot pink added even more of a do-it-yourself quality. She dreaded him seeing it. She covered it with a large gauze pad and secured the makeshift bandage with medical adhesive tape from the Boo-Boo Box.

"All done," she said.

Noah's eyes eased open to look at her handiwork. The retort sat ready on her lips for when he commented what a messy job it was. He was lucky she'd done it for him at all.

He surprised her, though. He stared down at his arm as if it were some interesting, rare animal he'd never seen. "Thanks, Mac."

She plopped out two Tylenol from the first-aid kit. "Here."

"Nothing stronger?"

McKenzie shook her head. He accepted the pills and swallowed them without water. Then, he dumped two more from the bottle and downed those, too.

"Taking that much can't be good for your liver," McKenzie said.

"Neither is a bullet in the arm," he murmured. "Two more only makes it extra strength, like a prescription." He closed his eyes again.

McKenzie watched him, wondering if he'd be able to sleep. In a minute, however, he spoke. "You know, even when I go swimming now, I still expect to feel Cody at my back when I break the water's surface."

McKenzie didn't know what to say to this. Noah's lips were dry and cracked, and his hands clutched the side of the sofa. She perched on the edge of the sofa next to him to listen, folding her hands in her lap to keep from reaching out to touch him.

"SEALs have the name because we're comfortable in all of those environments," he rambled with a slight slur to his voice. "Sea, air, and land. But, we're all most at home in the water. I heard Cody didn't swim anymore. That part of his life was over, I guess. Or he wanted it to be over, anyway. For me, it's impossible to imagine not being in the water. It's so perfect, so calm. Some people think of the ocean as a scary place teeming with the unknown and dangerous, but to me, it's the perfect hiding place."

He opened his eyes and looked into McKenzie's. "I wish I was there now." His eyes fell shut.

Her hand stretched toward his arm and traced the line from his bicep to his elbow. Two of her fingers stopped in the crook and changed directions, following the arm folded across his stomach. Oh, God. His stomach.

Her middle finger found its way onto his abs, then mapped its way around the hard lines of muscle. They tightened underneath her as his chest rose. Her hand followed the movements, caressing the indentation in between his pecs before travelling back toward his stomach again.

His hand jerked toward her abruptly, grabbing her fingers in his. "Stop, Mac."

Thinking was for people who didn't feel this tingling in their skin. Her body urged her to lean down toward him. She pressed her mouth to his ear. His face was only inches away from hers, so close she could feel his lashes flutter against her. "I don't want to stop."

Without warning, Noah's arms seized her, holding tight around the small of her back as his lips grappled with hers. She arched instinctively, which pulled her face away from him.

It didn't matter. He kept toward her, his mouth furious with need. She kissed him back as every inch of her body burned, drawn to him. His fingertips rolled up her back to her neck. They kneaded the base of her skull while his mouth worked from her lips to her collarbone.

His fingers ran around the neckline of her shirt, dipping beneath it, brushing her skin. Her back arched further to urge him to touch her.

Please!

As if he'd read the thought, his hands disappeared from her neckline and were suddenly under her shirt. His palms pressed just above her rib cage for a moment before he reached behind her to the clasp of her bra. Her shallow breaths caught in her throat entirely as his fingers moved at her back.

Then, her bra came free. His hands were on her, but only for a moment before he demanded more. She let her shirt be ripped over her head and helped yank her arms free.

One hand cupped a breast as his mouth sank greedily over the other. McKenzie's head fell back, and she raked her fingernails up his back so hard she could hear the sound.

Noah moaned in delighted surprise. His arms wrapped her shoulder blades and hurled her to the ground. The hard landing left her breathless, but in the next instant, he was on top of her. Her body screamed for him and nothing else.

She reached for his belt buckle, but he wrenched away from her. Instead, he tore open her zipper with a harsh jerk. The jeans slid from her hips, and cool air met her thighs.

Noah stared down at her legs. His mouth closed, and his jaw clenched as he forced hard breaths through his nose. Wordlessly, he reached to his back pocket and pulled out his wallet.

He threw his head back in defeat. "Oh, goddamn. Not my regular wallet."

"I...I have—" McKenzie stuttered. Her hand stretched toward her purse, but pinned beneath Noah's legs, she couldn't reach it.

The words were enough that he understood. His fingers grabbed at her purse, and the contents spilled across the floor. "In the billfold," she panted.

In seconds, he had the condom and was working on his own belt buckle. She bucked her hips underneath him while she

219

watched him push his jeans and boxers down, open the condom, and roll it on. *Now.*

She lurched forward and took hold of the backs of his thighs, pulling him toward her. Noah obliged and shoved her cotton panties aside with two fingers.

With a single thrust, he pushed all the way into her. Her mouth fell open, but no sound came out. Her teeth grazed his shoulder in front of her.

He reared back and drove even deeper.

Her hips lifted into him as one of his hands reached underneath her to draw her to him. They rocked together, his hands clutching her to him as if he were drowning and she was his only hope of salvation.

Her climax built so tightly she could hardly breathe. Her toes furled into the carpet as waves of pleasure crashed over her, pulsing in time with him.

Noah groaned, his head thrown back, teeth bared. After a long moment, his head collapsed forward onto his chest.

McKenzie saw the room spin. She shut her eyes to ease the dizziness as she felt his weight lift from her. For a moment, she lay there, listening to their gasping.

When she was confident she wouldn't pass out, she sat up and fumbled for her clothes. Noah was already sitting back against the couch in his boxers.

"That's one way to not think about a bullet hole in the arm," he muttered.

"I do what I can," she replied. A sly smile crossed her lips. Then, "You should rest."

Noah didn't argue. He forced himself off the floor onto the couch and lay back. McKenzie ran her fingers through the dusty brown of his hair.

"Sleep," she said, tracing her hand down over his eyelids.

He closed his eyes. "I'll try."

McKenzie went into the kitchen and fired up her laptop. This house was only inhabited a few months out of the year, so internet service was unlikely. With some luck, though, maybe she could bum wireless off a user nearby.

Sure enough, her computer picked up one of the neighbor's unsecured network signals, and her browser connected. She logged into her e-mail account, and her inbox popped up. She stifled a scream. Her chest constricted as she double clicked the message. Her eyes darted back and forth across the page. This couldn't be real.

The e-mail was from Pierce.

Reading the e-mail felt like deciphering a foreign language, her emotions bubbling to the surface and scrambling her brain. He'd sent it before he arrived at the motel that night.

Concentrate, McKenzie.

As she read her best friend's words, she could hear his voice in her head. Tears leaked down her cheeks and splattered the keyboard.

> McKenzie-
> I'm sending this in case I can't find you or something worse happens. Jessie's dead, and I'm not sure how or why. She was on to something. Whatever she knew, she was in over her head. I've been trying to figure out exactly what it was, but in case I don't, use her email. Newshound26.
> See you soon. Keep Safe. —P

Keep safe. Damn it, Pierce. Damn it, McKenzie.

A volatile combination of anger and excitement clenched at her gut. Pierce had given her a way to find out Jessie's source. And maybe to find his killer.

McKenzie clicked a few buttons to recover her old e-mails and get Jessie's e-mail address. When she did, she typed Jessie's e-mail provider into her browser, plugged in Jessie's screen name, and pecked out the letters Pierce had gifted to her: Newshound26.

McKenzie stared at Jessie's inbox, which was rife with e-mails from Morton Gaines, as well as several from other co-workers at the *Herald*. A number of e-mails in the days leading up to Jessie's death came from an address McKenzie didn't recognize at all. The subject heading was always the same: "water."

It was such a weird title for an e-mail. It had to be a code for something. Sure enough, when she started pouring over the messages, they were all from someone feeding Jessie information about the assassinations, in particular, information on how the killers were associated with the SEALs.

The sender's e-mail account used Gmail, which unfortunately made it almost impossible to trace. McKenzie looked back at the timestamps on the e-mails. The person always e-mailed in the wee hours of the morning, but the times varied drastically from message to message.

McKenzie opened the very last "water" e-mail. It was the single communication sent by the mysterious sender that Jessie had never had the chance to open. She skimmed the message. This time, she didn't care if Noah had fallen asleep or not.

"Noah. Noah, get in here!"

"What?" he said followed by a yawn. He clambered to his feet in the other room.

"What's wrong?" he asked, bleary-eyed.

McKenzie hurried to catch him up before reading the latest e-mail. She explained how she'd obtained Jessie's password from Pierce, told him about the weird messages in Jessie's box.

"Someone was spoon-feeding her information." McKenzie waited a moment, afraid of her next words. "Jessie never knew it, but this last e-mail has Kimberly Lawson's name in it."

"What in the name of kickboxing Christ?"

"Exactly," McKenzie went on, too full of anxious energy to slow down to let his brain catch up. "I saw her name, then all of the sudden, I realized something. Look at the way it's signed."

Noah's eyes widened as he tried to wake up. He scanned the page to the end. "So?"

McKenzie slapped her palms on the table. "So," she replied, mustering patience, "it's signed Uhlig. We've seen that name before. It was one of the files on Kimberly Lawson's hard drive."

"Well what are you waiting for, Mac? Let's put the damn thing in and find out what Uhlig has to do with this clusterfuck."

Noah pulled up a chair while Mac hooked up Kimberly Lawson's hard drive. Every time they turned up one layer, there was one more underneath. Worse, every new twist ensured he would have to make a move he *really* didn't want to.

"Okay, here it is," Mac said. "Marie Uhlig."

She clicked through the files. "It looks like she was involved with the Shen years ago. Here, look at this." She pushed the laptop toward Noah so he could better see the scanned-in newspaper article currently on the screen. It was an obituary.

The blurb was tiny, only a few sentences, but he read it aloud. "Marie Uhlig, thirty-four, died Wednesday evening in her New York home. She is survived by a brother, Asher, and her two sons, Fabian and Robbie. In lieu of flowers, donations can be sent to the American Cancer Society."

"Thirty-four is really young," Mac said. "The thing about donations makes it sound like she must've had cancer."

"Or someone wanted to make it seem like she did."

Over the course of the next couple of files, they learned that Marie Uhlig, in life, had acted anything but sickly. She'd been the chief organizer of a riot protesting a bill that would make abortion illegal. On a less public scale, she'd been the contact person for many of the Shen's dealings, a position not unlike the one Kimberly Lawson had recently held.

"If she was going through chemo during all of that, I'm Santa Claus, Frosty the Snowman, *and* the Easter Bunny," Noah said.

"So how did she really die?" Mac asked.

"I have a guess or two," Noah answered. "I doubt finding out how she died so many years ago is really going to help us much. If she's dead, I'd bet a couple hundred she isn't the one sending Jessie e-mails."

Mac's head tilted. "I see your point. Too big of a coincidence, though. The names, I mean."

"How about the sons?"

"Let's see what else we can find." She typed "Uhlig" into the box to search all files. A list of documents pooled on the screen. Mac scrolled through them. "Oh, boy. That's interesting."

Christ on vacation in the Philippines. There's the understatement of the year.

Almost every document containing the name "Uhlig" was listed in a file titled with someone else's name, a name all over the news because she'd recently been blown to smithereens.

Ikram Totah.

Nothing should be a surprise by now. It really shouldn't. The number of dead bodies McKenzie was now connected to could no longer be counted on one hand. She was officially wanted by the FBI. Yet, her mouth hung open. The contents of these documents stunned her as much as if she'd just found out she was adopted.

"Looks like you'll be springing for the expensive box of wine this New Year's Eve," Noah said dryly.

He was right. Discovering the Shen's connection to the assassinations had been an article that could thrust her into the dream of front page by-lines. But this—this would keep her there.

The first section of the document contained biographical information on Ikram Totah and her rise to political standing in the Middle East. The second segment, which McKenzie now scanned, detailed open threats made on Totah's life. Some of them were the standard hatred expressed toward every figure in the public eye even in the U.S.: religious organizations who disagreed with her policies or those in support of opposing candidates. The most outspoken threat, however, was from Dahir Al-Musari.

The terrorist was well-known for being an Islamic extremist. Al-Musari particularly hated the progress of women in the West and the way recent conflict in Middle Eastern countries had resulted in more liberties for women there, as well. He happened to be the man who publicly took credit for having Totah killed.

Within the profile of Al-Musari, Fabian Uhlig was listed

under the heading of "Possible Associates". His name also appeared to be linked to another document. McKenzie dragged the cursor over the name and double-clicked.

A personal file on Uhlig popped up on the screen, complete with a list of known contacts and last known whereabouts. "He grew up in his mother's home in New York, started college in the U.S., but then dropped off the radar at twenty-one."

"To get involved with one of the most screwed up bastards on the planet," Noah said.

"It seems impossible," McKenzie said. "This guy Uhlig is involved with an anti-feminist group who kills one of the most well-known women in politics. If they're anti-feminist, they'd be anti-Shen, yet he was sending Jessie e-mails with information regarding the assassinations and the Shen's involvement. He'd be the last person in the world with access to the inner workings and plans of the Shen. How would he know anything about who killed the president and vice president if the Shen orchestrated it?"

"Because he's a damn ninja, that's how," Noah answered. "What about the other Uhlig?"

"Other?"

Noah's hand covered hers in order to take over the mouse. "There's a brother, right?"

"Oh, yeah," McKenzie said. Her heart picked up speed at Noah's touch.

She scrolled through Fabian Uhlig's file back to the section marked with personal ties. "Siblings. One. What the heck—"

"Whereabouts not known," Noah read out loud.

McKenzie leaned back in the chair so hard she almost tipped over. "Brother dropped off the radar, too. How do we find him?"

Noah grimaced, then rolled his neck slowly. "I have a feeling I know someone who could find us information. But first, we have to find *her*."

CHAPTER FORTY NINE

Day 7: Early Morning (PST)
Los Angeles, California

YOU HAD ME right there, and you didn't even realize it. Could've been the promotion of a lifetime. Stupid pigs. Proof of why your emergency response systems don't work.

Lucas cruised down Santa Monica Boulevard in the stolen BMW. God, this night was delicious. Palm trees dotted the skyline; people lined the streets as they waited outside nightclubs and bars. He laughed out loud, wind from the open window rushing into his face. Guys would stand there for hours trying to get inside to writhe in one square inch of room, sardines in an oil of their own sweat, so maybe they could brush against a hot little blonde in a glittery tank top. The lucky ones might end up next to a girl who'd had one too many apple martinis and was ready to stick her tongue down a throat or two.

His blood surged at the thought of the firemen at Uncle Sal's turning to get back in their truck to radio that the emergency call had ended up being a false alarm. Had to have been fate that the fire truck got there first, but even if it hadn't, he'd have taken care of it. He made his own luck.

He eased the BMW to the curb, sliding the passenger's side window down. A brunette in a purple fake leather mini skirt, see-through blouse, and white platform wedges sauntered toward him. Her nose twitched where it came to its pointed tip. "Nice car."

"Want a ride?"

She opened the door and climbed in. No questions. Didn't

even occur to her the fancy vehicle might be stolen. Lucky for her, he had millions waiting on him in the Caymans. A few hundred was well worth it, especially right now.

And for the moment, he actually intended to pay her.

He pulled around the corner, trying to ignore the glow of her silky thighs in the corner of his eye. Damn. Walking away from those idiots at Sal's was like a light beer compared to the pure heroin of blowing off Seymour's head while his Secret Service looked on, helpless, but still, it was a buzz. Once he got those platforms up behind this chick's head, the world might just be perfect.

The parking lot was fairly dark, but Lucas didn't need light to smell. Her scent wafted to him on the soft breeze in the air. He was hard already.

Hope you're ready for this, honey.

He paid for the hotel room in cash. Was it a good idea to choose such a high end place? Probably not. But damn it, he deserved those feathered pillows after today. Brian Varnes was too in love with his precious *family* to risk not following through.

Cody flashed in Lucas' mind. Yep. Love. Such a weakness.

Lucas swiped the keycard in the door, and the little green light blinked.

Time to go.

The woman tossed her purse onto a chair. "First things first," she said, voice thick with Boston accent, "Cash is up front. Not negotiable, handsome."

He rolled his eyes.

Handsome, indeed.

The pale pink lipstick made her lips look small and thin, but he'd bet her mouth wasn't as tiny as it looked. And if it was, too bad. It would accommodate him, whether she liked it or not. "Of course."

He produced a roll of bills from his wallet and counted them out into her hand. The smile that played across her face stretched wider with every fifty he laid there. Probably thinking what she could do with that later.

Colby Marshall

"Congratulations," she said. "You just bought yourself a fuck."

The numbers on Officer Quinn's digital watch ticked another minute away. He tapped his fingers against the cleaning cart, which he'd been hanging out with for a few hours in that hotel hallway waiting for this sting operation to show some results. He'd done this enough to know exactly how much time he had before Officer Troy had done her job, and that was the number of minutes it took for the flavor to chew out of a stick of Juicy Fruit gum.

He still tasted something other than cardboard, so it wasn't quite time for the call yet.

"Hey, Quinn," the cop next to him said, slapping his arm with the back of his hand. "Wasn't that our guy?"

Quinn's gaze followed the other officer's finger to the elevator doors. They were already sliding shut, but he caught a glimpse of the guy before they closed.

Shit.

His feet scrambled under him toward the hotel room.

What the hell?

The master keycard the front desk had supplied him slid through the slot. The door clicked open. Quinn kept his hand on his gun even though he'd just watched the guy he'd need to use it on get on the elevator. Maybe the guy had caught a whiff of something "off" about Officer Troy and left before getting his pants unzipped.

As soon as Quinn turned the corner, though, he knew how wrong he was. Officer Troy lay sprawled on the floor, handcuffs still resting in her open palm. Her head was turned at a bizarre angle, eyes wide.

Quinn fumbled for his radio, almost dropping it twice before he managed to depress the button. "Officer down. Officer Troy is down. Suspect last seen on east elevator heading toward lobby."

All the muscles in his face clenched as his gaze fell on Officer Troy's neck again, the skin pulled tout where it was snapped,

228

quick and clean. He pushed the radio button once more. "Suspect on foot. Consider him armed and dangerous."

Lucas came to an intersection and changed directions to wherever the little white man in street crossing light said it was okay to walk. Pausing wasn't an option, but neither was getting stopped for jaywalking. At the rate he was going, that would be the next thing he'd be arrested for. Damn it. If only he had the car.

Plan, plan, plan.

Stealing a car would make things worse. Cab or bus. Something. Get a few miles away from the damned sting operation he'd fumbled into. He trotted across a crosswalk despite the oncoming traffic.

That's when he heard it.

"Stop right there!"

His legs pumped faster. There was no blending in any more. He'd been made. Time to evade. Survive.

The Pacific Ocean stretched parallel to the road Lucas turned down. He never looked back. He already knew more about them than they did about him. There were three. Two in uniform, one in khakis and a polo, the taller of the two uniforms fastest.

Too bad for him.

Lucas breathed rhythmically, in through his nose and out through his mouth. At the same time, he commanded his feet to be slow, steady, deliberate. On his right, a string of shops lined the street along with a row of cars parked flush with the curb. A tow truck beeped as it backed up toward an old Buick. People milled about outside the pub at the end of the row, enough bodies that the cop wouldn't have a clean shot. Sometimes, things just worked out for the best.

Lucas darted into the pub, letting the door swing hard behind him.

Ready or not, here you come.

Quinn was several blocks away when the closest uniform radioed in his visual. "Suspect entered Blackhead Pub on right front corner of building. Going in.''

"Wait for back up. Repeat, wait for backup,'' Quinn replied, but static crackled from his radio. He glanced around. Televisions lined the storefront behind him. Something in the electronics store was interfering with his signal.

Shit!

Quinn was the closest backup to the pub. He ran as fast as he could, but his lungs felt as if there was a buffalo sitting on his chest. God, those days of running miles every morning at the Academy seemed so long ago. His vision flashed to his partner lying on the floor of the hotel room. They'd been working the prostitution sting for several weeks and hadn't had so much as a penknife pulled on her. He should've been paying better attention. If he'd watched closer, he could've done something.

A few blocks away from the pub location, Quinn's walkie crackled to life again. "No visual on subject inside the pub,'' the officer panted. "I don't know where he could've gone—''

As the officer spoke, he heard the pub door swing open two blocks away, the uniform rushing outside to search the street.

Faster. Come on, Quinn.

The officer glanced into windows of the cars lining the street. The perp had probably snuck out the back door of the pub, hopped in a cab, and was now halfway back to his home in the Palisades, if his BMW was any clue to his lifestyle. Still, Quinn's stomach rolled. Something didn't feel right about this.

Quinn was still a block away when the uniformed officer ran past a Buick hooked to a towing rig. He stopped at the hood of the Buick and cocked his head, then backpedaled, slow. What was he—?

The cop's eyes were still locked on the Buick, but Quinn had the wider view as an arm shot out from under the tow truck. The knife sliced both the officer's hamstrings. The force of the swipe dropped him to his knees, his torso stick straight. Quinn couldn't focus on the officer, though, because something—or some*one*—dropped from underneath the truck.

"Look out!'' Quinn yelled, but it was no use.

The figure landed in a crouch underneath the truck but never stopped moving. He went to his left knee, his right leg stretching out to give him balance. His head bent at an unnatural angle to keep from hitting the underside of the chassis, he twisted his torso clear of the truck. With a quick jab, he drove his knife into the officer's thigh.

Quinn still had half a block to go. He seized his gun, but there was no possible shot. He was too far, the cop too close, the truck too low. *No!*

Even from this far, the glare of the streetlight spotlighted Quinn's view as the perp's grip shifted on the knife handle, the blade still in the officer's leg. His palm covered the handle as he squeezed and ripped downward. Blood spurted out of the officer, crimson spraying the white hood of the Buick in front of him.

"We need an ambulance!" the officer behind Quinn hollered into his walkie.

Quinn clicked his radio, too. "Officer down," he yelled while he watched, helpless, as the suspect took off running.

The uniform was still on the pavement in front of him, the suspect already another block down. Damn, he was fast. If Quinn stopped to check on the officer, the guy who'd just stabbed him—the one who'd killed his partner in the hotel room—would get away. Mother Mary, he'd never seen so much blood around a single body in his life.

The uniform behind him would stop and check on the officer. Quinn kept running.

One street between him and the ocean. That was all.

The plainclothes cop yelled to the other uniform, but Lucas couldn't make out what he said. Probably something about splitting up to come at him from another side. That would be a good plan.

If they weren't chasing *him.*

Lucas launched himself into the road. The beams of an oncoming bus flashed from yards away. The driver laid on the horn to warn him. He put on a last burst of energy and rocketed across into the brambles lining the road.

The cop in street clothes had gotten caught by the stream of traffic. Lucas turned to his left onto a block back toward the hotel. He ran on the short grass, his steps quick and soft. A parking lot for a different hotel loomed up on the right. He crashed through the manicured bushes lining the lot, but as he did, the other uniformed cop surged from out of nowhere through the matching shrubbery on the other side.

Lucas wheeled on one foot at a ninety degree angle and dove underneath the first car in the lot. The cement skinned his elbows, but he dug them in nonetheless, pulling his body under the vehicles, a snake. He weaved through a tunnel of tires, changing direction every two cars or so. The footsteps of the officer clambered around him. Dumb cops couldn't make themselves compact unless you tossed a chocolate-covered Twinkie under a car and said, "Fetch."

He slid from underneath a silver Mercury and was on his feet. The end of the hotel lot spilled into a breezeway toward the elevators, but no way was he going to box himself in inside a building when the water was so damned close. Past the elevator, a fence blocked off the pool area. Lucas closed in on it fast. Too fast for details like gate latches.

Every muscle in his body tensed.

Keep your arms and legs inside the vehicle.

His right foot found the flower pot at the edge of the fence. It provided just enough leverage to propel him over the gate before the pot shattered underneath him. Air rushed into his face, drying his eyes out. He slammed the cement. His ankles seared, and shock waves stung his knees. The few people around the pool gasped in horror, but he didn't hang around long enough to bother noting what they looked like. Rats in the common pool at a dumpy place like this at this time of night made piss poor eyewitnesses. The cop on his tail was a much bigger issue.

A wooden gazebo stood between the pool and the beach. Lucas took the stairs two at a time, elbows pumping hard for momentum. Squeals behind him of, "He went that way!" spurred him harder.

Get to the damn water.

At the last stair, the gazebo plateaued in front of him. More stairs loomed in his view only a dozen feet ahead, the trail leading to freedom. Below him, the wood pounded with the cop climbing.

No more stairs for me, thank you.

Lucas rushed the rail of the gazebo head on and grabbed it with both hands. His momentum carried him forward over the railing. He pushed with all his strength to make sure his head cleared the drop. His triceps were on fire.

Tuck and roll, tuck and roll.

There was no helping the over-rotation. His body hit the beach face first, and he choked on a mouthful of sand. Palms pressed to the mounded white grit, he hefted his frame from the ground and spat hard at the same time. He couldn't see, damn it. He twisted the inside of his shirt up to his face to wipe his eyes with the clean underside of his clothing.

His eyes opened to the waves crashing in front of him.

Forty yards. Go.

"Hold it right there."

Lucas didn't have to turn around to feel the gun trained on his back. He stilled and let his fingers splay, hands out from his sides.

"Don't move. Keep your hands where I can see them," the officer commanded. "Now put them behind your head. Interlock your fingers."

Slowly, Lucas turned to face the officer. As he turned, hands raised high in defeat, he used every tiny step of the turn to ease himself a centimeter closer. The cop had a clean shot. Nowhere to hide.

"Don't come any closer," the cop yelled, his voice cracking at the last word. He switched on his radio. "Have suspect at Hapley Inn on Shelby Boulevard. Backup requested."

The guy was young. Green. Lucas' eyes found the barrel of the gun trained on him, honed in on that small black hole lit under

233

the globe light from the gazebo. *Ten, nine...*

The hole shifted a fraction of an inch to the left. A tremble. The call had to be made now. Assess and contain.

Green, loose cannon, or green, I'm not gonna shoot anyone?

Lucas inhaled. The officer's fear breathed into him like a drug. *Go time.*

He charged at the cop and lunged hard into him. His palm found the hand with the gun and forced it upward just as the cop's finger snagged the trigger in panic. Lucas overtook the hand and squeezed, popping off rounds. The first shot would've given away their location to anyone nearby. Might as well empty the thing.

As he finished, Lucas let his hand slide to the cop's wrist.

Grip, bend.

The cop groaned, his arm twisted behind him as if Lucas was arresting him.

"Didn't you see your buddy?" Lucas breathed into his ear. "Should've left well enough alone. Then you could've gone to his funeral."

Lucas reached to his pocket for his knife, but the sheath had slipped down into his pants leg during the fall. No matter.

He ran forward full speed, giving the cop no choice but to move his feet, too. After a few steps, the cop was tripping over himself, being pushed through the sand like a strange snow plow. The stairs of the gazebo were straight ahead, the sound of the waves rolling in Lucas' ears.

The cop tried to put on the brakes. He dug his heels in, whimpering.

Lucas wrenched his arms harder behind him as they approached the stairs. The guy had become dead weight, but Lucas had eyes only for the railing. His right hand let go of the cop's wrist at the last possible moment and grabbed the back of his skull. With a final shove, they came to the stairs. Lucas' palm slammed the bridge of the cop's nose down into the wood, grabbed his hair, and dragged his face downward so that splinters drove upward through his nostrils into the vulnerable tissue of his brain.

At the end of the railing, Lucas yanked the cop's head out of the wood and threw him onto his back in the sand. The dead cop's face was already swelling blue from blood pooling in the pockets underneath his eyes, the skin of his nose stringing in shreds over his cheeks.

"That must've hurt," Lucas said as he took a second to retrieve his knife and put it back where it was easily accessible. "Ouch."

Flashlight beams flashed from behind the gazebo. Someone else was coming. Time for a change of plan.

Quinn could hardly breathe when he made it to the beach behind Hapley Inn. The suspect—with the uniform cop in pursuit—had cut across the traffic. By the time he got around, they'd disappeared. He'd gone with his gut and taken the right while the uniform took the left.

Now, he radioed in the "officer down" call on the beach. He couldn't stop kicking himself. If he'd moved left, this twenty-five-year-old kid might not be on his way to the morgue tonight. This was supposed to be a simple arrest, and somehow, it had turned into a bloodbath. Who the hell was this guy?

The beach unfurled in front of him. He scanned all angles, particularly the line near the road where the light pooled on the sand. Nothing. He turned ninety degrees toward the coastline. It was so dark he couldn't see where the sand ended and the water began.

A flicker of white caught Quinn's eye back toward the hotels. He jerked toward it, but nothing moved. The row of lounge chairs built into the ground were so low it seemed it would be impossible for anyone to use them as cover, but Quinn's gut told him to keep staring there.

He kept his focus trained on the chairs as he started forward. The hairs on the back of his neck prickled. Someone was there. He was sure. Removing the gun from its holster boosted his courage, but just in case, he clicked the safety off.

As if the safety had been a magic button, a figure suddenly

sprang from the ground behind the chairs and ran the opposite direction.

"Hold it," Quinn yelled, despite it likely being wasted breath. The guy had just killed three cops. No way would he allow himself to be brought in.

Quinn didn't have a prayer of hitting him. The bastard leapt over the lounge chairs and changed angle and direction at random every two steps.

Quinn's feet picked up, heavy in the sand even though the white mounds didn't seem to slow this guy at all. He wouldn't lose him this time.

The perp banked up the side of the beach through the tall grass.

Quinn followed suit. The brambles pricked and stuck to his calves and ankles. It was all he could do to keep moving, they stung so much. His eyes burned, but he refused to blink. He had to keep this guy in sight.

Ahead, the perp ducked under the ties of the pier. Quinn expected him to head for the road. However, the guy seemed so caught in the moment he didn't think hard enough about his next move, because in the next instant, he was sprinting full force toward the end of the pier.

Gotcha.

Quinn drew nearer to the pier. How long would it take him to get to his cuffs? Normally, with a gun on a suspect it wasn't something he thought about. With this guy Quinn took nothing for granted.

The detective straddled the ties the same way the perp had entered. He raced to the end, gun still aimed. The guy, cornered, had turned to look back at Quinn, a pleased smile on his face. It would be so easy to shoot him, to say he resisted arrest.

"Put your hands above your head!"

The perp laughed, his feet still carrying him backward toward the pier's edge. "Good try, detective."

"There's nowhere to go. We can do this the easy way or the hard way," Quinn shouted.

"How long before they assign you a new partner?" the perp asked, his voice radiating sick, smug pleasure.

"You son of a—"

But before Quinn could finish, the perp turned and dove clean off the pier, dropping thirty feet before plunging into the water.

Quinn ran to the end of the pier, gun on the spot where the subject had been standing only moments before. It didn't matter, though. There was only one place he could've gone.

The detective peered over the edge, but the thought of jumping after the perp died the second he saw how high the drop was. His head spun. He straightened up.

How in God's name—

He pressed the button on his walkie. "Perp in the water off the Eighth Avenue pier. We need Coast Guard."

Any minute, he'd hear the choppers clipping above the shoreline, searching for the suspect. Quinn stared into the black water that stretched into nothingness so far below. No normal person could survive that. Somehow, the thought didn't make him feel a damn bit better.

They weren't going to find this guy. Not this time.

CHAPTER FIFTY

Day 7: Early Morning (PST)
Los Angeles, California

"I ASSUME YOU have the documents I requested," Uhlig said after he sat down across the desk from Ms. Jarriel in her office.

"Yes," she replied. She passed a stack of papers. "Passenger manifests for all flights on record with the passenger names you listed."

"You've been most helpful," he said, shaking her hand. Without anything further, he stood and walked out of her office. He needed somewhere quiet to pour over the lists, but at the same time, he couldn't wait. There was a nice lobby downstairs. He'd take the elevator and sit and go through what he needed.

As the lift doors shut, he thought back on the day the man he'd hired to watch his brother called to inform him of what his sibling was up to. Sure, Uhlig left to do what needed to be done, but he couldn't leave his brother entirely. This was evidence why.

"He met with someone today in Los Angeles. A girl. I've tracked her down. Her name is Kimberly Lawson. She's Shen," the source said.

Uhlig's heartstrings had pulled taut. So, he was in bed with the enemy.

"What did they discuss?"

"We weren't able to obtain clear audio, but there was an envelope exchanged. We don't know what was in it. Immediately following the meeting, he went to the airport and boarded Delta Flight 415 to New York City for the convention."

That was last year, ten days prior to President Seymour's appointment of a liberal judge from Massachusetts to the Supreme

Court, effectively tipping the numbers of the highest court toward Democratic leanings. It was also the moment Uhlig realized he had to start keeping an even closer eye on things. Up to that point, he'd been very clear with his contact: he wanted information, but he wanted it an arm's length away. He didn't trust himself to be any closer.

Which was why that day, when Uhlig asked the contact for a phone number, he had known his brother was about to spiral out of control.

Uhlig reached the lobby and parked on a bench between two potted palms. He sifted through the passenger manifests, which were much more recent than a year ago. The man who had killed the President of the United States had used six different names in the past four months, the most recent on a flight to California. Los Angeles.

Uhlig piled the papers together and folded them into his jacket. The ride would give him some time to think about his next step. At this point, he had no clue where to start to find the shooter once he arrived. He was only sure that after what Lima Olmstead had whispered with her dying breath, everything had become much more complicated.

After all, the assassin was probably the only man left alive who knew what Uhlig's brother had done.

CHAPTER FIFTY ONE

Day 7: Early Morning (PST)
Brian Varnes' beach house, Los Angeles, California

MCKENZIE WATCHED NOAH pull up his e-mail account on her laptop. His fingers flew across the keyboard, searching his mail for a particular sender's name. No results.

"I figured. Haven't spoken to her in a long time," he said.

Was that regret touching the edge of his voice?

He started typing again, this time searching in the white pages for another name. Before she could ask, the cell phone was out. He powered it on and dialed the number on the page. "Ebbs? It's Hutchins. I need a favor, but you can't ask me what it's for."

McKenzie read the name on the page Noah searched, but it wasn't Ebbs. Fake names, IDs, guns in lockers in airports. This was insane.

Meanwhile, Noah replied to the muffled voice on the other end of the phone. "It's Jig. I'm looking for her."

He listened for a moment, then gestured like he was writing to McKenzie. He wanted a piece of paper. McKenzie touched the mouse pad on her computer and clicked the little icon in the corner of her screen to cause a sticky note to pop up on the monitor.

Noah typed, but it wasn't a phone number. It was a website. "Yeah, I understand," he said. "Thanks. I owe you one with no questions attached." He hung up.

"So?" McKenzie asked. Noah was already plugging in the website. A prompt glowed on the screen asking for a name and password. "Who's Jig?"

He inserted the other two words he'd typed while on the phone, and some kind of database loaded on the screen. Without looking at McKenzie, he scrolled the page. "Jig is the nickname of an old colleague of mine. Let's just say she and Pierce might've had a good bit in common."

McKenzie's eyes burned at the mention, but she blinked the tears away. There would be a time to lose herself in her grief, but it wasn't now.

Noah shook his head at the screen. "He said it would be a long shot. Said she doesn't keep a phone on her anymore."

"Huh?"

"Jig. She's..." he said, his voice trailing as he seemed to be lost in a memory. "...a character. Dang it, Jig."

"Would she be near a computer now, do you think?" McKenzie wondered out loud.

"What?"

She reached across him and opened the Skype application on her computer. Excitement bubbled in her chest while she put in her handle and password. "If she's anything like Pierce, the phone wouldn't be the only way to get in touch with her."

"Not bad," Noah answered.

"You sound so surprised," she said, smirking. "Any ideas what to search?"

Noah tweaked his head side to side. Then, without question, he said, "Jig 1444."

McKenzie pecked out the name and hit search. A listing popped up in the window. She raised her eyebrows. "Good guess."

Noah grunted. "Not a guess."

"Even better, it looks like she's online."

Of freaking course.

Noah typed into the Skype instant messaging window, all too aware of McKenzie looking over his shoulder. The fun never ended.

Jig?

The tiny pencil jerked on the screen to signify she was replying. How was he about to explain this?

>*what's a jig?*

He could feel his face reddening. Without considering who he was talking with, he typed:

>*Jesus Christ and Sting in concert. You are.*

The pencil scribbled again, then a word appeared on the screen:

>*noah?*

"How does she—"

"Because, Mac, she's a freakin' wizard." His fingers ran across the keyboard again:

>*So, it is you, then?*

>*ask a stupid question…*

Touché. "It's her all right," he mumbled, though he knew Mac had figured that much out already.

>*i feel special, seeing as how half the country is looking for you.*

Noah replied:

>*And we both know you could probably find me for them.*

She typed back:

which is why you must have a pretty good reason for looking for me.

Noah rolled his neck from side to side.

I need something.

The pencil pushed again.

viagra?

You know better.

Behind him, Mac gasped. *Oh, damn. There's a human behind you, you asshole. Try some tact.* Before Mac had a chance to ask questions, Noah typed again. This conversation needed to get back on track, and fast.

I need some information on someone.

what's in it for me?

Noah cocked his head, then pecked out letters:

Karma?

No response came at first. "Did she leave?" Mac asked.
He shook his head. "No. She's still there."
Sure enough, a response appeared on the screen:

ah, what the hell. i haven't done a good deed in a few years...

Noah shifted in his seat. Details or no details? Better to give less. She wouldn't ask. If she was curious, she'd find out anyway.

I need to find the children of someone named Marie Uhlig.

spawn of one uhlig, marie. sit tight. let me work some magic.

For the next twenty minutes, McKenzie stared at the screen, willing Noah's mysterious contact to return. A couple of times, the little Skype pencil moved but then stopped abruptly, erased, and disappeared again.

"If the Shen's people couldn't find Marie Uhlig's other kid, what makes you think this chick can?" she asked, irritated. Couldn't she hurry up?

"She's good at what she does," he replied.

McKenzie twitched at the glassy look that crossed Noah's face. "Apparently."

The second Noah turned to respond, the pencil reappeared on the screen. "She's answering."

there's only one birth certificate in public record for marie uhlig. it's for fabian r. uhlig.

McKenzie's head fell forward. Another dead end. However, she raised her eyes at the click of the keys, curious what Noah was responding. She read:

We know she had another child. At least one other.

On the other end of the computer, Jig was writing again.

true. i said he was the only birth certificate in public record. lucky for you, i'm 1337.

You're what?

Jig typed:

> *1 3 3 7. Leet. as in…fuck. never mind. let's*
> *just say i'm badass.*

Noah gestured to the computer as if to say, "So…" He waited a second. Then, when she didn't reply right away, he sent back:

> *Suspense is killing me.*

McKenzie's heart flitted inside her rib cage. Was it really possible they were about to know?

> *you're not going to believe this one. if i had any*
> *morals at all, i'd sell this shit to the enquirer.*

Noah plucked at the keyboard.

> *Thank Jesus on stilts you're ruthless and lazy.*

"Just get to it already," McKenzie said, her voice strained with anticipation.

Noah looked over his shoulder at her. "If you're about to storm the beach and you're on your last round, don't shoot at the sand."

McKenzie stared at him. "Ever the philosopher. But why would you know you were about to storm a beach and let yourself be on your last round?"

Noah cracked a smile. "Right you are."

His patience paid off, though. By the time she fixed her eyes on the monitor again, Jig had started to answer. She typed and erased several times before the message finally appeared on the screen.

> *can't find the birth certificate, because it*
> *doesn't exist. not with marie uhlig's name on it*

anyway. but a sealed adoption record does. marie uhlig, deceased mother of one son in the foster care system, adopted by his foster family. once i had the kid's name, i pulled his birth certificate. mother listed as marie, all right, but not uhlig. she's listed as marie frame.

"Frame?" McKenzie read out loud.

Noah was already typing a reply along those lines.

What makes you say I wouldn't believe that? Should the name Frame mean something to me?

While they waited for the answer, McKenzie searched her brain for where she might've heard the name Frame. She'd heard so many names the past few days she couldn't keep them all straight. Still, it was possible.

No amount of rehashing could've prepared her for the next message.

probably not, but the father's name might.

"Does she want us to beg? Christ in Jerusalem," McKenzie said, throwing up her hands.

"God rolling in dollar bills, I'm really rubbing off on you," Noah answered, clicking the keys. "Still, leave the references to his holiness to me until you get a better hang of it."

Please, Jig, before I'm using the Walmart scooter to do my grocery shopping.

Her reply came back.

some people are so sensitive.

Noah sighed.

How about if I said please?

Jig responded:

> *lol. okay, okay. but make sure you're sitting down. i don't even know how you found the name uhlig. it still freaks me out.*

Noah answered:

> *Noted.*

There was another short pause before the pencil on the screen moved again:

> *dad is listed as a guy by the name of royal.*

Gears shifted and clicked in McKenzie's brain one after the other. "Robbie Royal—"

Noah leaned his chin onto a fist. "Robert Royal," he supplied through a strangled half-laugh that sounded exactly the way McKenzie felt.

She swallowed hard. "The President's Chief of Staff."

CHAPTER FIFTY TWO

"WAY I SEE IT, only way to find out anything for sure is to find Lucas," Noah said, punching a text message into the phone and hitting send.

He knew it was true. That psycho was the only one who really *knew*. Whether or not he wanted to beat the shit out of Lucas for what he'd done to Cody, their team, that woman in Pakistan, Mac—well, that was irrelevant.

"That may be, but he could be anywhere."

Noah shook his head and held up the cell phone. He'd traded phones with Brian Varnes before leaving Sal's, and Brian had just replied to his text. "We've been trying to find Lucas, but you're forgetting he's been trying to find *us,* too."

Day 7: Morning (PST)
Los Angeles, California

The only thing Uhlig knew with any certainty was the specific time the shooter had flown into Los Angeles. That would be the only way to locate him now. This caused another major snag.

So now, tedious as it was, he sat in the middle of a fast food chain restaurant with free internet, waiting for an e-mail to come through. He knew his next step from here, which meant planning wasn't necessary. Unfortunately, that left his thoughts to lick at his insides. He had nothing to do to pass the time besides turn his cell phone over in his palm again and again. He would not call today. It would solve nothing.

After what seemed like an hour, the icon popped up on his screen to let him know his e-mail had come through.

Uhlig opened the document, glanced over it, then hit forward. He snapped the laptop closed and scooped it up along with the passenger manifesto papers. On his way out the door, he pressed another button on his phone for a different contact.

"Yeah?" a voice picked up on the third ring.

"It's me," Uhlig said. "Get to your computer. I sent passport and boarding passes for you. I need you to search airport security footage on the date of the boarding pass. Find the guy in the picture. Anything that points to where he went after he left LAX."

"On it," the contact replied.

Uhlig snapped the phone shut. If news of him killing Xavier hadn't gotten back to Al-Musari yet, it was only a matter of time before that phone call did. Once Al-Musari knew Uhlig was off course and using his people for his own agenda, he'd be hunted just like the man *he* was now tracking.

And when Al-Musari's lackeys found him, the only question was whether or not they'd torture him before they killed him.

The image he'd seen on the e-mail document burned in his mind. The face of his prey. *Better find you before they find me.*

Day 7: Morning (PST)
Los Angeles, California

Sweat dripped from Lucas' brow. Hot as hell inside this cab. Damned cabbie needed to rely on more than the cracked windows.

He had to get to his next job. The last thing Lucas needed was someone on his tail because he hadn't finished the job he'd been hired to do. Sure, he'd killed officers involved in a prostitution sting and was on the run from those cops now. Still, he was pretty confident he could hide with the best of the best; he was no moron. Whoever hired him had known to hire him, after all. If anyone came after him, they wouldn't exactly be the LAPD.

Sleep is for the dead.

It'd be easier to disappear once he was in Europe. Then, he'd worry about tying up loose ends here. Varnes would run, of course, but he'd come back home after a while. Whether he'd managed to off Mr. Perfect Noah Hutchins or not, Lucas would visit Varnes at home and pop a bullet into his skull anyway. Therapeutic.

Lucas' cell chimed, and he flipped it open. "Yeah?"

"Hello, there."

His face burned as if it had caught fire at the sound of Hutchins' voice. "You're about the last person I expected to hear from."

"I bet," Noah said.

"What terminal, sir?" the cabbie asked through a thick accent.

Lucas gestured for him to keep going toward the Sky Ways terminal. He gritted his teeth. If this ass wasn't in control of the car and him confined to the back seat, he'd kill him, too, just for breathing.

"Come to think of it," Lucas drawled, "how did you get this number?"

"Why, buddy? Worried?" Noah was quiet a minute before he continued. "I nicked Brian's phone after I beat the shit out of him, if you must know. Varnes is a good fighter, Lucas, but you've always known I was better."

"Than some."

"What's the matter, Lukey? I'd think the minute you knew I managed to escape Sal Becker's you'd be feeling out how to find me. You haven't asked a single assessment question yet. No new booby traps?"

"Ah, believe me, Hutchins, I'm coming for you. I have some other business to attend to, but don't you worry. I'll be back."

"Sounded like he was at the airport," Noah said as he ended the call. "I heard someone ask about a terminal." He was already rushing out the screened door of the beach house, keys in hand.

"Where are we going?" McKenzie asked. Despite the questions, she snatched Kimberly Lawson's hard drive from her laptop and shoved it in her jacket pocket. She grabbed her purse and laptop, followed him to the minivan, and climbed into the front seat.

"I told you. The airport."

"No, you told me *Lucas* was at the airport. You didn't tell me *we* were going there," McKenzie said, her voice rising in panic. She rubbed her upper arms to try to warm the chill creeping over her. Still, this could be what needed to happen. It might be the only way.

"He's not about to ride off into the sunset and not give us another thought. He *knows* that *we* know who he is. He killed the president for God's sake. Do you think he's willing to let us keep breathing when we know that tiny, insignificant fact?"

McKenzie nodded. It might be a month, it might be a year, but Lucas would find them. He'd be after them until he was sure they no longer posed a threat. "Do we have any idea which airport he's at?"

"I'm heading to LAX. It's the one that makes sense," Noah answered.

He careened the minivan through the roads like it was a Corvette. McKenzie's stomach swished inside her. "I may throw up."

"Well, if you do, make sure to do it out the window. It'll be hard to be inconspicuous in a crowd if you smell like puke," he said without any hint of joking. "Tell me something. I can't wrap my mind around why a presidential advisor would be supplying information to a reporter. He had to have something to gain from it. Or maybe Jessie had some kind of tie to him?"

McKenzie's stomach pitched forward as Noah threw the steering wheel back and forth to make sharp turns, not even braking when he wheeled the van into a street on the right hand side. She bit her lip hard to keep from yelling out.

"Somehow I doubt Bert Royal happened to be Jessie Cartwright's long lost third cousin," she said through clenched teeth.

"Me, too, but I can't imagine why he'd contact her at random. I mean, why her?"

McKenzie pursed her lips and mumbled, "I don't know."

She closed her eyes for the duration of the ride, because her stomach couldn't stand watching the road blur past her any longer. Noah's foot seemed magnetized to the accelerator, and that van wasn't made to be driven at that speed.

"You'll have to go in and watch when we get there. I'll make the call to tip off security, but I fit the damned profile, too. I won't be any use to us detained."

McKenzie's stomach knotted. "Then?"

"Text me where he's headed. I'll catch up as soon as I can make a move. You put Brian's number in your phone, right?"

"Yeah."

"If anything goes wrong inside, whatever you do, don't give yourself away. Don't get too close to him. Period. The disguise might get you past some people, but don't trust it to work on Lucas, Mac. Don't."

They rumbled up and down lanes of the parking lot at LAX, but there wasn't a vacant spot in sight.

"Where's my parking angel when I need her?" Noah said. As soon as the words were out of his mouth, a car a few spaces down began to back out. "God as a real estate agent. Thank you, thank you," he said as he pulled in. "Go," he commanded.

She scrambled out of the van, adrenaline surging. She carried her laptop with her, a standard traveler. Her legs pumped toward the building.

Don't think. Don't think. Don't think about all the ways this could go wrong.

Inside the airport, she followed the signs toward security. In her worst nightmare, Lucas had already made it through. If he had, the police would get him first or he'd go down fighting. The best scenario in so many ways, and yet, she couldn't stand it. Her chest tightened.

I have to know.

She moved close to the security line, squatted, and pretended to look for something in her laptop case. A solid two minutes ticked by. Then another. Nothing happened.

Then, one by one, TSA officials began to pull men from the lines. Young, clean-cut men in their late twenties, early thirties, give or take a few stragglers.

Her hand clenched around the cheap, untraceable phone, her only weapon. Her gaze darted across the crowd. *Come on.*

So much movement, people bustling about. Confusion, anger from some of the men.

Out of the corner of her eye, she caught a man in jeans and a ball cap ducking under the far left ribbon of the security line. He calmly walked toward the exits, backpack over one shoulder.

Had to be.

She followed a few good car-lengths back. He'd notice if he had a tail.

Keep your steps even. Hurrying will tip him off.

Lucas pushed through one of the glass doors, turned right toward the shuttle bus stop. McKenzie's heart galloped. Keeping him in sight, she typed on the phone, but the stupid keys were too different from her own for texting without looking.

Lucas boarded a shuttle. They would lose him.

Before she had a chance to change her mind, she pocketed the phone and stepped onto the bus, too. She kept her head bent. He was at the back. She sat at the very front, face turned toward the driver.

Don't look back at him. Don't you dare.

She fumbled with the phone in her right pocket. The words "park shuttle" would have to be enough. The center middle button felt like it had to be either power off or send. If fate planned for her to make it through this day, it had better be send.

The bus rumbled, and they started down the road toward the parking areas. McKenzie shifted, then stopped herself. Giving them away at this point would be brilliant of her.

Where are you, Noah?

Then, she caught a glimpse of Lucas in the rearview mirror. He sat still on the very back row, looking out the windows like any normal plane passenger having just arrived home from a trip, maybe on his way to his kid's softball game.

After what seemed like hours, the shuttle eased to a stop in the B lot of the parking area. McKenzie's stare never left the mirror.

The only other passengers on the bus—a skinny brunette in her twenties and a man who could be her father—stood. The driver rose to lift the girl's suitcase off the racks.

Cold eyes met hers in the rearview mirror.

McKenzie stiffened, a seen rabbit. She dropped her gaze to her lap, breaths catching hard in her chest. *It's just a coincidence.*

Hand still in her pocket, she turned the phone over in her palm, counted to ten.

Please.

The driver was back in his seat.

McKenzie slowly looked back up and into the mirror.

Lucas stared back as though he'd never looked away.

CHAPTER FIFTY THREE

MCKENZIE LEAPT FROM her seat as the driver pressed the accelerator. The rapid thud of footsteps was her only warning. The next instant, her cheek was on fire, and she flew into the seats on the right side of the bus. Her head conked the metal rail.

A crunch. A shout.

A thud.

Dazed, McKenzie lifted her face toward the window in time to see a blur hurdle over the body of the bus driver, which had tumbled out the door. The blur went straight for the driver's seat, but Lucas, now in the captain's position, floored the accelerator.

Lucas grabbed at the lunging figure with both hands. His fists clenched Noah's forearms, twisted him to try to eject him from the bus.

Noah seized Lucas' shoulders and used his backward momentum to pull him with him. They both hit the floor. McKenzie clambered over the thrashing bodies in the center aisle, each grappling for the upper hand. No matter what else happened, the bus was still rolling.

McKenzie reached the steering wheel just in time. She jerked the wheel to miss a parked soda stock truck. The bus' wheels screamed against the pavement. McKenzie's entire body leaned with the bus onto its left side. Her eyes squeezed shut involuntarily as she braced for impact, but she forced herself to open them.

Can't avoid other crashes if you can't see.

She stretched her right foot for where the brake should be, but the driver's seat sat way too far back for someone of her stature. Grunts from the back of the bus told her the fight continued, but she couldn't do a damn thing about it. Only drive, try to stop this contraption, and hope Noah was the better fighter.

They were on a straightaway now. If nothing came into their path, she could make it to the brake.

McKenzie sank down and strained for the brake pedal. She dipped further in the seat, and her foot made contact. Pumping it three short jabs first to try to slow the beast, she then forced all her weight onto it. The bus groaned, its momentum fighting her command.

The bus recoiled. McKenzie gripped the sides of the driver's chair to keep from crashing forward into the steering wheel when it made its final halt.

Keep steady.

She could barely see the parking lot over the steering wheel, but she didn't dare shift to look either at where they were or what was happening behind her. Stopping was good. Not knowing where the park or the emergency brake was? Another story.

The gear shift on the right side of the wheel seemed like that of any other vehicle. The punches of Noah and Lucas her background music, their cussing spiking her blood pressure, McKenzie arched her back to keep her foot on the brake as she gripped the shift. She depressed the end button and shoved upward.

She eased her foot up as little as possible. No movement.

They were still.

McKenzie ducked under the front dash and fumbled in her jacket for the cell phone, but it had fallen out when Lucas hit her into the seats. Her hand closed around Kimberly Lawson's hard drive. She shoved the precious find deeper and dared to peek toward the back where Noah and Lucas battled.

The two squared off at the rear. Lucas stood at the very end of the bus, blood streaming from multiple cuts, his face a twisted mask of raw fury. His eyes gleamed with a single-minded, unholy sort of madness. Noah's back was to McKenzie, blocking the killer's route to her. They dove in toward each other, arms and heads locked like boxers in a ring. After a brief struggle, both broke apart at the same moment, propelling backward. Noah landed butt first on the floor, but Lucas' back slammed the end wall of the bus. The momentum bounced him back toward Noah.

Noah surged up from a squatting position to his feet, using the power of his legs to thrust his fist swift and hard. He jabbed at his opponent.

His adversary, trained in the exact same way, hit back. The fight had the surreal air of having been choreographed. Blood and sweat sprayed from both of them in time to the animal grunts and growls, the dark, primitive beat of skin thudding against skin.

Here in the bus, SEAL battled SEAL, two caged beasts fighting for escape. Noah regained his footing. Took a step forward. He curved his open palm and thrust it into the base of Lucas' throat. The assassin tumbled to the ground and brought his hand to his neck for a moment, stunned.

Lucas hopped back to his feet and threw a punch at Noah. His right fist connected with Noah's left cheek. Noah wobbled, off-balance. As quickly as he wavered, though, his weight distribution stabilized. He came at Lucas again.

Noah swung his foot out to kick Lucas' shins, but the assassin was too fast for him. He grabbed Noah's foot and twisted. Noah's body swirled in an effort to break Lucas' grip. When he couldn't, his legs flew out from under him. In the second Noah took to recover his bearings, Lucas stomped hard on Noah's face. The sickening crunch of Noah's nose breaking hit McKenzie's ears. Blood spurted across the metal floor.

McKenzie gasped, the rasp of the indrawn air raw against her dry throat.

Until this point, Lucas had ignored McKenzie's presence. Now, he looked up at her. Sweat ran in rivulets from his bald head, blurring with the blood from the gash under one swollen eye. His chest heaved as he wiped the back of his hand across his mouth then spat out more blood.

She tried to duck under the dash, but it was too late. His eyes narrowed. He stepped over Noah, who lay half-conscious and moaning on the floor.

Lucas' movement toward McKenzie seemed to galvanize Noah. McKenzie watched his chest rise and fall with the second wind stirring in him. Noah rolled onto his belly, brushed the blood from his eyes, and army crawled behind Lucas. He snaked across the floor, fast and silent.

Even as her chest clenched with fear, McKenzie held Lucas' gaze with her own.

Hold his attention. Please, God, don't let him turn around.

She cowered beneath the seat, her heart hammering at the glint of silver in the corner of her eye. Noah had flipped open his knife.

McKenzie saw the reaction on Lucas' face as he heard the snick of the knife clicking into place. Too late. He turned to see Noah flash below him. Noah stabbed Lucas' calf and wrenched the blade back out in one fluid motion.

Lucas bellowed, low and thunderous. He reared his fist back and smashed it into Noah's jaw, sending Noah flat on his back once again. "You are *such* a pain in the ass!"

"Oh, and you're just a basket full of kittens, aren't you?" Noah said through gritted teeth. Smearing the wall with bloody handprints, he pulled himself to his feet.

Noah plunged his knife toward Lucas, but it was a blind stab. Blood matted his face, oozing down his forehead. Noah reached up to wipe the stream away, still wielding the knife in a wild attempt to keep Lucas at bay.

Lucas reached into his pocket, then clicked open a knife of his own. "So you want to play dirty," he snarled. He shoved the blade at Noah.

In lashing out with the blade in his right hand, Noah had opened his left side to attack. Lucas' jab went straight into Noah's left shoulder. Noah let out a guttural, primal yell, his voice taut with the fury of a wounded animal.

"Oh, sorry," Lucas sneered. "Did that hurt?"

Lucas lunged again. This time the blade sliced a jagged cut up Noah's cheek. Blood poured from the wound.

McKenzie's heart thumped, frantic. Nothing she could use

for a weapon that she could see, and Lucas' fist across her face had told her his strength would best her no matter what. Still, she had to do something. Surely the bus driver or the father and daughter he'd let off at the last stop would have sent up flares.

Noah had now collapsed into an unmoving heap on the floor. McKenzie was no match for a SEAL, but she could buy Noah some time until help arrived. Was he even still alive?

Now.

She charged forward and swung her foot through Lucas' legs with as much momentum as she could muster. Her foot connected with his groin. *Yes!*

A long time ago, Uncle Sal had pointed out a pressure point to use if she was ever attacked. Now was the time. While the killer's knees buckled, she jabbed her fingers into the groove behind his ear.

Lucas' face contorted as he whirled around. His fist clocked her in the face, and McKenzie's cheek exploded with pain. Her eyes slid out of focus. She kicked out at him with her right foot, aiming for where Noah had stabbed his shin. Lucas caught her foot just as he had Noah's. He twisted.

Her leg burned as if it was stuck in a relentless machine. She screamed and squirmed against his grip, but he wrenched it once more. The sound of all the pencils she'd ever snapped while deep in thought jumped into her head as she heard something pop inside her knee. Pain seared up her leg as if her blood had caught fire. She tried to stand, but her knee had the sturdiness of Jell-o.

The coppery taste of blood hit her tongue, and her stomach rolled. McKenzie turned onto her belly so she wouldn't choke if she vomited. She dry heaved, concentrating hard on not letting her head smack the bus' floor.

"Not quite as much of a badass as you thought you were, huh?" Lucas jeered. He spit some of his own blood onto the ground beside McKenzie. He stood above her, wielding his knife. "Now, what to do?"

Lucas grabbed McKenzie around her middle, hoisted her in a fireman's hold, and dragged her off the bus. She urged her legs to kick.

Move, dammit.

Nothing. They wouldn't respond.

One more stair and Noah would be out of sight. He lay unconscious—or dead—on the ground, covered in blood.

Her hope plummeted.

Lucas carried her toward the parking deck. She didn't have the strength to fight back. She could only pray that back on that bus, Noah's heart still beat.

CHAPTER FIFTY FOUR

Day 7: Afternoon
Los Angeles, CA

"DON'T HANG UP," Uhlig breathed into the phone.

He'd checked into a hotel near LAX and relaxed on the bed. He watched CNN's coverage of the presidential press conference while he waited for his contact to get back to him with information about where to start looking for the assassin. Yet with no warning at all, something had clicked in his head. The voice in the background of his phone call to Robbie weeks ago. He knew who it belonged to. It was the same voice he'd heard a year ago in the background of a recording of another phone call of his brother's. A phone call recorded the same day his brother met Kimberly Lawson.

All day, Uhlig had tried so hard to keep from picking up the phone, but suddenly, the call seemed not only a good idea. It seemed vital. His brother was in much more trouble than he'd ever fathomed, and he had imagined a lot. This—well, this was unspeakable.

Now, he could hear breathing. Though the person Uhlig knew to be on the other end of the line didn't reply, he didn't hang up, either. Uhlig spoke quick words while he still had the chance.

"I know. And when I say I know, I mean I know *everything*. Not just what you wanted people to know. But don't worry. I promised Mama I'd always take care of you, and I will now. I swear it. I'm at the Hotel Versailles in L.A. If there's any way you can, meet me here. We'll get you away. I promise it on my own life, brother. If not, I'll be in touch."

He closed the phone, too afraid to keep his brother long. He couldn't risk scaring him off. He prayed he'd listen to him, let Uhlig help him.

Amidst the complete chaos surrounding his brother, he needed help—and family—more than ever.

Day 7: Afternoon (EST)
in flight, Air Force One

"Madame President, everything is under control. My agents are at LAX, but so far, no sign of them," General Helms said.

Elaine sat on the sofa in her office aboard Air Force One. The state of the art communications system made the lousy plastic handheld sets on the backs of regular airplane seats look like something made by a toy company.

She was en route to London to meet with Britain's Prime Minister the next day. As soon as her aide left the room, Elaine had planned to make a very necessary phone call. The aide no sooner set down a cup of hot tea in front of her than Helms called. The country didn't stop just because she was in the air, and apparently neither did Noah Hutchins.

While she sat on a plane with a perfect safety record, the airport in California was flying straight to hell. General Helms informed her that the FBI agents following Noah Hutchins had tracked him to LAX. The agents lost Hutchins in traffic. Minutes later, airport officials received an anonymous tip that the president's assassin was inside LAX. Ten minutes after that, local 911 operators took a phone call from someone who'd just stepped off a park and ride shuttle when someone threw the driver out of the bus and took off with a passenger still aboard.

The agents had been given the green light to move in. They'd found Noah Hutchins, beaten and stabbed several times, on the floorboard of the abandoned bus. The perpetrator—and McKenzie McClendon—had vanished. Staff was now busy closing off all exits to the airport and searching the area, but so far to no avail.

"Doesn't sound like you have things under control to me. Ground the flights," she ordered, even though it probably wasn't a call she could make. Could the president usurp the authority of the FAA? She shook her head. Who knew? So far, her tenure as president had been one crisis after the next. The list of fires she needed to put out seemed to grow with every breath she took.

"I assure you, Madame President, the proper steps have been taken. We're doing everything we can."

"So Hutchins is in on it, then? Why have we *still* not brought him in?" Elaine asked. Her hands shook. She sat on the palm not holding the phone so she didn't have to look at it trembling. The physical manifestation of her anxiety only multiplied her jitters tenfold.

General Helms coughed into the phone. "Noah Hutchins isn't involved in the assassinations, Madame President."

"With all due respect, General, I think we have plenty of reason to detain him for questioning."

Helms coughed once again, and Elaine's temper flared. "Don't you have any cough drops, General?"

"Madame President, Noah Hutchins isn't responsible for the killings. We know he's not, because we know him too well."

Elaine gripped the phone with the same ferocity she'd held it the night she heard the president had been killed. Her knuckles whitened as blood flowed out of them.

"What do you mean, General Helms?"

"After Lieutenant Noah Hutchins left the SEALs, he made a comfortable living running a shooting range near his hometown."

"What difference does it make whether he ran a shooting range or a pet shop?" Elaine asked. "Make your point, General."

"A year later, he left the firing range and disappeared. In short, Noah Hutchins went MIA because he was working for us. For the CIA."

"What?" Elaine blurted out, all dignity of office forgotten.

"We needed someone. A sniper."

"You're the damn CIA. You could've had anybody."

"Exactly," Helms said. "We needed someone good. Someone better than good. We needed the best the country had to offer. We went to the FBI, Army, Navy, every branch. In the military, we heard two names over and over. Hutchins and Randolph. Even a few Army officers who didn't know them by name recommended two Navy guys with reputations of being able to blow heads apart from almost a mile away. According to high-ranking officers, the pair was the best there were."

"Wait a minute. You'd heard of Randolph before any of this happened?" Elaine asked in disbelief. A million questions smoldered in her throat.

"They were both part of SEAL Team Six. We never approached Randolph. He was discharged for mental reasons, so he wasn't exactly qualified anymore for jobs of the sensitive nature we had in mind. Whoever we chose had to be able to handle the work physically *and* cope with the pressure. We went to Hutchins."

Her cheeks burned with fury. She was the leader of the free world, and she'd had no clue Hutchins was a member of the counterterrorism force within the SEALs and already on anyone's radar before the killings. The Director of National Intelligence had kept this little fact neatly folded and tucked away. What other "tidbits" of the investigation had he not found convenient to divulge?

"Why are you just *now* telling me all this?" Elaine demanded.

The smugness in Helms' tone was unbearable. "I shouldn't have to remind you, *ma'am*, the government is bigger than the presidency."

It was a simple statement, and yet it was filled with so much animosity that Elaine could practically see the smirk on Helms' face over the phone.

He continued. "Hutchins hasn't worked for us for a while now, but we didn't have a reason not to trust him. He's been loyal to the country even after we failed his team. The man has a level of control you rarely see even in the military."

Elaine said nothing.

How does this make sense? What does this mean to the investigation? To me?

Helms spoke again. "That's why, the whole time, we believed he'd lead us to the killer. He's better than we are. After all, when we needed dirty work done, *we* went to *him*."

CHAPTER FIFTY FIVE

Day 7: Early Afternoon (PST)
Los Angeles, California

STILL OVER LUCAS' shoulder, McKenzie squinted as the sunlight hit her face. Lucas carried her through double doors at the top of the parking garage. She forced her eyes wider to try to assess where she was. Blue sky met her field of vision, and rooftops peppered the skyline. She could see the airfield off to her left. How they'd arrived here, McKenzie had no clue. Had she passed out?

Lucas threw her onto the ground like a stack of lumber. Her tailbone ached with the blow. She tried not to look at him, but she could feel his eerie stare on her.

"The big question is, what do we do with you now?" he said.

McKenzie shook her head, which only increased her dizziness. "I don't know."

"Well, I guess if you don't know, then we can get this over with."

Lucas whipped out his knife, the blade still smeared with Noah's blood. McKenzie's skin crawled at the thought of the tip penetrating her flesh.

"Please," she squeaked. "I'll do anything you want."

One of his eyebrows lifted. McKenzie immediately regretted her words. She needed time, though.

"Okay, then." he said, but he continued to point the knife at her. "We'll save your pretty throat for later. I *am* a bit curious how you managed to find me. How did you know I did it?"

McKenzie narrowed her eyes. "Did what?"

"Oh, now. Do you really think you have time to play stupid games with me? You know good and well what I'm talking about. Now, you start explaining, or I start chopping."

McKenzie scrambled to organize what she knew and what she'd guessed. Why bother lying to him now? The psychopath was going to kill her as soon as he finished questioning her, anyway. If she talked as long as possible, there was a slim chance help might arrive before he left her to bleed out the way he'd done so many others. After all, she wasn't even sure if she could stand on her damaged knee, much less escape a trained ex-SEAL.

She licked her dry lips. "We talked to Cody's mother when we first reached California. She told us he was hanging around with some girl named Kimberly Lawson, but that was it. Once we had the name, we tracked her down to ask her about her relationship to Cody. She didn't tell us anything, but I had a feeling she was hiding something. I decided to go back and talk to her again. The night I went to her house, we—" The image of the dead executive replayed like an endless movie loop frozen in her brain. "She was dead."

"Go on," Lucas said. A thin smile crossed his face.

God, he's enjoying this, isn't he?

McKenzie fought waves of nausea. From the look on his face, he relished the memory of watching Kimberly bleed to death on the floor.

"Noah followed me there and saw her. He said he recognized your style."

"Style?"

"Yeah," McKenzie stammered. The knife held her riveted, a cobra ready to strike if she made a single wrong move. "He—he said you were the only guy he knew that killed that way. Something about the femoral artery. That's how he knew it was you."

Lucas grunted. "I'll be damned."

"That's the part I can't figure out, by the way."

"What?"

"Why you killed Kimberly Lawson."

"I'll ask the questions here, if you don't mind."

But McKenzie kept going. She had to risk it. It might be her only chance to know the truth. Even if she—like Jessie Cartwright—died for knowing it.

"I've worked out why you wanted Cody to be your second sniper," she said, "and why you had to dispose of him. But I still have no clue why you went back for Kimberly."

"Haven't you learned by now that all this curiosity isn't very good for you?" Lucas said.

His smirk was unmistakable. So were the half-mad glimmer in his eyes and the flush of excitement on his cheekbones. The bastard was enjoying the thrill of reliving his masterpiece. He loved the chance to show off for someone, to brag about his cleverness.

McKenzie squared her shoulders. "Look, we both know I'm not leaving this roof alive. I've seen your face. Why not tell me the gory details? Let me have the satisfaction of knowing the real scoop before I depart for that big newspaper office in the sky."

As McKenzie expected, intrigue flashed across Lucas' face. He was as cocky as Noah said. He wouldn't pass up the opportunity to boast his biggest triumph.

"All right then," he said. "Ask away."

McKenzie exhaled. She'd bought herself a couple more minutes. "If Kimberly knew everything about you—your role in the assassination of President Seymour—you'd have never let her live in the first place. And yet, you did for a time. On the other hand, if she knew nothing—couldn't identify you specifically, or somehow implicate you—she wouldn't be dead right now."

"You're observant, aren't you? If I didn't have to kill you, you'd make a fine detective. It must run in the family."

Her spirit panged at the mental image of Uncle Sal.

Reporter. Detective. They're not so different. Both of us only want to know the truth. To turn over the rocks, shine a light in the dark places. To get some damned justice in this world. For somebody.

"Cody Randolph was the best damn sharpshooter I've ever come across," Lucas said. "Aside from Noah. Neither of them missed a shot. I knew I didn't have a prayer of persuading Noah. Sometimes I think the boy *shits* righteousness. I knew Cody wouldn't do the job for pay." He shrugged. "So I started watching Cody for something I could use. His friends. His family. Learned a long time ago that with people like Brian Varnes and Cody, you have to find a weak spot. Then when you do, squeeze." He let out a laugh. "I never dreamt he'd have a skeleton *that* huge in his closet. Got pictures of him cozying up to a bona fide pro-life, deer hunting, anti gay marriage Republican governor. He was screwed in more ways than one."

"I knew that much." At his glare, she hurried to probe further before he had a chance to get angry. "You still haven't explained Kimberly Lawson."

"You're too persistent for your own damn good," he said, but he kept talking. "One day when I was staked out to take photos of Cody, I saw what I thought at the time was a tail. For all I knew, the damn FBI was watching me. Or watching the governor and his boy toy, Cody. Hell, it could've been the opposition, trying to dig up some dirt. All I knew was there was a woman who seemed mighty interested in the same target I had my eyes on. I managed to leave my car without her seeing me. She was out of her own car with a camera. I grabbed her in the sleeper hold until she passed out. Dug through her stuff to see if she had anything on me, but all I found on her camera were pictures of the governor and Cody."

"What?"

Lucas nodded. "Yep. She was on a stakeout of her own, only her recon had everything to do with the governor and nothing to do with a former SEAL. As it turned out, the Shen were using the governor's little affair as blackmail to keep him from signing certain legislation into law. I doubt she knew anything about Cody Randolph other than that he and Governor Bartley were doing the nasty."

"Wait—it was the *governor's affair* that drew the Shen's attention?" She shook her head, more confused by the second. Lucas killed Kimberly Lawson because of something unrelated to the assassinations? Kimberly had hired him to commit them. Hadn't she?

"Once I knew she wasn't a cop, I didn't mind leaving her there unconscious. Later, I started worrying she might remember me, especially after the hit on the president and vice president went down. What if she'd come around while I was looking through her pictures? Gotten a look at me? She'd been attacked while stalking Bartley and Randolph, after all. She might hear Randolph's name and connect the two things. Paranoia can be an occupational hazard. Best not to leave any loose ends." He shrugged again. "It's not the kind of risk I'm willing to take."

McKenzie forced herself to ignore the implication. She was the one who was a risk to him now. Confused or not, she had to keep talking if she wanted her chances to stay alive. "You arranged the extra sniper. Even with two gunmen, it had to be almost impossible to execute the shots at the same time."

Lucas grinned, his ego effectively stroked. "Even more than you realize, I think. Secret Service protection on the president and vice president extends about 900 yards. That's almost a mile radius around the president. Moving in close enough for an accurate shot wouldn't be feasible. But when someone from the inside hires you, chances are they have other people on the inside, too."

McKenzie's mouth fell open. "Are you telling me Secret Service were in on this?"

Lucas shrugged. "I'm telling you I was where I needed to be, and so was Cody. The spots for the sniper nests were conveniently overlooked. Maybe even cleared."

McKenzie shook her head in disbelief. The depth of this was a never-ending nightmare of corruption. Was there nothing that couldn't be bought if the price was right?

Lucas spoke again. "Wind speed, altitude, humidity, air temperature. They all have to be compensated for. Both of the targets were in motion, so their foot speed had to be taken into account. The shots had to be aimed a centimeter in front of their position in the scope. Have you ever seen what a fifty caliber rifle will do to a skull from a distance, McKenzie?"

McKenzie shook her head slowly. A tear slid down her cheek. Too much. It was all too much.

"The forehead doesn't have a little dot the way it does if a person is shot from a few feet away with a pistol. Like say, your uncle." He pointed his fingers at her head like a pretend gun and pulled the pretend trigger. "At that distance, the head is more like a watermelon exploding from the inside out."

McKenzie's neck burned with anger as her Uncle's face, Levi's, flashed in her memory. She swallowed the bile that rose. She imagined Cody Randolph pulling the trigger to protect someone he loved. He'd had to watch Vice President Tifton's face blow apart. Unlike the bastard standing in front of her, Cody wouldn't have taken any pleasure in the sight. McKenzie clenched her teeth. Her head throbbed from the earlier blow Lucas had landed to her face. She touched a hand to the bruise blossoming on her cheek.

"Now there's something I've been meaning to ask *you*," Lucas said. "Noah said you two fought Varnes at your uncle's. Yet, your pretty face didn't have a scratch on it until I touched it."

He squatted across from McKenzie, the flat of his blade cold on McKenzie's undamaged cheek. "Were you lying to me, McKenzie McClendon? I don't like to be lied to."

McKenzie yelped, her cheek burning as Lucas traced a shallow line toward her jaw line with his knife. He shifted behind her and yanked her to her feet, clapping a hand over her mouth. She writhed under his grip. *Someone help me!*

"I guess Varnes and his family are a few more wildcards I'll have to deal with when I'm finished with you," he hissed into her ear.

The knife at her neck touched the purple welt it'd left the night before Pierce died. She grimaced. Her feet shuffled underneath her even though running was no use.

"Drop it," a voice yelled from the other side of the roof.

Lucas whirled around, bracing McKenzie in front of him as a human shield. A man in an FBI jacket faced them, his Glock

271

trained.

"I don't think so, buddy," Lucas said.

Lucas' knife dug deeper into McKenzie's neck. Droplets of blood seeped out and trickled toward her shirt's neckline.

She sipped air, hard and fast. If she breathed deeper, the knife would slash her throat.

The FBI agent didn't have a clear shot at all, but McKenzie didn't trust him not to try for it anyway. Not only that, but his finding them seemed to be a stroke of luck. Whether the agents had split up to search the buildings surrounding LAX or he was on random patrol, this agent didn't look like he had any backup whatsoever.

Lucas must've assumed the same thing. He edged toward the agent—and the only exit from the roof. He hauled McKenzie along in front of him. "You want to take a shot, buddy? Go ahead. I'm sure she won't mind."

Lucas' breath was hot on McKenzie's ear when he laughed. She could feel her pulse throbbing in the hollow of her throat, beating against the steel. If she didn't act now, while she had help, she had no chance.

Despite her ongoing dizziness, she oriented herself to where Lucas' feet lingered behind her own. She let her legs drag nearer to his until her ankle brushed against his. With a quick internal prayer, she stomped as hard as she could on the instep of his right foot, the same side of his body where he held the knife.

It didn't do much, but he was distracted enough to slacken his grip. In the millisecond of relaxation, McKenzie dropped out of his arms and hit the pavement like a kid practicing a fire drill.

Unfortunately, the gunshot she was expecting from the FBI agent never came.

The agent stalled. He took a moment he didn't have to register that the hostage had been released. Lucas capitalized on that extra pause and lunged into him. The agent's gun flew across the roof. The pair tangled in a bizarre wrestling match. Their feet scuffled atop the roof, their heads and arms locked together like battling gladiators.

McKenzie stumbled to her feet and hobbled across the roof in the direction the gun had sailed. She'd never used a gun. Hell, she didn't even know how to aim. If she shot, she'd risk shooting the only person on this roof who could save her.

One problem at a time.

The two men scrambled, coming dangerously close to the lip of the roof. The agent swung his foot forward in an attempt to clip Lucas' legs out from under him, but Lucas was faster. He moved to the side and thrust the knife forward. The agent dodged, and the knife stabbed into the empty air where his arm had been only seconds before.

The cop threw a hard punch that collided with Lucas' nose. Blood streamed from the killer's face. Lucas answered with his own jab to the agent's jaw. The FBI agent staggered backwards, the low side of the roof brushing his legs below his knees.

McKenzie spotted the gun lodged in the narrow space between the ledge of the roof and a radiator box. She plunged her hand behind the radiator. If only she could recover it without shooting herself in the process.

She curled her palm around the butt of the gun. No way her finger was going anywhere near the trigger, even if the handle was the easiest part to grasp. She pried upward with every bit of strength she could muster, but it wouldn't budge. The wall was right behind her, and she saw an opportunity there. She sank into it, sat down, and pressed her back against the ledge of the roof. Using her feet for leverage, she tugged on the gun.

The weapon popped out, but as it did, it slipped out of her sweaty palms. It dropped deeper into the crook between the wall and the radiator. On her knees, wincing from the agony of her injured leg, she squeezed into the space behind the box.

McKenzie fumbled for the gun in the corner. As her hand clasped around the cool metal, she watched in horror while the agent swayed backward toward the roof's ledge.

His arms windmilling, he caught his balance and rocked forward. He used the momentum to go at Lucas again. He battered Lucas' stomach with his head and was rewarded with a grunt.

Lucas swung his arm back, a ray of sunlight catching a flicker of steel. Before McKenzie had a chance to yell a warning, Lucas plunged the knife into the agent's leg. As Lucas slashed the blade downward, blood spurted from the agent's femoral artery. Lucas ripped the knife from his opponent and shoved him hard in the chest.

For an awful moment, the world froze. The agent's legs toppled over his head and straight over the ledge. He drifted through the air for a long second, a lifeless dummy. McKenzie winced at the sickening crunch of his body against an awning below them.

On the roof, Lucas put his hands to his knees and gasped like a competitive swimmer breaking the water's surface. McKenzie's leg seared with pain, and her head swirled.

Please. Just stay turned away. Just for a few seconds. Don't look at me. Don't turn around.

She edged toward the door where the agent had entered. The staircase led to safety.

Her heart, however, had other ideas. The weight of the gun in her hand called to her. Images burst forth in her mind: Kimberly Lawson. Cody Randolph. Pierce. Uncle Sal. Levi.

Noah.

For all she knew Lucas had killed him, too. The last time she'd seen him, his broken body lay crumpled on the filthy floorboard of a bus. If by some miracle he lived, Lucas would come after him. Again. Just like he would go after Brian Varnes and his family. She couldn't let his children end up like Levi.

She leveled the gun at Lucas. Her hands trembled.

He had turned around. His eyes found her.

His face was covered in blood, but still, his expression mocked her. His laughed, cold and dry. "You gonna shoot me?"

"You're damn right."

She pulled the trigger.

Her first shot was wide to the right, but she shifted the gun sideways a few inches to compensate. She fired again before she lost her nerve. The blasts rang in her ears. Her hand vibrated so much it was as though an earthquake rattled the foundations of the building beneath her.

The second shot was true. Lucas clutched his gut as he went to his knees. McKenzie fired again, this time hitting him in the thigh. He fell backward onto the cement.

A sound was still coming from Lucas. Another laugh? She tiptoed toward him, the gun still aimed in case he jumped.

He didn't.

The killer stared into her face, a weird, manic smile plastered on his own. "I didn't think you had it in you."

A trail of thin, red-filled saliva ran out of the corner of his mouth. He let out a grunt mingled with a cough. His eyes rolled and then refocused. He was dying.

The thought suddenly terrified her. With him, all the answers would die, too. He couldn't die. Not yet. Not before she had the truth. Her words flew out faster than she could think. "Kimberly Lawson. You didn't kill her because she was the one who hired you to kill President Seymour?"

Lucas' pupils slid in and out of center. They were beginning to look glassy and far away. He cough-laughed again. A bubble of blood popped from his lips.

"She?" he whispered.

Then, for a moment, his eyes cleared. Registered the implication of McKenzie's words.

"Heh," he rasped. "Kimberly Lawson was screwed long before I killed her."

Lucas Crawford gurgled, then spoke no more.

CHAPTER FIFTY SIX

Day 7: Evening (GMT)
London, U.K.

"WHAT IS THE status of the UNSUB?" Elaine asked. The Unidentified Subject was, by all evidence, the man who shot the President of the United States.

"Dead on arrival, Madame President," General Helms replied.

"And Hutchins?"

"He's been taken to the best trauma hospital around, but they don't know his chances yet. He lost a lot of blood."

"The reporter?"

"Okay, I think. The ambulance is taking her to the hospital to have her checked out. Our people are following. We'll question her again as soon as she's examined, but she explained how it went down. Seems cut and dry."

"Thank you, General," Elaine said before hanging up the phone.

Jet lag was already catching up to her, but she couldn't rest. By the time Elaine had arrived at the hotel in London, President Seymour's killer was dead on a rooftop in Los Angeles. Was it possible the whole thing could be over?

Day 7: Afternoon (PST)
Los Angeles, California

Uhlig paced the room, trying to put together a plan from the shattered pieces he'd been left with. Each minute that passed without action—planned, reasoned action—was another minute in which something else could go awry. Everything was so wrong now, but there had to be a way to control it, to stop the spiral toward utter disaster. A way to make sure his brother was covered even if something happened.

With every second his brother didn't show, Uhlig's certainty grew that something *would* happen. Call it instinct. Call it paranoia. To Uhlig, however, it was experience.

The news coverage on the television had shifted abruptly to reports claiming that the FBI had stormed a parking garage near LAX and removed a body assumed to be that of President Seymour's assassin. Other unconfirmed reports said the former SEAL and *Herald* reporter wanted by the FBI were rushed to the hospital in the chaos.

That's it.

Uhlig yanked out his cell phone and, with trembling fingers, punched the numbers as fast as he could.

Day 7: Late Afternoon (PST)
Ronald Reagan UCLA Medical Center, Los Angeles

McKenzie changed into the faded blue gown the nurse had handed her, a second gown put on backwards like a robe to protect what little modesty she had left. Technically, she needed a hospital gown about as much as she needed the fluids they insisted on putting in her arm on the way to the hospital. She'd be out of there as soon as they stitched up her cheek. But her gore-spattered clothes had been so miserable, the cold congealing blood plastering them to her body. She hadn't been able to stand them anymore. As soon as they pronounced her in stable condition, the Feds would be all over her. Bad enough she'd be interviewed in a butt-ugly gown, but better than enduring the questions while her blood—and Noah's—formed an indelible crust all over her.

She fingered the hard drive inside her bloodied jacket, pulled it out, and tucked it underneath the cheap mattress of the ER hospital bed. Then, she stuck her clothes in the plastic bag they'd

277

given her for her personal items.

The doctor came in, checked her over, and pronounced her in stable condition. He explained the FBI agents were adamant about questioning her if she was at all physically able. He sewed the gash on her cheek closed, uttered some vague reassurances that the scar would eventually fade, then added to her misery with a couple of injections. She heard him say something about tetanus. Pain killer maybe. Hell, it might've been an anti-bubonic plague shot for all she knew. The adrenaline rush of the rooftop ordeal was rapidly wearing off, leaving behind a creeping lassitude. She had to hold it together. Just a little longer.

The minute the doctor cleared her for questioning, two agents entered the tiny room. She was asked to sign a voluntary consent form so they could search her personal items, which she signed. They'd have a warrant in ten seconds flat anyway.

After that, Agent Number One questioned her while Agent Number Two dug through her stuff. Someone had retrieved her purse from the bus, but her laptop case was nowhere in sight. Probably off being searched somewhere.

Her face flushed while she answered their questions. As she told them about how she and Noah found Lucas and almost everything she knew about Kimberly Lawson and the Shen, the hard drive practically burned her rear end through the mattress. Obstruction of justice: a great charge to add to her growing list of felonies. Still, she had to look at the thing before she gave it up. After what Lucas said on the rooftop, she had more questions than ever.

Thankfully, even if she still had a lot to answer for, finding the president's killer bought a decent get out of jail free card. The Feds thanked her, told her they'd be in touch. Soon after, she signed the forms officially releasing her from the hospital. A nurse was nice enough to lend her a pair of hospital-issued scrubs to change into to avoid her bloody clothes.

The instant the nurse exited, McKenzie breathed a sigh of relief as she yanked the hard drive from under the mattress. She wrapped it in her hospital gown and tucked it safely into her plastic personal item bag.

Even if she was free to go, McKenzie wasn't ready to venture far from the hospital yet. Not while Noah was still in critical condition, and not while her knee, though now back in place, was so sore.

The shopping center nearby seemed like a good idea and was within walking distance. First, she stopped into a discount store and bought clean undergarments, a T-shirt, and a pair of elastic-banded khaki capris. Not stylish by any standards, but they beat the scrubs. She changed in the tiny stall of the store's bathroom, dumping the ratty scrubs into the plastic hospital bag with her bloody clothes.

Next, she wandered into an electronics store. Now that the FBI was the proud owner of her laptop, surely the *Herald* wouldn't mind if she charged a new one to their account. After all, it was kind of like workers' comp.

When she got back to the hospital, she checked on Noah's condition. Still in surgery was the only thing the nurse at the desk would tell her. It'd be hours before there would be any news.

Rather than pace the waiting room, with its dog-eared magazines and unwatched television blaring an inane game show, she headed downstairs toward the cafeteria. She rushed through the line, not even caring what kind of cardboard pizza they handed her. She'd have skipped it entirely if her stomach wouldn't have murdered her.

She settled in at a corner table and booted up the new laptop. Finally, a quiet moment to think about what had been gnawing at her since the rooftop.

Kimberly Lawson hadn't hired Lucas.

As soon as the laptop's screen came up, she pulled the hard drive out of the bag. The rush that had come every time a clue snapped into place during their hunt for the killer wasn't there this time, but she plugged in the little black box anyway. The chances of knowing the full truth might've died with Lucas, but she had nothing better to do.

Absently, she clicked the folder titled "Archived Footage."

The window opened, and the screen filled with video clips, the most recent at the top. She glanced through the names, but nothing looked interesting or Shen-related. They were titled things like GRMStudiosStaffMeeting01 or AssistantNotes4B.

McKenzie's finger was moving to close the window when her sightline caught FredericksKellyOffice. FredericksKelly. The names she and Noah had used when they'd first found Kimberly Lawson. She clicked the video.

Kimberly's office filled the screen. McKenzie saw her own countenance beside Noah's. The sound on the laptop was off because she couldn't turn up the volume in the hospital cafeteria with so many others around, but she didn't need it. She'd been present for the conversation.

Kimberly Lawson taped her meetings.

McKenzie's curiosity sped up. The idea seemed crazy at first, but then again, the woman had been a part of a secret society involved in all sorts of underground dealings. It made sense she'd want everything someone told her on record, not just in case something happened to her, but as reassurance if her other methods of, say, blackmail fell through.

McKenzie clicked the videos open one by one. If nothing else, it would pass the time. After viewing a few unrelated meetings, she scrolled down the list for anything interesting. Ten or twelve videos. Nothing. Executive meetings at her movie studio or clients coming in to sign contracts. Irrelevant. She watched footage of what appeared to be Kimberly firing a woman. It didn't seem immediately pertinent, but McKenzie made a mental note to come back to it when she had sound. She jabbed the button to open the next video, and her eyes almost ejected from their sockets.

She stared into the face of Bert Royal.

Sound, sound, sound!

McKenzie looked around the cafeteria, frantic. There. A teenager huddled in a chair in the corner, listening to his mp3 player. She picked up her laptop and carried it over to him. With her free hand, she tapped his shoulder.

His eyes flicked open, staring at her with the classic teenage look of, "What the hell do you want?" He plucked out an earphone. "Yeah?"

"I'll give you five bucks for the buds," she said.

The kid laughed. "Five bucks? Man, dude, I can't even get a new pair for that. Twenty, maybe."

McKenzie dug in her wallet for bills, but she only had a fifty.

"Don't have change," the kid said, grinning.

Desperate times.

She ripped the earbuds from the kid's hand and gave him the money. "Easiest money you'll ever make."

"Nice doing business with you," he replied, but she was already heading back toward the other side of the room with her computer.

She jammed the buds into her ears and stuffed the jack into her laptop. The greetings were clipped, tones serious as Kimberly Lawson and Bert Royal launched into their business.

"What assurances do I have that you can convince the president to appoint Pembry to the Supreme Court?" Kimberly Lawson's voice rang in McKenzie's ears.

Royal shifted on the bench where he sat. It looked like they were in a park somewhere. The camera took him at an angle that suggested the laptop sat in Kimberly's lap. "Pembry will be a done deal if you say the word," he replied, not facing her.

"I don't trust your word," she answered in a hard tone that didn't entirely match the one McKenzie had heard in her office. This one was colder, harder. All business.

"It's a one time offer, Ms. Lawson. You can either muster some faith or turn around and leave." Royal's hands swiped over his pants, but as quick as the gesture happened, he stopped. "But I should remind you that as soon I get the money, I have no reason to screw you over."

Kimberly grunted her sarcasm. "Sure. You have no agenda."

Still, when she spoke again, it was with certainty. "Ten million is the offer. Not a penny more."

"I think that'll do," Royal said.

"The money will be transferred this evening. Don't make me regret this."

Royal slid an envelope into her hand. "You, either."

The footage abruptly cut off. McKenzie yanked the buds from her ears. Confused, she replaced the earphones and replayed the video once more. In the middle of it, however, her gaze drifted to the timestamp in the corner.

Justice Pembry had been appointed to the Supreme Court by President Seymour the week before the assassinations. Pierce had told her Kimberly Lawson's bank account had become millions poorer that same week. McKenzie had assumed the missing money was used to hire Lucas.

She stared wide-eyed at the image of the president's Chief of Staff on the screen, unable to believe it even after everything that had happened the past few days.

Kimberly Lawson hadn't hired anyone to kill the president. She'd paid for a Supreme Court appointee. Someone else had hired the killer and used her as a cover.

Kimberly Lawson—and by extension, the Shen—had been set up to take the fall for the most notorious assassinations in history.

CHAPTER FIFTY SEVEN

Day 7: Evening (PST)
Los Angeles, California

ROBBIE WASN'T COMING.

Uhlig could wait no longer. He'd taken every precaution he could, but he had to move. All the years working for Al-Musari to try to find the man who killed his mother had taught him being still was to be avoided at all costs. Hell, it was why his mother had died, too.

Tears stung his eyes as he gathered his humble belongings in the room, realizing he had nowhere to go. There wasn't a reason left. No task to be performed. He'd finally reached that place in life where he'd done everything he could do, and now, it was just him. A shell.

Don't think about that now. You have to get out of here.

Uhlig yanked the handle and wrenched the hotel room door open.

He barely had time to register the .357 pointed at his head before it blew him away.

Day 7: Evening (PST)
Los Angeles, California

Noah's eyelids fluttered like moth wings against a screen.

"So you're coming back to earth, huh?" McKenzie whispered.

His hand was clammy in hers. His other arm sat snug in a sling. Lucas' knife had ravaged the muscle tissue in his shoulder, but it would heal.

"Jesus in a bowling league," Noah said. He opened the eye that wasn't swollen shut. "Will you hold up a mirror for me? I want to see, because I think I might've been punched in the face."

"You lost a lot of blood, but they think they've got you patched up."

He eyed McKenzie's cuts and bruises. "You look like shit."

"Always the gentleman."

Noah started to smile but winced as it pulled on his stitches. Then, his eyes clouded again. "Where is he?"

"Dead."

"How?"

She told him about the FBI showing up, about the battle on the roof. Tears stung her eyes as she relived the agent's fall. Then she described shooting Lucas Crawford three times with the agent's gun.

Noah blinked rapidly with his good eye. "I must be on some good drugs. I could've sworn you said *you* shot Lucas."

"I did."

"Damn. I didn't know you had it in you."

"Funny. Lucas said the same thing."

Noah grunted as he cocked his head on his pillow. He closed his eyes again, his discomfort evident.

McKenzie told him about her last conversation with Lucas on the roof, about finding the video on Kimberly's hard drive of her meeting with Bert Royal, and about all that had happened since then.

After she'd found the incriminating videos, McKenzie had called the FBI agent who'd given her his card. She told him about the Bert Royal video, but her other suspicions, she kept to herself. He'd met her at the hospital to confiscate the hard drive. Whether he bought her story about "forgetting" the hard drive, she'd never know, but what could he do? She'd called him to turn it in, after all.

She itched to tell Noah about the questions looming in her mind, but other things had to be addressed first. In order to tell him everything, she had to start at the beginning.

"How did Kimberly Lawson know who Cody was?" Noah asked.

McKenzie shrugged. "I don't think she did. Not in the context of blackmailing the governor, anyway. She'd been watching the governor, knew he was gay, but I don't think she knew Cody was his boyfriend then. That she was in that bar the night she met Cody could've been a bizarre coincidence, but I doubt it was. I bet she was there because she knew the governor would be. Even she said Cody was meeting 'Chris' that night. Governor Bartley's plans must've changed, and it just happened that she and Cody talked without her realizing who he was."

Noah's lips were dry, and flecks of blood cracked on them as he spoke. "I can see Cody doing that. If he saw someone alone, he'd strike up a conversation."

"It would explain a lot," McKenzie answered.

Noah coughed and shook his head. "I wish I'd known. Maybe I could've helped him. Done something."

"I think he did the only thing he knew to do," McKenzie replied.

"He took an oath to defend this country from all enemies, foreign and domestic." Noah's voice sounded distant. "I didn't know anything trumped that."

"He killed to protect someone he loved, Noah." McKenzie drew a shuddering breath. "Something that mattered *more* to him than his country. Maybe he felt he had no choice. Maybe the thought of what would happen to someone he loved if he *didn't* pull that trigger was too much for him. Drove him to do something he never in a million years thought he'd do. Wouldn't you have done the same, Noah? Protected someone you loved at any cost? Even if it cost you your honor?"

"I used to think there was no way, but now…" He sighed. "Mac, I need to tell you something."

Confessions of her own sat perched on the tip of McKenzie's tongue. Her new information continued to niggle at her mind. Still, she remained quiet and listened.

"I used to work for the CIA."

It was as though Lucas had come back to life and punched McKenzie in the gut.

"What?" she whispered.

"I was a ghost. A sniper."

"What do you mean?" she asked, even though she knew full well what he meant.

For once, there was no trace of Noah's trademarked sarcasm in his response. "I eliminated people if the government needed them gone. No questions asked. I felt it was a service to my country. After all, how different could the CIA be from the military? I did what they asked, because I believed whatever— whoever—they targeted was a threat to our nation."

McKenzie's chest tightened with doubt. The two of them were so good at keeping secrets from each other. "Why are you telling me this now?"

"Didn't it seem odd to you that the FBI wasn't on to us sooner than they were? Every time we were chased, it was by the local cops. More than likely that was only because it hadn't trickled down the line that we were to be left alone. The Feds only came looking for us because they had to, what with cars exploding in front of motels and all that. The big guys—the government-issue ones—tried to give me room. They knew I'd find him."

McKenzie's desire to reveal her suspicions died in her throat. She'd trusted Noah. She might've loved him. Now, distance stretched between the two of them. Nothing was sure anymore.

"They're planning to keep you for a few days to make sure you're stable," she said. She patted his hand while she stood.

"Mac, I should've told you before now."

"It's okay. I understand."

She did understand. Better than he knew.

"We found him," the Secret Service agent said over the phone. "He was armed, so we took him down hard."

"And was it who we thought?"

"It does appear to be Fabian Uhlig," the agent replied.

"Very well, very well," the voice responded.

"Not quite," the agent countered. "There's one more thing you should know. We checked his belongings, including his cell phone. About an hour ago, he made one final call."

"To whom?"

The agent hesitated, then replied. "The *New York Herald*. The voice mail for McKenzie McClendon."

CHAPTER FIFTY EIGHT

Day 8: Morning (GMT)
London, U.K.

A KNOCK SOUNDED on the door of Elaine's suite. "Madame President?"

She'd only sent for him sixty seconds ago, but Bert Royal had already arrived.

Here we go.

Elaine recounted the story General Helms had told her, ending with the assassin's death. "Hutchins is out of surgery. He's pretty banged up, but he's going to make it."

"And McClendon?" Royal asked.

Several advisors entered the room along with four of Elaine's Secret Service. Her eyes shifted toward the Secret Service agent nearest her.

"Funny you should ask that, Bert. The reporter had some interesting things to say about you."

Bert Royal's eyes widened. "What do you mean?"

"She says she has evidence you were involved."

"Madame President, you can't think—" his voice rose in panic, but he stopped talking as the agents closed in on him.

Royal spun away. His eyes were wild, like those of a rabid dog staring into the headlights of an oncoming car. He reached to his side, the perfect place for a holster.

"Gun," one of the Secret Service agents yelled.

Elaine's body slammed the ground as a Secret Service agent threw her down to shield her. Another agent drew his weapon.

Bert's hand brushed his gun.

The Secret Service man popped two bullets into his chest. The Chief of Staff lay still on the ground.

"Are you all right, Madame President?" the agent who had tackled her asked.

"Yes, yes, I think so," she said. She wobbled to her feet. Bert's dead frame stared at her from the floor, his eyes holes in which she might get lost.

This wasn't supposed to happen.

"Katherine," she said to an aide, her voice shaking, "cancel everything on the schedule after the conference with the Prime Minister tomorrow. Have the plane ready to head back to D.C."

Katherine nodded, but another voice sounded. "Madame President, I'm sorry to interrupt, but we have a situation."

Elaine closed her eyes. She allowed one of the Secret Service agents to guide her from the suite and into an adjacent room. "What now?"

"The shuttle *Galaxy* has exploded in space," the aide replied.

Disbelief rose in Elaine like steam from a kettle. Even with the dead body of a friend sizzling in the next room, the chaos continued.

Unholy.

The press secretary spoke up. "We'll prepare an address about the *Galaxy* within the hour, Madame President."

Elaine blew out a slow, cleansing breath. "We'll have to make a statement about what happened here tonight. Somehow."

"I'll take care of it, Madame President."

"Thank you," Elaine replied. She turned back to Katherine. "Make sure my calendar has some time when I return. I want to meet with this reporter as soon as possible."

CHAPTER FIFTY NINE

Day 8: Evening (EST)
Washington, D.C.

MCKENZIE LOOKED AROUND, appreciative of the statuary and priceless paintings as she was led through the White House by the woman who'd been sent to greet her. They weren't headed toward the Oval Office, but toward the president's private study.

"The president instructed me to bring you here," the new Chief of Staff said as she steered McKenzie through the twists and turns of the hallways past Secret Service agents. "We're so glad you could come. The president is anxious to speak with you."

I'll bet.

The president's packed calendar couldn't allow for many of these civilian meetings. McKenzie was getting the full-on rock star treatment.

The Chief of Staff rapped her knuckles on the door. As she swung it open, McKenzie caught her first glimpse of President Elaine Covington. She sat behind her desk in the Treaty Room. Light from the Victorian chandelier overhead glinted on the glasses atop her nose.

"Madame President, McKenzie McClendon of New York," Nikki Carrol introduced her, though McKenzie was quite sure the president knew who she was. She'd instructed Carrol to escort McKenzie to her private study, after all.

"Of course." President Covington smiled. Her face looked more like that of an aging librarian than the commander of one of the most powerful armies in the world. "It's nice to meet you in person, Ms. McClendon."

The president nodded to her Chief of Staff. "Thank you, Nikki."

Carrol recognized the dismissal. She tipped her head and backed out of the room, pulling the door closed as she left.

As soon as the door clicked shut, President Covington said, "You've been busy, Ms. McClendon."

McKenzie stifled a chuckle. "To put it mildly, Madame President."

"I'm glad you're safe. You've been on a dangerous road."

"That makes two of us."

"My aides tell me Lieutenant Hutchins is recovering nicely."

The president gestured to the chair opposite her. McKenzie obliged.

"He'll be all right. Nothing a few weeks of rest won't fix," McKenzie said. Her heart fluttered. It was a reporter's dream come true to be sitting in the White House across from the first female president in the history of the United States.

"Yes, I'd like a chance to thank him personally at some point," the president said with another smile.

The awkwardness of the moment crowded in on McKenzie. She and the president were making small talk. Incredible.

"I owe him a lot for finding the truth," the president said.

And so they came to it.

McKenzie swallowed hard. "Funny thing, the truth."

The president cocked her head and folded her hands in front of her. She smiled, thin-lipped, and nodded. "I knew it."

"That's why you wanted to see me in your private study, isn't it? So we wouldn't be videotaped?"

"You're astute as ever, Ms. McClendon."

McKenzie leaned back in the chair.

Exude control. Don't look like you're about to faint.

"You planted a good trail."

President Covington's smile turned down at the corners. She stared at McKenzie, scrutinizing. "You give me too much credit. And obviously it wasn't good *enough*."

Ah, confirmation.

"How did you get Bert Royal to betray his friend?" McKenzie asked. She matched the president's intense gaze. "He sowed the seeds of the faux conspiracy by baiting Kimberly Lawson into shelling out millions to steer a Supreme Court Justice appointment. That way, to anyone who found their interaction, it would look as if Kimberly Lawson financed the assassination plot. How was Bert Royal sure he could get Seymour to appoint Pembry? He had to know Kimberly Lawson would screw him over if it went wrong."

Elaine shrugged. "Pembry was a done deal with Seymour long before Bert made the deal with Ms. Lawson. We could safely use it as bait. She'd never have to know it would've been a sure thing without any money whatsoever."

"Royal also must've arranged for Cody Randolph and Lucas Crawford to penetrate the security radius. He had to have been the one who passed the assassins information about President Seymour's and Vice President Tifton's movements. Otherwise, they wouldn't have had clean shots at the exact same time. I thought Bert Royal and President Seymour were close."

President Covington unclasped her hands, then twined her fingers together once more. "Bert and I met at a State Dinner several years ago. Suffice it to say we became *better* friends than he and President Seymour. Hell, framing the Shen was *his* idea. He knew all about the little society. Said they'd be the perfect group to push this off on. This type of thing is right up their alley. Not to mention, he was more than happy to help further his mother's cause."

McKenzie couldn't help a laugh. "Yeah, I'm sure his mother would be thrilled he had his own brother killed." Fabian Uhlig's death had made the news the same day as Bert Royal's.

"You give Bert too much credit, Ms. McClendon," the president said. The woman's eyes turned cold. "Fabian knew too much. He was a danger. Still, Bert had no intention of harming him. But I figured what Bert didn't know wouldn't hurt him."

"Hurt him?" McKenzie scoffed. "He's dead!"

"Unfortunate," Elaine Covington replied. "If Fabian Uhlig

hadn't called you to make sure an unbiased party knew the truth, Bert could've hung around forever."

"So there was no car crash?" McKenzie asked. This had been the White House's official story about Bert Royal's sudden death.

"Don't believe everything you read," President Covington said.

McKenzie made no remark. The courage to probe even deeper boiled under her skin. "The Shen were a nice touch. Convenient, too."

"It was almost too perfect. Americans are chomping at the bit to believe in conspiracies. What better way to mask one conspiracy than to cover it with another?"

McKenzie nodded. "And Jessie Cartwright?"

President Covington cocked her head for a moment in confusion. "The other reporter?"

"Yes."

"Ms. Cartwright was putting together pieces that were dangerous to me. That's all I have to say on the subject. I have no idea where she was getting her information, although now, I'd venture a guess that Fabian Uhlig probably made a few misguided attempts to out the Shen for what he believed *they'd* done."

"So you had her killed."

President Covington looked straight into McKenzie's eyes. "Women in politics is a tricky thing, Ms. McClendon. Look at Bhutto. At Totah. In this world, you either get killed trying to get into office, or you *do* the killing and actually make it there."

"Tell me, *Madame President*," McKenzie said without bothering to disguise her contempt. "What's to stop me from writing about everything you're telling me right now? It's the biggest story a reporter could imagine."

"Because you know it could be quite hazardous to you."

McKenzie raised her eyebrows. "Is that a threat?"

President Covington remained quiet. She reached down to something beside her. Before McKenzie realized what was happening, a bag lay on the desk. The president unzipped it, revealing banded stacks of U.S. currency.

"Write the article you set out to write about a violent feminist group hiring an assassin. That way, everyone can be happy. You have your big break, a lot of cash, and you don't have to look over your shoulder." President Covington gave her a shark's smile. "You've already exposed the conspiracy of the Shen to make the first woman president, but you haven't written the inside scoop from the president herself about how it feels to be in that position. All my thoughts, my plans, my hopes... You could have that, Ms. McClendon, along with a front row seat at every presidential press conference in the future."

McKenzie wrung her hands in her lap. This couldn't be real. The offer was a dream.

The story she'd written about the Shen was already out there. Retracting it now would be a major setback in her news career. She'd take a lot of flack for jumping on the Shen story before she had all the facts. After all, it was an inaccurate report of one of the biggest stories in history. Her credibility would be in the dirt. Right now, no one knew the story was wrong but her and the woman sitting in front of her.

Noah's face flashed in her mind, the hurt in his eyes as he talked about his time in Afghanistan and his dead teammates. She thought of all she and Noah had been through together. Of the way he'd trusted her. Protected her.

Made love to her.

He'd been hurt and betrayed when he discovered his best friend had killed to keep a secret that mattered more to him than his loyalty to his country. Yet, if she hid the truth about Elaine Covington—lied for money and prestige—wouldn't it be the same thing as Noah hiding the truth about his involvement with the CIA? Noah understood the need to keep some things secret. Didn't he?

The image of Noah fighting Lucas Crawford on the bus flashed before her. He'd been prepared to die for her. How could she keep something of this magnitude from him after all that?

The shadow of distrust crept into her. He had deceived her, as well. The whole time they'd been running, dodging, taking blows, and sleeping side by side, he'd been aligned with the very same government now headed by a woman with no conscience.

McKenzie leaned forward and grasped the handle of the cash-filled bag.

"I knew you'd make the right choice," the president said.

CHAPTER SIXTY

Day 10: Morning (EST)
New York City

THE DAY AFTER her groundbreaking story appeared in the *New York Herald*, Noah showed up at McKenzie's desk. She sat with her head propped on her fists, reliving the morning. Her coworkers had flowed in a steady stream to congratulate her. In front of her was a celebratory bag of Skittles from her desk neighbor, who had no idea how thick the irony of his present was. It had taken days to wash out the Skittles hair-dye job Noah had done on her.

"Long time, no see," Noah said.

She hadn't returned to California after her meeting with Elaine Covington. Noah had dozens of people watching over him in the hospital, including Cody's mother. He didn't need her. She'd flown straight home to New York to write the story of a lifetime. At night, she paced her apartment, empty and lifeless without Pierce's laughter and vibrant presence. She'd poured herself into the story, staving off her grief. So much loss.

McKenzie smiled up at Noah, even though her heart beat faster than it had on the rooftop across from Lucas. She folded her arms, trying to look natural despite her shoulders tensing. He'd never been the man of the purest intentions she'd thought him to be. He was a government-trained killer who made a living shooting other people. Was he really any different from Cody or even Lucas?

From Elaine Covington?

"I'm glad to see you up and about," she said. If nothing else, this was the truth.

His arm was still cocooned in a sling, and he limped like a senior citizen. His face was bruised almost beyond recognition, and one side remained puffy and swollen. She noted that they had matching gashes across their faces, which were perhaps the ultimate testament of the journey they'd been on together.

Whatever else happened, they shared the scars.

"It's been a rough week, but I'm back on the old feet again." He gestured to the newspaper open on her desk. "I guess kudos are in order."

She shrugged. The money paid to her in exchange for the interview with the president herself wasn't even close in worth to what it had cost in her soul. She'd never believed herself to be someone whose integrity had a price.

She looked at her toes to avoid those cool blue eyes.

"Mac, I came to say I'm sorry."

"For what?" she asked, even though she knew.

He continued. "I should've told you the second we made it out of that police station why they weren't chasing us."

McKenzie didn't speak. What could she say? Whether or not he'd told her he worked for the CIA didn't matter. Nothing would've changed. Pierce would still be dead, and she'd still be a sell-out. Sometimes, it was so much easier to not forgive when you couldn't forget.

"Anyway," he said after the awkward silence, "I'm leaving. I took a job. The FBI needs a new sharpshooter."

At this, McKenzie looked up. *After all this, he's still loyal to his country. The past two weeks didn't change a thing.*

"I'm leaving tomorrow for Washington," he said. "I wanted to say goodbye. Mac, I know it's a lot to ask, but if you can ever trust me again, give me a call. I'll miss you."

With that, he turned and walked away.

Day 10: Late Afternoon (EST)
New York City

McKenzie slouched at the kitchen table. The lack of Pierce's presence left a deafening silence in the room. She drank her coffee. Caffeine wouldn't be conducive to sleep, but she'd run on the stuff for so many days, going without a cup every few hours meant a killer headache.

Not long ago, she and Pierce had sat at this very table. Pierce had encouraged her not to be so quick to dismiss Noah's plea for help. Pierce had always been good at pointing out views others were too shortsighted to see.

"I don't know, McKenzie," he'd said that day. "You might be going about this thing all wrong."

McKenzie slammed down her coffee cup, grabbed her jacket and keys, and ran out the front door.

Day 10: Late Afternoon
Astoria, New York

Noah's back was to her as he loaded boxes into his Jeep. She inched up behind him. This was feeling like less and less of a good idea.

"I knew you'd make it," he said without turning.

"How did you—"

"Plenty of people have snuck up on me. Compared to a lot of them, you're really bad at it. No offense."

McKenzie grinned and plopped down in the open back of the Jeep. "Noah, there's a lot you don't know. I couldn't let you leave without telling you the truth."

The information spewed from her like an uncorked champagne bottle. She told him about the last thing Lucas said before he died. She recounted finding the video and her meeting with President Covington. She told him all about how the politician had arranged for the president and vice president to be assassinated to catapult herself into the presidency, and how she and Bert Royal had leaked a false trail to the Shen as a cover-up.

McKenzie admitted to Noah that she'd been offered—and had taken—the bribe money.

He didn't say anything for a long moment. Her neck burned like a schoolgirl caught by her teacher passing notes. When he spoke again, his voice was quiet, one secret-keeper to another. "The question is why are you telling me this now?"

McKenzie took a deep breath. "Because I love you."

Did I really just say that out loud?

Noah's face broke into a grin. He enveloped her in his arms. "Christ swinging from a chandelier. I think I might just love you, too, Mac."

His lips brushed the top of her head. "I've got a plane to catch," he said.

McKenzie hopped off the back of his hatch so he could close it.

"Thanks for being honest with me," he said as an afterthought, and then he climbed into his Jeep.

Her forehead wrinkled. "You're with the FBI now. You're not going to tell them?"

The roguish smile of a little boy caught in mischief stretched across Noah's face once more. "Nah. I don't have to. I have a really good partner. I trust her implicitly. When her back is to the wall, she always does what needs to be done. The right thing."

McKenzie watched him crank the Jeep. She ambled to her sedan, climbed in, and fired the engine. As Noah pulled the Jeep even with her car, he slowed and rolled down his window. She did the same.

"I'll call you once I'm settled," he said. "I know we usually do these things on a need to know basis, but out of curiosity, where are you off to now?"

The scenes played in front of McKenzie's eyes: Noah's first visit to her office. The day with Cody's mother. Kimberly Lawson's death. Jessie's. Pierce's. Uncle Sal. And little Levi.

Most grating was the memory of President Elaine Covington's smirk as the woman pushed a bag full of money at her to buy her silence.

"My office," McKenzie answered. "I have a story to write."

Acknowledgements

WHEN I SET OUT to write this novel, I had some of the story already in my head. However, I found I had many questions and doubts. Luckily, my life was never short of people to help me figure out the impossible and cheer me on. I have so many people to thank. I'm sure I will forget too many, so I apologize in advance. Please consider this a thank you to you, too.

First, to my editor, Pat Shaw, who believed in this book as much as I did, knew the characters in my head as if they were her own, and championed this effort every step of the way: I couldn't have asked for someone easier to work with, someone more "my style," or someone who would work with me to suggest revisions that resonated with me so whole-heartedly. You are such a gift.

To Ken Coffman and Chris Benson at Stairway Press for taking a chance on me and my work, and for your support and willingness to push this bird out of the nest and into the world. Not only have you made the experience of publishing a pleasure, but you've allowed me to realize a dream and share this little book with the world. For that, you have my never-ending gratitude.

Thank you to Simon and Guy for the brilliant cover design. I couldn't be happier with how it captures the mood of the story. My biggest thanks to Matt and the team at 27 Sound Entertainment for my brilliant website design and your patience to develop concepts based only on words like "badass."

Researching certain details for this story wouldn't have been possible without: Major Tom Greer, who has been a wealth of information; LTC (ret.) Robert F. (Bob) Koester, who was always ready to answer the many questions that cropped up in clarifying the confusing world of the Unites States Army; Major David Carter, one of the first Special Forces commandos and a former notifications officer, whose stories made difficult parts of my book more tangible. A special thank you to Former U.S. Navy LT Kory DeFore and his wife, Terah—your bravery showed me what military families sacrifice to do what they do. To the men and women in uniform who gave their expertise but must remain anonymous due to secretive occupations: thank you. And for the family of SGM Oscar Sapp, since he is gone and won't be able to read this himself: a special thank you to such a special man, who not only made the military come alive for me, but who also taught me that, "Good things come to those who wait, but better things come to those who get off their lazy cans and do something about it."

A host of others helped me with questions big and small. A huge thank you to Dr. Richard Elliot for hours in a coffee shop talking with me about things that, if overheard, would make other patrons run and hide. Thank you to Nadine Semerau and Tina Meyers for lending a hand on hotel expertise, as well as to Will Crews and Ian Owen, who have much more patience with Google than I do. I'm forever indebted to Dr. Katie DeFore and Dr. Khaled Al-Khasawneh for their assistance in afflicting characters with wounds and diseases in various writing ventures. Thank you to Joseph Zampa for taking some of my shadier questions, as well as to Herbie Hatlee for conducting a "for dummies" lesson for me on how flights and airports work. To Lindell Saloom for his language expertise in various works. To Doug and Margeaux Copeland, I am so grateful to have you both not only to answer my queries about all things police-related, but to call you friends and occasionally ask for impromptu photo shoots. Thank you to Nikki Vincent for being a super Vincent, as always. I owe a big thank you to Tiffany Lawson, an unsung hero of this manuscript, who made it so much better than it originally was.

I'm thankful to have a group of friends and readers who not only read this book in part or in full and gave suggestions to better it, but who also provided me with morale support. My Purgies and Pitizens are beyond compare. To Kelly, Jenna, Jennifer, Bob, Tracey, and Ami: you guys make my days easier and make me laugh hard. Thank you to Gretchen McNeil, without whom I might've never learned to pitch a book. To other beta readers Rick and Lisa, who may not have read Chain but who have helped me in endless other ways: I appreciate you. And to dear Bryn

Greenwood, I don't have words for all the words you've given me over time, all the questions you've answered, and finally, for recommending this book for publication. I couldn't have made it to this point without George, who has not only read nearly every word I've written the past few years (sometimes at great speed), but who has reminded me consistently to never give up and never give in.

Writing can be a solitary profession, and it's easy to see how some writers go crazy in the midst of their work. Thankfully, I haven't been alone during this adventure. To EJ, my wonderful mentor: words can never express how grateful I am to you. I'd like to thank Courtney Hatlee, Judy DeFore, Stacy Hinson, Emily Renstrom, Lindsay Yasin, Shirley Kitchings, Elaine Greene, Carol Atkins, Carol Cloud, Pat Marcus, and Danielle Thuen, readers extraordinaire who have helped me to keep different novels on track. To Frank DeFore: thank goodness this day came without you having to take this book around to folks in the rain in New York City, but I love you for the fact that you would've. To Dr. Dennis Ashley, if you hadn't kept me healthy and moving along, I might've never finished the editing of this novel, so I thank you. I'm forever grateful and filled with love for my theatre and dance families at Macon Little Theatre, Theatre Macon, and Hayiya Dance Theatre who keep me sane(r) than I'd be if I was a hermit all the time. Thank you to Brian for your support and faith in my writing, as well as for always asking me (in a British accent) how that novel's comin'. *Bows* to Meg, who listened endlessly to my rambling about whatever was frustrating or exciting me at the time. And to Tim, wherever you are, I thank you for everything you've done for me.

I couldn't have lived through the past few years or this novel—in concept or revisions—without Ashlee Haynie, who put up with endless whining and countless venting sessions, read every word I wrote, and found answers to some of the strangest internet searches known to mankind. I also appreciate you letting me name Elaine after you since, given the fates of the other presidents in this novel, you couldn't have known whether that would go well or not for you. And to JP, for lending me your wife whenever I needed her, I'm thankful.

To my Dad: thank you for your confidence in me, your love, your words of encouragement, and for holding doors open for me that would've otherwise slammed in my face. Thank you for hunting down interview subjects for me and reminding me I could do anything I set my mind to. But most of all, thank you for being the best dad a girl could have. I love you dearly.

To my Mom, my most devoted reader and biggest cheerleader: thank you for letting me give you headaches over talking through plot points, allowing me to cry on your shoulder when I was down, and for permitting me to scream in your ear when good news came my way. Thank you for making my dream your own, and for always helping me to realize that one day, it would come true.

To the newest addition to my family: I'm so proud to call you mine. You may not be able to read this now, but one day, I want you to know I sat feet away from you while typing this, and that you were loved then, too.

To David: I'm not sure where this book—or my writing career—would be if not for you. You reminded me how to just write, both for publication and because it was what I loved doing. You called me on my crap when I needed it, held my hand when I needed that more, and believed in me even on days when I didn't. I'm not sure if anything in the world says, "Thank you," quite like a book about an assassination plot, which is why this the perfect place to give you your dues. I love you, and I'm thrilled to call myself your Mrs.

Last but certainly not least, to those of you reading this book: I thank you so much for picking up my little tale. I hope it thrills and entertains you, and above all, I hope it keeps you reading late into the night.

Writer by day, ballroom dancer and choreographer by night, Colby is a contributing columnist for a local magazine and a proud associate member of International Thriller Writers. She's active in local theatres as an actress and choreographer. She lives in Georgia with her family, where she is hard at work on her next thriller.

www.ingramcontent.com/pod-product-compliance
Lightning Source LLC
Chambersburg PA
CBHW021207250626
47155CB00008B/2711